M000033649

TRAFFICKED

A Mex Anderson Novel

For Melody —
Don't be...

TRAFFICKED

A Mex Anderson Novel

Enjoy!

PEG BRANTLEY

BARK
PUBLISHING
LLC

TRAFFICKED A Mex Anderson Novel
Copyright ©2017 by Peg Brantley
Cover design by Patty G. Henderson, Boulevard Photografica
Edited by Peggy Hageman
Formatted by LiberWriter and Patty G. Henderson
Author's photo by Kelly Weaver Photography

All rights reserved. In accordance with the U.S. Copyright Act of 1976, the scanning, uploading, electronic sharing of any part of this book without the express permission of the author constitutes unlawful piracy and theft of the author's intellectual property. If you would like to use material from this book (other than for review purposes), prior written permission must be obtained by contacting the author through her website, www.pegbrantley.com

ISBN (electronic version): 978-0-9853638-6-4
ISBN (trade-paperback): 978-0-9853638-7-1

Thank you for your support of the author's rights.

The characters and events in this book are fictitious. Any similarity to real persons, living or dead is coincidental and not intended by the author.

Praise for Peg Brantley's TRAFFICKED...

Peg Brantley's TRAFFICKED is a heartbreaker, a thriller, and a hair-raising education, all at once. I wish I hadn't already read it, so I could read it for the first time again. — Timothy Hallinan, author of the Junior Bender and Poke Rafferty crime novels

The scourge of human trafficking is worldwide; yet, most Americans clutch the idea that it couldn't possibly exist here. Peg Brantley's chillingly honest, gritty novel moves readers to empathize with lives shattered by modern-day slavery. Through an accessible, awareness-raising narrative, Brantley spotlights a foul, hidden human crisis. In Americans' own back yard, not only can trafficking happen, it does. — Susanne E. Jalbert, Ph.D., Activist

With TRAFFICKED, Peg Brantley has crafted a thriller that's as moving as it is suspenseful. Beautifully written, and a vivid wake-up call about the reality of sex traffic here in the US. Highly recommended. — Dennis Palumbo, author of the Daniel Rinaldi Mysteries

Other Books by Peg Brantley

Aspen Falls Thrillers:

Red Tide

The Missings

Mex Anderson:

The Sacrifice

For the men and women who work ceaselessly to stop human trafficking in its tracks, and for those who strive to bring a measure of hope to its victims.

And always, for George.

Acknowledgments

Without the input of the following people, this story, if it got written at all, would have been far less. If errors exist, either in craft or research, the fault is entirely mine.

First my sincere thanks to Dr. Susanne E. Jalbert, who made it clear to me the story needed to be local. Because it is. And to my good friend, M.L. Hanson, who introduced us.

My humble appreciation to Detective Elisabeth Reid with the Colorado Springs Police Department. She pointed me in all the right directions at the best possible times. And to Heather Liggett, Victim Advocate of the Colorado Springs Police Department. You are my heroes. I can't hold you high enough.

Thank you to FBI Agent Ricky Wright for giving me a sense of what it's like to do what law enforcement officers do day in and day out to combat human trafficking, and then try and live a normal life by going to a Bronco game.

Thank you also to my sister, novelist Lala Corriere, for help regarding new forms of heroin, based on her research for her novel TRACKS.

Enormous gratitude goes to my beta readers: novelist Polly Iyer for her willingness to skewer my story where it needed it most; Kel Darnell for feeling free to tell me what she liked and what she hated, and to sit around with me (and a bottle of wine) and brainstorm all sorts of options; novelist Donnell Ann Bell whose thoughtful insights and encouraging words propelled me forward; novelist Sheila Lowe for her instincts and advice; and novelist L.J. Sellers who has mentored me from the beginning, whose suggestions I always consider seriously, and who was also instrumental in introducing me to Ricky Wright.

The talented Peggy Hageman edited this story and helped me move it up to another level. She's amazing. Early reader, John Gunkler, acted as my proofreader. We might not always agree about commas, but I'm grateful he caught those silly goofs that happen after editing and revising a million times.

Patty G. Henderson brought her skill and creativity once again to both my cover and the interior design. It's her work readers see first.

Speaking of readers (you know who you are), I hope your patience is rewarded. You certainly reward me with your kind words and reviews. I'm honored.

With this story in particular, I felt the solid support and belief of Bud and Judy Ham, Michael Ham, and Jandy Dugan. You guys rock.

And as always, without the sturdiness afforded my life through George's love, my days would be darker, my heart emptier, and books never written. You fulfill me in so many ways.

*3,287 people are **reported** sold or kidnapped and forced into slavery every day. That's almost 137 people an hour. More than 2 people every minute. **Reported.** What about those who aren't?*

—*Statistics from Force4Compassion*

CHAPTER ONE

JAYLA

Mama dumps her cup of instant coffee, laced with whatever booze she had on hand this morning, into the sink. "Jayla, I need you outta here by eight tonight."

A few years ago she would've just told me to shut my door and be quiet when she had a boyfriend over. At least then I could do my homework. Now she sees me as competition.

"Where am I s'posed to go?"

"Don't matter. Just want you gone by eight."

"Until?"

"Don't mess with me, girl."

"Fine."

"You gone then?"

"I'm gone."

Mama looked at me. "You know I love you, right?"

"Yeah, I know."

Mama does her best. Most of the time, anyway. She feeds me and clothes me except when she doesn't. Her focus has always been men and she only feels like she's worth something if she's got a man in her life.

Me she could do without some days. It isn't exactly that she resents my mind and desire to learn, it's more that she doesn't understand it. To her way of thinking my common sense is about as abysmal as my daddy's and she never fails to remind me of that fact whenever the opportunity arises.

I've seen my daddy exactly four times in my whole life. As a little girl, I pretended he had a very important job that kept him away from Denver for years at a time, and when he could come home, I was the draw. Not Mama or any cash she might happen to be flush with at the moment. He always brought me a stuffed animal of some kind. The last time I saw him, when I was thirteen, I gave it back to him and told him to keep up. I wasn't ten anymore. I think he got the message.

Because I want to keep Mama happy and make her proud of me, I do my best not to sound "white" when I'm around her. And I sure don't talk about a new concept I recently read about or some story that touched my heart with pure light. I talk about clothes and current music and what I need to pick up at the grocery store to fix the little kid's meals over the next week. What for Mama is normal and easy to wrap her head around.

On my way to the school bus stop I watch a gust of wind pick up a piece of trash and toss it down the street. The crumpled paper hits the pavement and skitters, wearing a little of it away with each contact. I feel like that every day. It's like I work toward this one life and then a gust of wind comes along and pushes me towards another one, scraping off a part of me every time. Sometimes I wonder what will happen when my bone is exposed. Is that when I die?

So where am I going to sleep tonight? I have a couple of friends I can check with. Trouble is, their families have as many issues, or more, than mine. I'll give Chris a call. Since he got his own place he's let me sleep on his couch a couple of times. I'll stay there if he'll let me.

* * *

"We'll be square then, right? I won't owe you anything? You'll leave me and my family alone?"

"That's the deal."

Chris hung up the phone. He couldn't believe his good luck. Just when it looked as if his days, hours really, were numbered, his luck had turned around. Who said being nice didn't pay? He'd let Jayla crash on his couch before when she had nowhere else to go. And tonight she'd be here again.

He knew better than to believe what he'd been told about why they wanted a girl—that they were engaging in a college prank—but he wasn't in a position to ask too many questions. And honestly, he didn't want to think about it too much. Jayla would probably be pissed at him for sure, but eventually she'd get over it. Instead of thinking how scared shitless she'd be, he concentrated on how years from now they'd share a laugh.

And in the meantime his gambling debt would be paid and he could get on with his life.

* * *

"Thanks, Chris. I mean it." I stow my backpack at the end of the couch that is my bed away from bed.

"No probs. What are friends for?" Chris grabs a dishcloth and wipes down countertops that already look pretty clean to me.

3

"Is everything okay? Do you want to talk about something?" I ask him as he rubs away at the shining surface and doesn't once look at me.

"Nah. I'm cool. I imagine it's an okay thing to be away from your moms for a while. Am I right?"

I think about this and wonder how much Chris suspects. Why is he asking this now? I don't want him, or anyone, to think badly about my mom. At the same time, it's clear she's the reason I have to find someplace else to sleep. "Even when you love someone, short breaks can be a nice thing."

"That whole absence makes the heart grow fonder thing? Or is it that your mom's heart is aimed in another direction?"

"Don't be mean."

"Sorry. My bad." Now he grabs a pan he's already washed and puts it in the sink, adds dish soap, and starts washing it again, still not looking at me. Something's not right.

"What's up, Chris?"

He gives the pan a final rinse and puts it back on the towel to drain. "You caught me. A friend of mine is coming by later and I don't want you to feel uncomfortable."

Heat flames my face. "Oh, uh... I'm sorry. I don't want to mess up your plans. I can—"

"No, no. Not that kind of friend. Just a guy. He wants to hang out while his wife has her girlfriends over to talk about books or something."

"Books? A book club? You know I love to read. Do they live around here? Maybe I could join."

"Maybe not books. Maybe only girlfriend shit." Chris opens his refrigerator and stares into it. "I've gotta go get some beer." He closes the door and looks at me. "You cool if I leave?"

"Why wouldn't I be?"

"Cool then." He picks up his keys and looks back at me. "See you in a few. If he gets here before I'm back, let him in."

"No probs."

I've known Chris all my life. He lived in the building next to mine. He graduated high school last year, has a great job repairing computers, his own place, and is attending night classes at Metro.

Something is bothering him. I can tell.

Is he feeling put out because I'm sleeping on his couch? Surely he knows I'd do the same for him if I could. I'll pin him down when he gets home with the beer. I'm sure we can work it out.

I spread my homework over the coffee table in front of the couch. There's a science test tomorrow and I have to get better than just a passing grade to keep my average up. Science isn't my best subject... unless it involves science fiction and then I'm all in. But tomorrow is all about protons, neutrons, and electrons in the real world, not a story world. Too bad.

The clock on the stove says forty minutes have passed. Where's Chris? Where was he going for the beer? Did he get mugged or something? Horrible images pass through my head.

I grab my backpack and head to the door.

The buzzer rings. Maybe Chris forgot his keys.

"You were starting to scare me," I say into the intercom.

"Excuse me? I'm here to see Chris Wilson. He's expecting me."

"Oh, sorry. Yeah, come on up." I press the button that opens the entrance door for the building.

Where's Chris? He only went out for beer. It's not like him to be gone this long, especially when he has a friend coming over.

I dig my phone out of my backpack just as there's a knock.

"Hi, come on in," I say to the rough looking man standing in the doorway. I'm surprised at his appearance and the fact he's so much older than my friend. "I'm trying to find out what's going on with Chris." I punch in the speed dial number and then turn away to better hear when he answers the phone.

"Hey, it's me—" I'm aware of a sweet-smelling cloth pressing up against my nose and mouth and there's something dark covering my head. "Chris!" My cry is muffled in the cloth.

"Hines would control his victim through beatings and through the use of drugs," the district attorney's office said in a news release Thursday. "At one point, Hines, who was in a halfway house, traded his victim to a pimp in Fort Collins so she could continue to support him while he was in custody."— Denver man gets 24 years in prison for sex trafficking in metro-area hotel rooms, *by Jesse Paul, for* The Denver Post, *December 15, 2016*

CHAPTER TWO

JAYLA

I wake up to a mantra in my brain. *This isn't good. This isn't good. This isn't good.*

My arms are folded in such a way that I can feel my heartbeat. If this isn't good, why is my heartbeat so steady?

The floor beneath me is cold and hard. A blanket has been thrown over me that stinks of body odor and urine and scratches my skin when my breathing causes it to shift.

Maybe the urine smell is mine. Please God, don't let it be mine.

Why is my heart rhythm so steady? I'm scared out of my fuckin' mind and my heart should be beating out of my chest.

When I try to change position my head screams out with the worst headache I've ever known.

What's happening to me?

Lying here isn't going to get me any answers. I throw the blanket off and rise slowly to a sitting position, focusing on my lap while I wait for the dizziness to pass. Feeling more settled, I raise my head and look around. I'm in a corner of a windowless room.

The floor, walls, and ceiling are all cement. A bare bulb hanging on a wire overhead doesn't cast enough light to illuminate the corners. But over there, across the room from me, I can make out a foot.

I'm not alone!

"Hey." Even speaking softly sends a shard of pain through my skull. "Hey," I try louder, ignoring the agony. The foot doesn't move.

From another corner, a man comes toward me out of the shadows and I instinctively go quiet.

This isn't good.

He takes a long look at me and leaves through a door I hadn't noticed before.

A minute later a woman rushes into the room carrying a bag or duffle of some sort. "Well, Jayla Imani Thomas, I see you've decided to join us."

How does she know my name? I remain silent, but can't help looking at the foot in the corner across from mine. Is that Chris? Is he dead?

As if reading my mind, the woman takes my hand. "Jayla, don't worry about the others in this room. They are safe, as safe as you are." She opens the bag which I can now see is a medical kit. "I'm going to take a few vitals to confirm you're in decent health and unharmed. Relax, this won't take long."

I stiffen involuntarily at her words. The man I'd seen is now standing, blocking the light, and holding a camera.

What the hell is going on?

"Move, asshole. I can't see what I'm doing." The woman's tone is sharp, different from the gentle way she's speaking to me. Is this something I can work with? My brain clears and I realize what a foolish thought that is.

My clearing brain brings paralyzing fear. This is real, not a movie.

The pungent odor of visceral fear is enough to send me into a gagging fit, but I manage to swallow it down. Focus. Pay attention. Figure out how to get out of here.

She takes my temperature and records it in a thick notebook. How many people are represented in those pages? Then she puts a cuff on my arm to get my blood pressure, and after that I peek through half-closed eyes while she draws enough blood to fill three vials.

The woman reaches out to touch my shoulder, almost like she's asking for permission. Sneaky bitch. "Jayla, honey? Can you hear me?"

Instinctively I start to clench my hands into fists but stop before it happens. I force a shallow nod. An arm wraps around me.

"You're safe, Jayla. You're safe."

Safe? I've dealt with Mama and her boyfriends and her booze and her drugs. Dealt with uncertainty and rejection. Yet I've never felt less safe or more confused. And completely vulnerable.

This isn't good.

"How did I get here?"

The woman ignores me.

"How did I ge—"

"You feel safe, don't you Jayla?" The woman's voice has a hard edge to it.

I shrug and dip my head.

"Excellent. I've got new clothes for you. Do you like clothes?"

"Uh-huh." Heaven help me if she knows I'm lying.

"Very well. I'll have your new clothes brought to you." She fishes in her pocket and presents a pill and a cup of water. "This will help you continue to feel safe. Take it for me, will you? I don't want you to be afraid."

Now I have an idea why my heart rate is so steady. Drugs.

I want to ask where I am. I want to ask why I'm here. I want to ask about Chris. I want to ask when I can leave.

I know I can't ask any of these questions.

The pill slips easily into the outside of my gum. I swallow the water and hand the woman the empty cup. "Thank you," I manage.

She smiles at me. "That's a girl. Someone will be here to pick you up soon. Be sure and have your new clothes on."

When she leaves I pop the pill out of my mouth and stick it in my own pants pocket. Will I be able to keep my old clothes? Who knows? Probably not. I might not be able to figure out what drug they're giving me, but it's clear it's to keep me calm. Sedated even.

I have to concentrate on not responding to anything that happens in any quick or instinctive way. Otherwise she'll know I didn't swallow the pill. But right now I feel like any tiny sound will catapult me to the ceiling. Reacting like that would take things from "not good" to "damn bad," and I can't take that chance. Not right now, anyway. I imagine hearing gunshots or explosions and merely gazing into the distance, practicing a calm response to anything and everything.

In order to survive I have to focus on appearing drugged.

A man comes up to me and I work hard not to cringe. He throws a bag at me and says, "Here. Put these on and make it quick."

I want to ask him where I should change but realize that where I am there is no such thing as privacy. I'm sure a drugged Jayla couldn't care less. My face burns hot with embarrassment.

Survive, Jayla. Survive.

Inside the bag are clothes Mama would never wear, even when she's in the hunt mode for a new man. Suddenly I think about the hookers I've seen around Denver and my stomach heaves. Had some of them been sitting where I'm sitting now? Had I judged them without knowing anything about how they got there? Oh God, is that what's happening to me?

"I said to make it quick, bitch. You're up next."

Up? This isn't good.

* * *

The man who brought me the clothes leads me out of the room. I watch for an opportunity to escape. It isn't happening.

Someone ahead and to the side is videotaping me as I make my way down the hallway. There are no doors. No exits.

No way out.

The clothes I'm wearing make me want to hide in shame. Give up. Let them win. But a stronger part in me says I can fight this. I can be the winner. I can walk away.

Walk away? Really? Could I ever simply walk away? Not likely.

I remember a movie I saw about a girl who was kidnapped. She survived because she went along with her kidnapper. I figure this is my only chance—to seem submissive. Compliant. But look for a way out.

I think I know what's coming. They'll do everything to break me.

Because I'm not going anywhere I choose. At least not today.

I know I'm strong. I want the hell out of here. I want my life, whatever it is, back.

Still, I believe I'm here for a reason. What the hell it might be I have no idea. They can throw whatever they want at me.

They can't break me.

At least I don't think so.

I put one foot in front of the other, recognizing for the first time how cold I am. The cameraman continues to film. As much as I want to flash a finger, I keep my head and eyes down.

I keep looking for a weak link. It isn't here.

My awareness remains my secret. My power.

* * *

A bald man with ice blue eyes yanks my arm. I tell myself not to flinch or show any reaction. After all, I'm supposed to be drugged.

"C'mon bitch. Ginger's waiting."

We move down a long dark hallway, bare bulbs throwing shadows onto the floor and walls. It's eerie and hypnotic at the same time. The smell of fear follows us.

He opens a door, nods to someone in the room then shoves me inside.

The dim lights in the room grow brighter until I want to shield my eyes. A woman with skin the color of pecans and beautiful auburn hair is studying me. Slowly, she circles. I can feel her looking at every inch of my body.

"You need to lighten up."

My hands fist. This from a sister? "Pardon me?"

"You need to put on a party-face. Look like you're having fun. Look like you'd be fun to be with."

What I *need* is to be studying for my science test. What I *need* is to be anywhere other than here and what I *need* is to make sure Chris is okay.

Inside I'm shaking. There's a roar in the room punctuated by the rapid beat of my heart. I want to cry. Never in my life have I been in a position even remotely similar. I'm a straight-A student, not a party girl.

I'm not equipped for this.

The woman, Ginger, is moving again. "Here. Take these." She holds out a couple of pills and a glass of water.

I shake my head.

"Trust me, honey. If you don't take these now, a couple of hours from now you'll wish you had."

For the first time since finding myself in this situation, whatever 'this situation' is, I make eye contact with another human being. At first, I see great sorrow in those deep brown eyes. And then that sorrow is replaced by something hard and cold. My chest tightens.

"Take 'em. Now."

I swallow the pills because she's watching.

"Open your mouth."

Ginger doesn't wait but brings a hand up to my jaw and pinches, forcing my mouth open. The forefinger of her other hand does a swift check along my gum line. She gives a satisfactory nod. "Smart girl."

I watch her. She's part of whatever is happening to me. Maybe she has some answers. I know I can't trust her but I don't have any other options at the moment.

"Ma'am?"

She laughs. It's a sad and sarcastic sound. "Ginger. Call me Ginger."

"Okay. Ginger, can I ask you something?"

"Ask it, girl. Don't waste my time."

"I'm worried about my friend."

Her head cocks to the side and her eyes pierce mine. "Friend? Another girl?" She bites the words.

"No. A boy. My friend is a boy. His name is Chris. I was staying at his place when all of this—"

This time Ginger's laugh explodes in relief. "You stupid cunt." She breathes the words.

"Pardon me?"

"Your friend Chris is who landed you here in the first place. He wanted cash and you were for sale."

"Chris wouldn't—"

"He could and he did. Deal with it." She clicks on her phone. "Your date will be here in about twenty minutes."

Date?

Even as part of me begins to panic, other parts of me are loosening up. Fading away. Moving to a zone where they can't be touched. The drug is taking effect.

Whatever it is, it's happening, and it isn't good.

While numbers of internationally trafficked children and adults are up, the majority of exploitation occurs within a country's own borders.
—Girls Like Us, *by Rachel Lloyd*

CHAPTER THREE

Six Months Later

"Damn reporters." Mex Anderson slammed his phone down. "It's been over a year. Why the hell are they still pestering me?"

The sun hung low in the sky, basking the deck in its rich glow. Deer were eating shrubbery while others drank from the gurgling stream about thirty yards away. Any other time he'd appreciate the peaceful view from his Aspen Falls home. Not now.

Cade moved behind his chair to rub his neck and shoulders. "This is what happens when you rescue the daughter of the head of a Mexican drug cartel from people who were about to sacrifice her—literally. A lot of reporters can't let a good story die."

"And Darius's book has fanned the flames."

"You could say that. But I know you don't begrudge him his success."

Mex sighed and popped his neck. "Guess I don't."

"So let it go."

"Have I told you lately how much you mean to me, Acadia LeBlanc?"

"*Mon cher*, sometimes you even come close to convincing me to make the extraordinary decision to move to Colorado permanently."

"But I'm also aware—"

"That I haven't sold my home in Louisiana while keeping my own place here in Aspen Falls? What I said is true. You've come *close* to convincing me."

"What'll it take?"

Cade stopped her massage and moved around to sit on his lap. The light from the fire pit reflected on the side of her face, the other side shadowed seductively. Her green eyes, highlighted with gold, made him want to disappear into them. Into her. She cupped her hands to either side of Mex's face. "I can't say. What I can say is that today I love being here with you. Today is perfect. Can't we let things move the way they move and not force anything?"

"Force?"

"Okay. Wrong word. But you know what I mean. With pasts like ours it takes awhile to believe in a future."

Mex had lost his wife and family in Mexico. After his family's massacre, Mex sold his property and invested in Silicon Valley startups before anyone knew where Silicon Valley was. He'd gotten out while the getting was good.

Cade had worked through losses of her own, first personally, and then professionally as an exit counselor for kids immersed in cults. Between the two of them, they had enough pain in their histories to keep a university psych class busy for years.

He grasped her hands in his. "You and I are two strong people. We'll figure this future thing out." He waited to make sure he had her full attention. "In our own time." Mex winked.

"Well, our time might be moving forward. A little." She pressed closer to whisper in his ear. "I'm selling my home in New Orleans."

Even while enjoying the increased pressure of her body against his, he pulled back. "Are you sure?" He searched those glorious eyes for an answer. Maybe she was finally ready to move in with him.

As if she read his mind, she shook her head. "I'm not ready to make more of a commitment, but sometimes we have to step out in faith. You taught me that. Right now, this is as much faith as I can muster."

The couple watched in silence as the sun set with magnificent color. After the fire died to flickering embers, they held each other as the cool Colorado high country night settled in.

Cade stood and held out her hands to Mex. "Let's go inside. I brought a bottle of champagne."

"To celebrate?"

Cade hiked an eyebrow.

"Celebrate what? What are we celebrating?"

"Today. Does that work for you?"

"It'll do."

Later, sleeping the smooth and contented sleep of an untroubled man, Mex's cell buzzed on the desk in his office. He didn't hear it. Which was a good thing because it afforded him one more peaceful night's sleep before everything changed.

Again.

* * *

Three Days Earlier

Donny clicked the screen closed on his computer and shoved away from the desk.

"Goddammit. Why didn't I see this coming?" He stood, batted the chair and watched it spin away before catching on a desk leg and toppling over.

He'd counted on her and she'd let him down. What a bitch. At least his hacking skills had paid off before he'd lost more time. His idea to check the Clerk and Recorder's office to determine the potential amount of her trust fund proved right, but not in the way he'd planned. He found the amount, but he found something else too.

Alexis won't see a dime until she's twenty-one. Twenty-one? Twenty-fucking-one?

He needed to put Plan B into action. The sooner the better. *Damn.*

It had been two years but he still knew how to get the word out. He logged into a chat site through a Virtual Private Network and made a mental note to change his preferred VPN the next time he went online. He didn't use it very much, but it still made him nervous to use the same one too often.

Donny left the same message he'd used two years ago. He'd know soon if it still worked.

It didn't take long. Less than thirty minutes later he received instructions to upload photos to an email account. Good thing he'd copied the best of her Facebook photos.

What he wanted right now was a beer. Instead he settled for vitamin water from the employee stash.

And waited.

"Look man, you have her photo. She's seventeen. She's hot. And feisty. Way different than most of the girls you get which makes her worth a lot more money."

"Feisty implies difficult to control," the man said. "Neither me or my clients are interested in procuring a long-term problem."

Donny paced, then sat back down at the communal desk and fiddled with a stack of paper, mostly gym membership applications. The pile reminded him of his own stack at home that contained nothing but bills. His eyes blinked Morse code while he tried to steady his breathing.

Desperation flashed through Donny's chest. This had to work. Stay calm. In control. He had what the man wanted, he knew it.

But while Donny talked on his personal phone he felt pretty sure the man on the other end had a burner. If a problem ever came up it would come back to him, but it would never get to the man with the throwaway phone. Hell, he didn't even have the guy's fake name, let alone a real one.

And this marked the third time they'd worked together.

"What are you willing to go?"

"Ten."

"Are you kidding me? She's worth forty to fifty, easy."

"Why are you willing to cut this *hot and feisty* asset loose?"

"Because she doesn't hit her personal jackpot until she's twenty-one. Too long, man. Not quite the asset I'd hoped for."

The man chuckled. "When can you deliver?"

"Tonight."

"I'll go fifteen."

"C'mon man. Thirty-five. You'll make out and then some."

The silence screamed in Donny's ear. He rolled his shoulders.

"Twenty-five. Three a.m. You know where."

The connection went dead.

Donny did a fist-pump. He knew they'd want her. He checked his watch. She'd be here in a few minutes. If he played her right, she'd be in exactly the right place at exactly the right moment.

And he'd collect twenty-five grand.

He shoved his computer into his gym bag and whistled while he walked to his locker. Before securing it he double-checked his supply of Rohypnol. You never knew when a roofie might come in handy.

Things were about to go his way, with a little time of his own to play with the merchandise.

According to the U.S. Attorney's office, she had been sold to him, for $1,200, in a package deal with her best friend. The vendor was Brian Forbes, a six-foot-five-inch, 40-year-old bodybuilder, whom local law enforcement understood to be employed in the bail-bond business.

—Sex Trafficking of Americans: The Girls Next Door, by Amy Fine Collins

CHAPTER FOUR

At the fitness center's second-floor overlook, Donny stood at the rail and observed Alexis Halston enter and walk to the women's locker room. He noticed she wore her signature eye makeup. To him it looked Goth but with a turquoise twist. The blue-green eyeshadow framed her eyes like a mask.

She strode with a straight back and just enough head and hip movement to look natural—as well as catch the eye of every guy she passed. Donny liked the way her hair swung loose. She always drew it back into a ponytail before they began their workout, so today he accepted this view of her free-style look as his parting gift.

Someone would pay big bucks for pussy with an attitude he thought, then quickly squeezed back the chuckle that bubbled in his throat. After a few more seconds of consideration, he decided that more than likely Alexis would end up with someone who liked the extra force required to get compliance. Donny shrugged. None of his business.

A few minutes later Alexis approached Donny while he lifted hand weights.

"Hey, beautiful! Right on time."

Alexis rewarded him with a distracted smile.

He slipped the weights back into their holder. "You okay?"

Alexis shook her head. "Same old shit, Donny. I wonder if my friends would be my friends if I didn't have money. And it isn't even mine. It's my dad's." She threw out her arms like throwing off a coat. "Sorry. Sometimes I think you're the only one who cares about me. You read me in two seconds. Why's that? I mean, why do you care?"

Donny cocked his head to the side and drew his lips into a small smile. "Maybe because it's easy?" He waited while the amber colored eyes connected with his, then watched as a slow flush crept into her cheeks.

Score!

"You ready to work out or would you rather take a pass today?" He took a risk to ask, but he had a backup plan in case she decided to leave. He figured she would want to be with him even if she didn't feel like doing squats.

"No, I'm okay."

"Maybe you can take out your frustrations on the punching bag."

Alexis smiled and nodded. "Sounds like I'm going to get a decent workout."

An hour later, sweat-soaked and flushed, much of the turquoise eye color long since swiped away on her towel, Alexis took a swallow from her water bottle. "Thanks, Donny. I needed this today."

"Glad I could help." He watched as she went back to the showers, then he jogged up the stairs to the administrative level.

In the employee locker room, he took a quick shower, brushed his teeth, put on street clothes, then tossed the roofies into his gym bag and zipped it up.

At the reception desk he leaned in to the young girl whose main job it was to sign members in and hook up non-members with a trainer to get them to join. "Got a call from my sister. Family emergency."

The girl pulled a schedule up on her screen. "You have Leslie Lewis at 6:30."

Donny worked to hide a smirk. Leslie Lewis was a fat bitch who thought her law degree made her smarter than everyone else and entitled her to automatic worship. He would not mind losing her as a client. "See if someone else can take her. If not, call her and cancel. I've gotta go."

"I'll do what I can as long as you understand it's your ass if she's pissed. And she will be pissed."

Donny looked at the young girl with the sweet face sitting behind the desk. He'd never really noticed her before. Now he saw her for the piece of shit she was, and briefly considered how much he might get for her before deciding she wasn't worth the trouble. Plus a missing girl every couple of years didn't raise too many questions, especially if they were from different gyms. Two so close together and he'd have detectives breathing down his neck faster than he could run fifty yards.

"Look, do your best for me, will you? I promise I'll make it up to you." He flashed his widest smile and winked as he headed toward the doors leading to the parking lot.

Once inside his car, he jammed the keys in the ignition and hauled ass. Parking on any of the nearby streets posed a problem as rent-a-cops patrolled the high-end neighborhood frequently. Rich people didn't want any cars parking on the streets their taxes paid for, especially a crappy seven-year-old Camry. He drove a half-mile away to a parking lot in front of one of three office buildings and found a place in a far corner where his car would be less likely to stand out when everyone finally left for home.

Donny grabbed his bag and looked around. A few people were coming and going from the buildings but no one glanced in his direction. He set off at a quick but steady jog, not wanting to call attention to himself. Once back at the center's parking lot and only slightly out of breath, he found Alexis's Porsche 911 Cabriolet and experienced immense relief that he'd beaten her to it.

Tossing his bag casually at his feet, he leaned against the hood and waited. He didn't have to wait long.

Alexis spotted him long before she got to her car. He saw her grin and then immediately downgrade it to a tiny smile. "What are you doing here, Donny?"

"I thought you could use extra attention this evening. Maybe a friendly ear." He took a breath, stalling to gauge her reaction. "Am I right?"

Alexis walked passed him to the trunk and tossed in her gym bag. "How did you know this was my car?"

"Now you're making me feel like a stalker."

"Are you?" She grinned.

"Look, Alexis. I became a fan—not a stalker—long before I knew you drove this car, or any car for that matter. I happened to see you get into it one afternoon is all." He smiled at her. "I think you want someone to vent to. If I'm right, I'm your guy. And I'm ready to go with you anywhere. My treat."

"Your treat? Really?"

He laughed. "Of course."

She looked around. "Where's your car?"

"In the shop. I took the bus in today. I'm hoping you'll give me a ride home later. I don't live far from here."

"You just don't want to ride the bus."

"Not true. I want to spend time with you. Away from exercise equipment and people scratching private parts of their bodies everywhere you look."

This time she laughed.

He knew he was in.

"We're in a technological age now where we have powerful computing devices that we can hold in the palm of our hand," said Sgt. Dan Steele, of the Denver Police Department, who supervises the Innocence Lost Task Force. *"Because of that, we have now seen traffickers and sex buyers alike looking at those devices and going, 'Wow, I can sit on my couch or I can sit in my car or I can stand on the street corner and I can pick and choose a person that I want to exploit. I can pick and choose if I want to buy someone, sell someone, exploit someone.'"*

—*FBI recovers 9 child sex trafficking victims in Colorado, Wyoming as part of national operation,* by
Jesse Paul, *for* The Denver Post, *October 18, 2016*

CHAPTER FIVE

ALEXIS

I shove down the blanket, suddenly hot and uncomfortable. I open my eyes enough to get my bearings. The room is gray-scaled with highlights of silver, a combination of moonlight and the ever-burning city lights that serve to ensure the entire Denver Metro area will never experience complete darkness.

I look around for a clock in the shadowed room and see a digital readout on the nightstand on the other side of the bed. 1:37.

Shit.

I might as well stay tucked in and go to school from here. Dad's not in town, as per usual, and even if Mom is, she's always so out of it she'll never know whether I came home. The only person who would be the wiser would be Marla when she comes to make up my bed and clean my bathroom. Our maid figured out a long time ago my whereabouts aren't newsworthy. At least not to Steve or Adele Halston.

Donny's apartment. It's weird but also nice to be here. I was happy when he invited me to go home with him after our dinner at Shanahan's. He gets me.

A warm feeling floods my body. Shanahan's isn't cheap by a long shot, and we consumed enough booze to set a record. My expensive fake ID had paid off again. I offered to buy but Donny insisted. Sweet. He cares.

His apartment surprised me too. I expected to walk into something that looked like a continuation of the fitness center—stacked weights and exercise balls at the very least. Instead, while not exactly luxurious, it's tastefully decorated with two or three passable pieces of art. Not collector's items, but not half bad.

I look next to me and Donny's not there.

Since I don't have pajamas and don't feel like marching around naked, I tug the duvet off the bed and wrap it around me as I leave the bedroom. Donny has to be here somewhere.

Trailing the ridiculous duvet behind me I see Donny out on the tiny deck off his living room. He's talking on his phone and smoking a cigarette.

A cigarette? Donny smokes? I can't decide whether to be disappointed or intrigued. Maybe a little of both.

Who is he talking to at this hour?

I shove the sliding glass doors open and Donny quickly kills the call. Moving to the rail, I lean over to see a jogging trail and bike path side by side, both of which make sense in this part of town. "Hey," I say.

"Hey."

"Missed you in bed. Who were you talking to?"

"A night-owl friend on the West Coast. He gets even less sleep than I do."

"Did you hang up on him?"

"Nope. We were done."

"I didn't know you smoked."

"Only when I'm anxious about something."

"You? Anxious?"

"Well, not normally. But my friend has a lot going on and wanted me to help him work through things."

I'm impressed. A guy who cares enough about someone else to talk with him at his hour? "Got another one?"

"Another one what?"

"Cigarette, silly."

"Not only do I have a cigarette for you, but I've been working out a particular drink recipe I'd like your feedback on. Are you game?"

"Sure. Why the hell not?" I'm too jazzed to go back to sleep anyway.

Donny lights a cigarette and hands it to me. "I'll be right back."

Comfortably settled into a chair, dizzy from the tobacco, I look out onto the perpetually backlit sky and take a deep drag on my cigarette. For the first time in a long time I feel like I'm in the exact place I'm supposed to be.

"Here, let me know what you think." Donny hands me a glass filled with a dark amber liquid, and sits on the chair next to mine. "Don't lie."

I swirl and sniff. "I don't usually drink bourbon."

"Don't worry. It's smooth, I promise. I added diet coke and my special ingredient."

"Are we gonna go like bunnies again if I drink this?"

"If I'm lucky."

28

"You mean if I am." I take a long healthy swallow, then shake my head. "Donny, this needs work."

He looks hurt. "Please. Try it again."

I attempt to hand him the glass.

"Please?"

I put the drink back to my lips and swallow. "I don't know, Donny. Not my drink. Sorry."

Donny grabs the glass from me and marches inside to the kitchen. He's acting hurt or pissed or something. Really?

"I'm sorry. I didn't mean to offend you." I watch his stiff back, but can't help but admire the firm butt it's attached to.

"Not to worry. I think maybe you should get dressed." He presses both hands onto the counter and tilts his head toward the ceiling.

"Donny, I said I'm sorry."

He turns to me. "Get dressed Alexis, or I'll dress you myself." He spits the words at me and throws the kitchen towel on the counter before walking back to the deck.

I follow him and pause at the sliding glass doors. "Can we talk about this?"

"Tomorrow." He's looking at the sky but turns back to me with a cold stare. "Or maybe fucking never. It's almost time to go and I'm tired of dealing with your drama."

In the bedroom, I turn on the light and blink at the glare. *Almost time to go?* What the hell does that mean? I grab my clothes and tug them on.

A tear slides down my cheek. I thought he was different. I thought I'd finally found someone I could talk to. Someone who could love me.

"Screw him. Screw this whole night."

I feel a little sick.

* * *

The I-70 overpass roared above Donny. Drivers flew by without even considering the dark places that existed below the highway they traveled. Underneath the racing cars and rumbling semis, almost subterranean, industrial yards surrounded three sides of the street. No trees or grass grew down here.

Back the way he'd come, sodium-vapor street lights cast shades of yellow over a closed bar. Everything else appeared shadowed and gray. Donny suspected that when and if a cop ever showed up down here, it was because there'd been a bloodbath.

Which, in light of his current mission, was probably a good thing.

He lit another cigarette.

Donny arrived ten minutes early to the meet. He killed the engine of the Porsche and pocketed the keys. It wouldn't do to have the car 'jacked while he waited.

He stepped out and took a look around the place that felt both familiar and threatening. The smell of cement, dirt, and urine assaulted him. Anything could happen in this deserted underbelly of Denver. If his contact, whatever his name was, decided to kill him and take the girl there would be nothing he could do about it. All Donny could count on, right now, was that maybe this guy might think they could do business in the future, which had held true so far.

And of course he was counting on the cash that would soon be his.

He'd never before considered where the girls he'd handed off had gone, but somehow Alexis had gotten to him. At least a little. He wondered where she would wake up tomorrow. Then he closed the door on those thoughts. They weren't doing him any favors.

The others he'd sold had been cows. Almost literally. There'd been nothing to them. Vapid. Scared. Stupid. Absolutely no awareness of what was happening to them. They'd been easy. How many? Four? Five? He couldn't be sure. The most he'd been paid was a thousand bucks. The least was his first one. He'd pocketed a fifty and immediately blown it, ironically, on a prostitute.

Alexis, with her attitude, had given him a challenge. A challenge he was happy to meet (and get paid for) but also a challenge that made him wonder if he should reconsider his options. If maybe waiting four years wouldn't be worth it.

He decided no. He could pluck girls like Alexis from expensive fitness studios or off the streets whenever he felt like it. In all likelihood she wouldn't have come to him, even at twenty-one, without a lot of legal crap designed to keep the money in the family. He was doing the right thing.

Donny heard the echo of the van's engine before he saw it. As it had previously, the van moved slowly down the other side of the viaduct. He leaned against the car and watched, knowing he was being watched as well. About a hundred yards away, the van turned left onto an intersecting street and then left again to work its way toward him. The driver killed the headlights but kept up a slow and steady crawl in his direction.

After it stopped, a large hooded man emerged from the passenger side of the van. He kept the door open between him and Donny while he stuffed something in his waistband, presumably a gun. Donny resisted reaching for the small of his back to touch his own weapon.

Not willing to make the first move, Donny waited. As he was shaking another cigarette out of the pack, the man stepped away from the van door, leaving it open.

"Need a light?" the man asked. His walk was all smoothness covering up both caution and a twitchiness Donny could pick up only from the fingers of the man's left hand drumming against his thigh.

"Thanks." Donny leaned into the flame.

"Give me your weapons."

"Wha—"

"Now. I don't know how the guy before me worked, but I want this to go without incident." The man's gray-blue eyes shone in the dimness like two high-beamed flashlights. "I promise, I'll give them back to you when we're finished here."

"But I don't—"

Before Donny could finish his sentence, the man spun him around against the Porsche and produced the gun from his waistband. Both of his arms were pinned with one meaty fist, and Donny thought his shoulder might be sprained, or worse. An efficient pat down didn't turn up anything else and Donny was released.

"Did you bring our package?"

Donny reached up and grabbed his shoulder. "I did."

"Condition?"

"Out of it."

"Out of it how, pretty boy?"

"Roofie."

"At least you're smart about something." He signaled the van and two more men slipped out of the sliding side door. One of them carried a large envelope.

"Let's make this quick. I assume she's in the trunk?"

Donny felt his face flash with heat. "She's in the backseat."

The large man laughed. "Well, for what you're getting paid, it's best not to turn over damaged merchandise."

The man not holding the envelope opened the door to the backseat and nodded before hauling Alexis out like a bag of dirty gym clothes. Donny felt himself flinch when her feet slapped to the pavement. Then the money man shoved the envelope into his chest before helping carry the dead weight of the girl to the back of the van.

"We'll see you again," the big man said as he handed Donny his gun. "And if this one turns out to be as lucrative as we think, we might be back with a special order. You'll be hearing from us."

Less than five seconds later the van was gone.

Donny kneeled outside the driver's door and pulled his thoughts together. A few minutes ago he thought he was dead. He figured he earned every dollar tonight. The dudes in this business were getting rougher. And the whole gun thing. If that hadn't happened his shoulder would be fine and he wouldn't have to think of an explanation for work tomorrow.

Suddenly that was the least of his worries. He cursed himself for not checking to make sure he had the money before the men and the van split with the cargo. Sliding into the driver's seat, he tore open the envelope. A quick perusal settled his mind.

He'd been paid.

He started the engine of the Porsche. While he would love to drive the magnificent car for a few days, he knew he needed to ditch it. One of the long-term parking lots outside of Denver International Airport would be perfect.

An estimated 200,000-300,000 adolescents are at risk in the US each year.
—Girls Like Us, *by Rachel Lloyd*

CHAPTER SIX

ALEXIS

What's happening? I groan.

Noise. Not from me. Sandpaper on my face. Can't lift my head. Nothing is right. Worst hangover ever.

I gag from the smell. BO, vomit, shit. Bleach. Smells like fear.

Where am I? This isn't right.

"Alexis." A woman's voice.

A hand on my shoulder, gently trying to wake me up. I'm not falling for it.

"Alexis Emily Halston, come on girl. It's okay. Wake up."

Something is whispering inside my head. *Be terrified. Terrified. Terrified.*

I push the hand away. Well, I try to. My coordination is off.

"'s th' fu'?" My tongue is twelve-feet thick.

"There's my girl. You're coming 'round. That's what I want to see."

See. Open eyes. Bunk beds. Metal bunk beds. Cement walls and floors. No windows. Screaming loud. Someone in another bunk. Three people here. Sounds like a dozen. Head pounding like a bitch.

Wait. Where's Donny? I try to lift my head that feels like a glob of granite and get nowhere. I close my eyes. Maybe this is a weird dream because Donny and I had a fight.

Sleep. That's what I need. *Sleep.*

* * *

The fuzzy bits of my brain are clearing. I can hear people talking. I'm pretty sure they're talking about me.

"She's fine. She exhibited an attempt at responsiveness earlier. A few more minutes should be enough for the drug to wear off."

"She has to get mobile. And pulled together. Buyers want to take a look in twenty-four hours. Could be a bidding war on this one."

"My usual cut?"

"If you have her ready in time."

"She'll be ready."

Before I can process this and understand what it means, another voice propels these words to the back of my mind. Someone is panicked. Afraid. A boy.

"No! No! You can't do this!"

A slap and the sound of a body slamming into something hard. It's all I can do to keep my eyes shut. Even if I open them there's nothing I can do.

"We can do whatever the fuck we want, you little shit. The sooner you learn that lesson, the sooner you'll get over your bruises."

The voice was breathy and rough. No accent. Hell, he even sounds a little like Mr. Larson, my algebra teacher from junior high.

What's going on?

"Here's your choice," the man with the raspy voice continued. "You can either be a pretty boy or do manual labor. Stay fresh and clean or give up bathing and privacy permanently. I'm willing to give you a try as a pretty boy because I can make more money off you. But don't confuse me with someone who gives a flying fuck. The minute you don't meet quota, whatever quota I set, I'll sell you off so fast the smell of Dial soap will be a distant memory inside a week. Either way you're gonna end up fucking assholes. Up to you, whether they're assholes in the city or in some fuckin' field."

Shit. Am I next? Not here. Not me. This can't be right.

And why me? I don't even hang out in the part of town where this might happen. So *not* Alexis Halston.

Relief and surprise flood me when I realize I'm still fully clothed. They haven't even removed my shoes. I push up from the cactus-blanket and swing my legs to the floor. A wave of dizziness crashes through my head and slams into my bones. I think if I don't lie back down I'm going to hurl. I steady myself. Breathe normally.

A door, twenty feet away. Gotta get out of here.

No one's watching. I stand and immediately want to barf. Be strong. The door's right there. No way I'm going to stay in this stink hole another minute.

I inch toward escape using the wall as support. I can do this. I have to do this.

"Where do you think you're going?" A well-muscled guy in a taut t-shirt stands between me and freedom.

"There's been a mistake."

He grins, showing perfect white teeth. He's clean. I bet he even smells nice. Not like the rest of the people here, myself included.

I try again. "Look at me. I know I'm a mess, but do I look like I belong here?"

He's still grinning.

"I can make it worth your while. I have money."

"Let me see it."

"I don't... I don't..." I feel a tear roll down my face. *Shit.*

My back against the wall, I sink to the floor. Bright Smile is laughing out loud.

I'm in trouble.

It's become more lucrative and much safer to sell malleable teens than drugs or guns.
—*Sex Trafficking of Americans: The Girl Next Door*

CHAPTER SEVEN

Present Day

Cade slipped off her jacket, tied it around her waist, then closed her eyes. Turning her face toward the morning sun, she reveled in the gentle warmth that awakened her spirit to the day. She rotated slightly and opened her eyes.

The scene before her took her breath away.

As much as she loved Louisiana, these Colorado mountains stirred her soul. At once, they called to her inner strong adventurer and illuminated her insignificance. They beckoned her to discover their sweet beauty and recognize their capacity for violence. Nature lived in both Louisiana and Colorado, but in Colorado it seemed bigger, more vibrant.

It was almost eight o'clock. Her morning habit was to take a hike whenever weather permitted. She began the walk back to Mex's home. Constructing the house had been the dream of Mex and his late wife, Maria. Mex had survived the horror of murder—his family's murders—in part by building it. A fabulous property, every inch boasted views and quality and craftsmanship, as well as sadness and loss and a dream forever dead.

Back at the house she busied herself in the kitchen and decided it would be a fine morning for mimosas. She checked the fridge. No champagne. There were two more possibilities. The wine cellar in the walkout level or Mex's office refrigerator. The office was closer.

When Cade walked into the room, Mex's cellphone was vibrating on his desk. By the time she got to it, the phone had gone silent. She opened the small refrigerator and extracted a bottle of champagne. As she left the office, she grabbed the phone and looked at it.

Fourteen missed calls. All but one were from the same number. Someone with a Denver area code wanted to get in touch with Mex Anderson. Badly.

Cade put the phone near Mex's favorite place to sit in the kitchen. He loved the views from this room. Who wouldn't? Floor to ceiling windows that looked out on everything the high country had to offer. Wildlife, mountains, blue skies.

She inserted a pod of bold coffee into the Nespresso machine and stood back to receive the first fragrant burst of heaven. After the coffee finished brewing, she emptied the full capsule container into the recycle bag, added warm cream, then settled in to wait for Mex. If there was an emergency, and with thirteen calls an emergency was a good bet, mimosas might not be appropriate. An emergency also meant Mex could use a few minutes to enjoy a bit more of the morning. Cade didn't know exactly when she'd become this protective, but she had.

Mex walked in to the kitchen. "Enjoy your walk?"

"Always."

She waited for him to make his coffee selection. The tough guy tended to like a lighter coffee choice and she loved to tease him.

When he sat down, she barely glanced in his direction. "Think maybe that's got too much kick, Kemo Sabe? Don't want you overdoing it or anything."

"Watch it, woman. This helps me stay calm and in control. You don't want me amping the meter."

Cade laughed. She loved everything about this man. Except maybe his house. The house was Mex Anderson's Taj Mahal, and Cade felt Maria's presence everywhere. "I was going to make mimosas, but those might have to wait."

"For what?" He waggled his brows. "Do you have something in mind that involves heavy breathing?"

"You wish." She flicked a finger toward his phone. "I think you should see who's been trying to get hold of you. If it's your other girlfriend, tell her I'm on to her and her hours are numbered."

Mex keyed in his voicemail number and put it on speaker. "Just in case you're even half-way serious."

The flight attendant's instincts told her something bad was happening on that airplane. [Shelia] Fedrick says she was able to tell the teenage girl to go to the bathroom, where she had left the girl a note. The teenager responded on the back of the note: "I need help."... The group Airline Ambassadors is hoping to train more flight attendants to be as vigilant as Shelia Fedrick was on that 2011 flight. The nonprofit is training flight crew to spot signs of human trafficking, like passengers who appear scared or drugged, have visible bruises, or aren't allowed to speak for themselves, NBC News reports.—Flight attendant says she saved girl from human trafficking with a secret note, by Alex Martichoux,

San Francisco Chronicle, *updated February 6, 2017*

CHAPTER EIGHT

The first voicemail spilled into the sanctuary of the kitchen. "Mr. Anderson, my name is Steven Halston. My daughter has been missing for three days and I want to hire you to find her. Call me as soon as possible." He sounded like a businessman calling to discuss a fine point in a contract negotiation.

The tone in the next message, roughly one hour later, was slightly more stressed. "Look, Mr. Anderson. I can pay you whatever you want. You found that drug cartel girl, and my missing daughter can't possibly be more difficult to locate. Call me."

Mex skipped to the last recorded communication, expecting to hear that the wayward daughter had turned up and that he should ignore all the previous messages. Something like, "I'm so embarrassed, blah blah blah. Please disregard everything. I'm sorry. I look forward to running into you on the golf course one day."

Instead, he heard sobbing. "Please. They found her car." The next bit was unintelligible. Then, "I know I've been a lousy father, but she shouldn't have to pay for that."

Mex disconnected and sat the phone back on the counter. He looked out the window, lost in a father's pain.

Cade slipped a warm poppy seed muffin in front of him. "You're gonna need your strength, and this is all we have available at the moment."

Mex shook his head. "Damn." He pushed the phone away.

"What are you doing? Why aren't you calling him back?" Cade sat next to him, her entire body on high alert.

"I can't do this again."

"Bullshit."

"She's just another runaway."

"You won't know until you meet with the man," Cade said. "And you won't be able to live with yourself if you don't."

"Fuck," Mex said as he reached for his phone.

* * *

"Hey, it's me," Mex said when Darius picked up. "I need you to get me everything you can on a guy named Steven Halston. He's the father of a missing teenage girl. I've talked to him and think he's legit. You've got a contact in the Greenwood Village PD, don't you? Can you contact him to get us up to speed on the case?"

"Hi, I'm fine. Thanks for asking. And you?"

Mex rolled his eyes. "Sorry. I'm also fine. Did you notice that tomatoes were on sale at City Market and isn't the weather wonderful?"

Darius chuckled. "My Greenwood PD contact moved to Chicago."

"You got someone else?"

"Easily done. What's up?"

"I don't know. Maybe nothing. Feel like a trip to Denver with Cade and me?"

"Like old times, huh? When are you leaving?"

"In about thirty minutes."

"Wish I could, buddy, but I'm heading out tonight for a two-day signing stint in California."

"Do you have time to check on Halston for me?"

"No problem. Give me fifteen. The Greenwood PD info might take longer. Give me the details."

While Mex told him what he knew about the missing girl between bites of poppy seed muffin, he made himself another coffee. Cade signaled from the hallway asking if he wanted to take an unopened bottle of his meds with him. He nodded and then answered another question from the journalist turned true crime writer.

Fifteen minutes later Mex received an email from Darius. Steven Halston was the managing partner of Halston & Barrow, an international law firm with offices in fifty cities including Dubai, Milan, Hong Kong, and Singapore. Mex wondered why Halston would choose to live in Denver, but it didn't take long to get his answer. At least in part, Steven Halston liked being a very big fish in a medium-sized pond. His name was associated with at least seven boards of major corporations headquartered in Denver, and linked prominently with the same people over and over again who all appeared frequently in the society pages for their philanthropic gestures.

Halston's twenty-fifth wedding anniversary was a big enough story to warrant a full-page spread in *The Denver Post*. Mex wondered if the law firm had paid for the coverage as a soft-sell piece. He looked for more information on Adele Halston but the pickings were meager. There were a few photos of her at charity events in which she looked disconnected and bored. Mex felt an immediate sympathy for the sad Mrs. Halston. He didn't see any mention of children.

Mex sent a return email to Darius, thanking him for the information and asking for more on the wife.

Cade had made reservations at the Ritz-Carlton. They would have everything they needed from the parents this afternoon so there was no reason to book more than one night. They'd have dinner at Elway's. Mex could already taste the steak.

"C'mon, Cowboy. Let's hit the road," Cade called as she walked out the door to the garage.

Mex followed and tossed his gear in the back of the black Range Rover.

They were forty minutes into the four-hour drive when Mex's phone rang. He hit the Bluetooth button and the jazz they'd been listening to was replaced by Darius's resonant voice.

"Adele Halston is just this side of a ghost, my friend. She was active and social her entire life as a debutante, and for a few years after she married Steven. There were reports that she was pregnant, even a fuzzy picture of her at a garden party with a child on her lap, then nothing."

"I can't use nothing," Mex said.

"Nor will you have to."

Mex knew his friend. "What do you want?"

"If this is another epic kidnapping, I want in."

"So you can write another book that will make you money at the same time it makes me miserable?"

"Yep."

Mex sighed. "Tell me what you've got."

"Alexis was not the Halston's first child. Samuel Halston, named after Steven's father, was kidnapped when he was three years old from the Wash Park ice rink, which is near where the young couple were living at the time."

Mex reached out to grab Cade's hand. "I'm betting there wasn't a happy ending."

"The boy's body was found a week later. He'd been sodomized and murdered."

"He was fucking three." Mex could barely press the words out.

"Yeah, Mex. He was."

Silence filled the Rover. Then he felt the loss. And the guilt. Antonio.

Darius's soft voice gently shoved the silence into a corner. "You know I would've told you anyway."

"I know."

*There were 8,042 reported cases of human trafficking in the United States last year—the most ever, according to a report released last week by the nonprofit organization Polaris. Most of those came through calls to the National Human Trafficking Hotline **[1-888-373-7888]**, which was established by the federal government in December 2007 and is operated by Polaris in a public-private partnership.—Flight Attendants Fight Human Trafficking With Eyes in the Sky, by Jacey Fortin,*
    for The New York Times, *February 7, 2017*

CHAPTER NINE

Two Days Ago

ALEXIS

I took a shower earlier. Is it morning? Not possible to tell in this windowless prison. They gave me makeup but it's used. I get that now's not the time to be bitchy. Now's the time to play along. To figure out where the hell I stand. But still.

A guy is here with a camera. Are you kidding me? He centers me in front of a sheet that's been strung against one of the cement walls.

"Look," he says, "I'm not looking for *Vogue* or *People* or even a driver's license photo."

He shoves me against the wall. A creepy smile plays on his lips, sending a shiver down my spine. "I need to prove you haven't been hurt. That you're good to go."

For a split second I imagine bashing my head into that white sheet, coming away bloody and battered, but I know it wouldn't matter. I'm either screwed as "good to go" or I'm screwed to suffer another form of humiliation.

I think about Donny and then blow his lying face out of my thoughts. If I ever get out of this, Donny will be the first person I look up on my revenge list.

When I was in the shower I fantasized. I go all kung-fu (no idea where that came from) and escape this horror show. I could've gone to the cops, but instead I track down Donny. He opens the door to his apartment and the expression on his face when he sees me is priceless. The only question I have is whether I'll kick the shit out of him or sell him into the same place he sold me. One would give me immediate gratification; the other would take time but be pure justice.

The flash goes off. Once. Twice. Three times. After the last flash, the photographer gives a nod to one of the guards, then leers at me. I can't move.

"I agreed to take my payment in pussy."

The guard hauls me behind a cheap curtain. This is not my cue to resist. "Any noise from you and you'll wish you didn't have a throat." He throws me down onto a floor mat in the corner and I back into it for a weird sense of security.

I consider what the photographer has at stake, so when he comes in, drops his pants and begins to come down on top of me, I pull my leg back and kick him in the nuts as hard as I can. When he's done screaming I lean into him and say, "If I'm not 'good to go' asshole, you'll be running for your useless life. I suggest you sit back and be thankful you still have one."

The photographer draws his fist back and strikes a blow to my upper chest, a second punch to my side. "Some things are more important than others, bitch. You'd best learn your lesson." He continues with his punishing blows.

Terrified. I'm aware I'd blacked out. For how long?

He's gone.

Terrified.

My chest burns with every breath. I move my legs, my arms, testing for pain. While everything hurts, there's no sharp pain indicating a break, nothing that indicates I was raped.

Is this what my life has become? Pain and fear and survival?

My parents can't help me now. Money can't help me now. I've gone down the rabbit hole. Whatever made sense before no longer does.

How long has it been? I have no idea.

These people, whoever they are, are trying to break me, and the only way I can think to survive is to treat it like a game. A game that I will not lose. A covering of fear and anger and determination descends on me.

I struggle to stand, the burning in my lungs makes me want to hurl. A hand reaches through the curtain and forces it open. Three more girls are shoved in with me. No one seems to notice the photographer as he leaves.

The man who'd brought the other girls looks at me. He points his finger. "You. Come now."

If he would have simply walked me down the hallway to the staging area, we might have been okay. But the creep had to try and haul me. By the time we arrived, he was bleeding and I was pissed. Not my fault.

Bright lights flood my eyes. Beyond the blinding white, there are people. I can smell sweat competing with cologne. I've gone from pissed to full-blown angry. A moment later, sounds register. I'm being auctioned. Oh, God, how did I get here?

People were bidding. Like slavery days. Only it's today.

And they're bidding on me.

There can be no keener revelation of a society's soul than the way it treats its children.
—*Nelson Mandela*

CHAPTER TEN

Mex took a sip of coffee and placed his travel mug back in the holder. He and Cade were just outside the Golden area, west of Denver. They had another thirty minutes or so, depending on traffic, to get downtown to the Ritz. Their drive had been mostly quiet with a mix of blues and jazz for company, allowing each of them to reflect. Madeleine Peyroux played softly in the background.

Mex touched the steering wheel button to turn off the music.

"I love her," Cade complained.

"I want to talk before we get to Denver."

"I'm listening to you. Exclusively. But I could probably listen to Madeleine too."

"Odds are this is some kind of ransom play," Mex ignored her. "Daddy's got the money and they've got the kid."

"Maybe, but why hasn't he heard from someone? That doesn't feel right. It's been too long. Kidnappers who are looking for a payoff tend to act before worried parents can even think about contacting the authorities."

"So if it's not ransom, what?"

"Could be she was looking for a home. A place to belong. Get some answers, ya know?" Cade's voice grew stronger. "Could be we find out her home life sucked and suddenly there was a guy who made her feel treasured and promised her some kind of spiritual family. Enlightenment. At the very least people who appreciated her."

"A cult."

"Yeah, why not?"

"Why?" Mex asked. "What's their end-game?"

"Does Alexis have her own money or at least access to some?"

"Not that I know of. But it's worth looking into."

"I bet she has at least one credit card with a sweet limit."

"Okay, okay. Point taken. I'll ask." Mex shook his head.

"What? What's wrong with this angle?" Cade asked.

"Let's say she has a couple credit cards. Really? That's gonna make it worth the risk? It's all too easy to track unless they kill her and take off."

"That's not the way it works. They'll access what cash they can with the cards and then determine what other assets are in her name they can sell. Finally they'll appeal to Mommy and Daddy."

"And when that's over?"

"They'll find ways to use her," Cade reached for a piece of muffin from the bag sitting between them. "Does she have any special skills?"

"Not that I know of."

"We need to find out. Most cults are self-sustaining operations. She's too pretty to put to work in the fields, and I'd bet she knows how to clean about as well as I know how to man a rocket, but she could work in the office or something else. In fact, they'd probably use her first to see if she could recruit any of her friends. She has a nice face for promotional material."

"Okay," Mex picked up his mug and drained it. "There's still a lot we need to find out."

"When you're right, you're right." Cade turned the music back on.

They passed the 6th Avenue exit and Cade looked over at Mex. "What if it's none of the things we're used to dealing with? We're already pretty sure she didn't run away. But what if she wasn't kidnapped? What if she didn't join a cult?"

"Mr. Anderson, does your new case have anything to do with the girl you rescued last year?" The reporter shoved a microphone toward his face. The trees and flowers in the center of Denver's 16th Street Mall provided colorful background to the news bite.

He really wanted to call the reporter an idiot but reluctantly decided that wouldn't get him anywhere. "This case is totally separate. A young American girl is missing. Neither she nor her family have anything to do with Mexican drug cartels." He looked into the camera. "If you have any information that could help bring Alexis Halston home to her family, please notify the authorities at the number showing on your screen, or call me at 970-555-9786."

Mex had agreed to this news conference in Denver because he knew it could help the case. He also knew he'd get a slew of crap calls, but that was part of the job. Cade would help him sift through the messages from people who were only seeking attention. He also couldn't help thinking about the three-year-old boy Steven and Adele Halston had already lost. The connection to his own lost family seared his heart.

He'd been there. The memory whispered to him. He wanted to shut down and disappear. Instead he pried the whisper away with the promise to revisit it again later, when he had time to feel. When he had time to cry. When he had time to lose time.

"You were perfect." Cade hugged his arm as they walked away from the cameras and the talking heads.

"You know you're gonna have to help me field the crazies."

"A given."

"It seems to me I promised you fantastic Italian food."

"Also a given."

Twenty minutes later the pair was in a booth at Nonna's, a wonderful restaurant in an unassuming strip center at Leetsdale and Monaco.

"It's been a while, Mister," the waitress said to Mex.

"Not so long you forgot me, Patty."

"Not ever likely." She took their wine order and a starter of calamari then moved to take care of diners at another table.

While they waited Mex's phone buzzed. The call-ins were starting. He glanced at the numbers, but none were familiar. He and Cade would sort through them either tonight or tomorrow. While he knew one tip could make a difference in an investigation, he always felt like a puppet on parade at news conferences. Asking the crazies to contact him. Hoping for that one solid lead. Mex tamped down his hopes.

Patty uncorked their Primitivo and poured a sample for Mex. He took a sip then handed the glass to Cade. "What do you think?"

Cade smiled, took a sip. "Tastes good to me."

Three minutes later, dipping into the calamari, Mex's phone buzzed again. This time the number looked familiar. He scrolled through his missed calls to see multiple attempts from one source. He looked at Cade, shrugged, and took the call.

"Oh my God, is it you?"

"This is Mex Anderson. Do you have information for me relating to the Alexis Halston disappearance?"

"No, but I—"

"I'm sorry. I really don't have time to—"

"Wait! My daughter's missing too. And no one is paying attention."

"How do you know your missing daughter has anything to do with Alexis Halston?"

"I don't. 'Cept neither of them should ever've gone missing."

Mex glanced at Cade. Today, her green eyes were smudged with enough brown to make them smoky. They were watching him intently, willing him to do the right thing. And she'd only heard his side of the conversation. Even if he hadn't been inclined to continue, there was no way he could shrug this mother off when Cade was looking at him that way.

He signaled Patty. "Do you have somewhere we can have a private conversation?"

The waitress nodded and ushered them to the owner's office.

Once inside, Mex hit the speaker button. "Listening with me is Acadia LeBlanc, my partner. She may have questions for you as we proceed. If we believe we might be able to help, we'll meet personally." Mex reached for some paper and a pen. "Tell me about your daughter. Why shouldn't she have gone missing?"

When they finished, Mex clicked off his phone and laid down his pen. "What do you think?"

"I hate what I'm thinking," Cade said.

"Probably the same thing I am, but you go first."

"On the surface, we have two girls from completely different backgrounds. Alexis comes from an affluent two-parent family who live in what's considered a better part of town. And she's learned to manage independently when her parents don't have time for her. Jayla lives in affordable housing with her struggling mom and siblings from different fathers, and they've all learned to manage independently when Mom entertains at home. No connection, right?"

Mex nodded.

"But when you look closer," Cade's voice warmed to her topic, "when you look closer, they are totally similar. Two young people who feel disconnected. We know that Alexis's father is never home, always away on business. And don't tell me you haven't been able to intuit that her mom has issues of her own, issues that create a distance between her and her daughter. Drugs? Alcohol? Both? It's there." She paused and looked at Mex.

Again, Mex nodded.

"Jayla's family is as dysfunctional as Alexis's. Mom is worried about both money and men. Neither of these girls had an anchored home life strong enough to give them confidence to pay attention to their instincts when something or someone around them wasn't right."

Mex picked up his pen and scribbled. "Where are you going with this?"

"Same place you are." Cade shook her head. "We've got two girls whose lives might not be perfect, but who had no reason to bolt. Alexis Halston had privilege and position. Her parents might suck, but leaving them would mean leaving her meal ticket. Unless we learn something contrary to everything we know so far, she's not walking away from her family's financial support. Do you agree?"

"Yeah."

"And Jayla Thomas, also lacking a qualified parent, was doing well in school. She had hope for her future. She had challenges, but she was coping. Agree?"

"Yeah."

"So what do you have when young girls go missing involuntarily and there's been no ransom demand?" Cade looked at Mex. She waited until his eyes met hers. "What you have is a different kind of abduction. Trafficking."

"I was afraid you'd say that."

"So what do we do?"

"Let me think a minute." Mex got up and peeked out the office door. He caught Patty's attention and asked her to bring him a double bourbon. "This is gonna get tricky."

"Yeah. So what do we do?" Cade repeated.

"We need Darius to get into the trafficking system. Know the game. Know the players. And we're gonna need to get in fast."

"You told me he was leaving to sign books in California or somewhere."

"Never mind that. He'll want this next book. Leave him to me."

* * *

"Hey, man. I can't just up and leave," Darius said in his soft bass. "I'm contractually obligated."

"Your publisher is lucky to have you. You were doing fine on your own. Tell your publisher this is a one-time shot, and give them a first right of refusal on the new book. You want to be here because things are unfolding and you'll be at the center of the information."

"Big?"

"Big."

"I'll call you back."

Mex hung up the phone and paced. He hated it when the star in a movie had a "gut" feeling. It seemed like a weak way to work the plot. But now, his gut was singing. The disappearance of the girl from one of the wealthiest parts of town was related to the disappearance of the girl from one of the poorest. The connection between the two is that neither girl appears to have left voluntarily.

"C'mon, Mex. Let's go back to our table and order," Cade said.

Patty returned the calamari she'd kept warm in the kitchen. "You guys take the longest time to make up your minds about what you want to order."

Cade laughed while Mex looked at his cell, willing it to ring.

"We'll have two of the salmon," Cade decided for them. "Don't fuss with me, Mex Anderson. You should eat more fish." She looked at Patty. "And more bread, please."

Mex's phone rang. "Yeah, Darius. Are you in?"

"I'm in."

Mex smiled when he heard the excitement in his friend's voice.

"What's next?" Darius asked.

"Get the new contact with Greenwood PD immediately and exercise your DPD muscle. We've got another missing girl and need to know everything there is to know about trafficking in Denver."

"I hope you mean the human kind rather than the car kind. My publisher wouldn't be too happy to yank me out of book signings for a traffic report."

"I do. But I'm tellin' you Darius, by the time we're finished, you might wish for the car story." Mex took a sip of wine. "Get down to Denver. Tonight. Cade and I are at the Ritz-Carlton. We'll book a room for you, the one adjoining ours if we can. Tomorrow we're meeting with the mom of the other missing girl, and I want your eyes and ears there with us."

Mex was about to end the call when Cade got his attention. "Oh, yeah. How are your wife and the new baby doing?"

Cade rubbed her ear and smiled.

"We're all doing fine. Pamela's mom is here to help because of my book signing trip. She'll probably be glad to have me out of her hair for longer than a few days."

"Okay. Get here. Get as much sleep as you can. I'll want to get an early start, but I also want you on top of things. Breakfast at seven?"

"Can we make it eight? I probably won't hit the hotel until two or three in the morning. Explaining things to Pamela could take a bit. She's into these book signing gigs, even if she isn't actually there. In her mind she's got every book I sign as adding so much cash to pay for three college tuitions. And I want to make a few calls before I leave. With luck, I'll receive relevant intel overnight."

* * *

"PJ, honey," Darius said, "it's not like I'm losing any sales. Well, maybe a few. But not enough to cut seriously into our budget."

"But you were supposed to be there. Signing books. Not tagging along with Mex again."

"You forget, tagging along with Mex is what created the book I'm signing in the first place. Tagging along with Mex is what has gotten us this far, and what might give us the next income producer. And baby, two income producers are better than one."

"Does it really matter what I think? You've made up your mind."

Darius dipped his head before meeting his wife's eyes. "Yeah, I guess I have. But if you insist, I can make a couple of phone calls and everything will be back on schedule." He grabbed his wife's hands. "Up to you, PJ. I'm ready to do whatever you want me to do."

Pamela tugged her hands away and hugged her waist.

Darius waited. Hoping against hope, but ready to make sure the love of his life remained happy.

"Do you know one of the reasons I married you, Darius Johnson?"

"Other than you were madly in love with me? That you couldn't get enough of my sexy self? That you couldn't live without me? And we could do the PJ-DJ thing?"

"Other than those, one of the reasons was because when you were committed to something, when your moral compass stood solidly in one direction, you were fearless. Nothing else mattered." She grabbed his hands. "And I'll be damned if I make you reconsider your heart. You tell Mex he owes me. Again."

"You're okay then?"

"Yeah. I'm okay. Unless you get killed. Then I'll be pissed and there'll be hell to pay."

Darius grabbed her face and kissed her. Hard. "Have I told you lately that I love you?"

"Not enough."

As he reached the door, she called him back. He knelt beside her, certain she'd changed her mind. Instead, the woman of his dreams whispered, "Don't say a word to Mama. She pretty much thinks you're a shit for going to a couple of book events in California. She doesn't have to know anything about this."

Darius kissed her again. "I agree. Mum's the mama-word."

The state capital is the nation's bull's-eye: one long day's drive to Juarez or Saskatchewan; 10 tedious hours on the Great Plains to Kansas City, Mo.; 13 brutal hours across the desert to Phoenix. Denver is a convenient hub for the comings and goings of kids indentured to magazine sales crews or migrant farm workers in bondage to debt.

—*Moving in the Right Direction, by Leslie Petrovski, January 30, 2014*

CHAPTER ELEVEN

Greenwood Village was a high-end community in the metro area. Located south of the City and County of Denver, it boasted upscale businesses and expensive residential areas. The zip code itself could take a boring, old tract home and put it out of reach of most buyers.

The police department had fewer than ninety employees, including administrative staff, and only two of them were minorities. While the department might work in an affluent and relatively crime-free area, every employee took their job seriously.

Detective Les Franklin, one of the minorities, copied information from the Alexis Halston incident board to a notebook. Right now there was only one board and it was pretty empty. They were three days in and scratching for anything that could turn into a lead. By the end, there would be multiple boards, and there would be no way to copy the data because there would be too much information thrown up in sloppy handwriting and cryptic shorthand. Sometimes the simple act of transferring details of a case onto paper gave him ideas to explore. He needed ideas on this one. The pressure to get fast answers was enough to create brain-freeze.

An hour ago his commander called and told him to switch on the news. Steven Halston had brought a PI into the case. Franklin wanted to check out this Mex Anderson character. He found some PIs easy to work with, assets even, but a lot of the privates felt they needed to earn their fees. Ultimately they got in the way, bungled evidence and jeopardized not only the legal case, but sometimes even the prospect of finding whoever or whatever they were looking for to begin with.

The detective closed his notebook and booted up his computer. Did Mex Anderson have any inkling of how law enforcement worked?

Thirty minutes later he'd learned about Mex's law enforcement life in Mexico, how he'd refused the cartel bribes and lost his family as a result. There was more meat to the stories about Anderson tracking down the missing daughter of a drug cartel leader. Franklin searched in vain for a connection between the murders of Anderson's family and the drug lord he helped, but he found nothing, and finally ordered a copy of the book written by Darius Johnson about the rescue. *Murdered Family, Missing Girl* seemed to be selling well and had some good reviews.

It looked like this Mex Anderson might be one of the asset PIs. Les Franklin would give the ex-cop a few days to make contact. He had a few things to follow-up so it wasn't like he'd be losing a lot of time. In a couple of days, if he didn't have anything more to go on, he'd reach out.

One cop to another.

The defendant was chewing on her finger, had her hair pulled back into a tiny pigtail, and spoke in a high-pitched voice. She was 10.

—Selling Atlanta's children: What has and hasn't changed, by Jane O. Hansen, Special to CNN

CHAPTER TWELVE

JAYLA

"You. Cherie! Get in the van. Don't worry about your shit. We've got supplies."

I hate that name. *Cherie*. Like I'm some kind of French cherry. I laugh to myself. It's a sick laugh that makes me sad. Even when it's all in my head.

Inside the van are five other girls and two boys. We're sitting on two long benches facing each other. I have no idea where we're going and I don't even care anymore. It takes about twenty minutes for us to be on our way.

No one looks at anyone. We've learned that melting into the shadows means we might be safe from being used as an example. From a fist making contact with our skull. We're silent, lost in our own memories. Our own pain. Our own fears.

The thing about these road trips is that on one hand, I'm not walking a track, not pacing up and down one piece of street looking for johns. On the other, they give me time to think. Walking I do numb, and the hookups with the customers even more so. It's the thinking that's painful. Or it can be if I get surprised by a random memory.

Highway sounds are rumbling underneath the van. We're moving pretty fast, but I'd lay odds we're not speeding. A window would be nice but too risky. I focus on the sound and imagine the scenery flying by. The road motion is calming and I lose my resolve not to think about anything.

I miss me. I miss Jayla. I put her away a lifetime ago. Ha. Six months. At least I'm pretty sure it's been six months. I've tried to keep track. The best I can say is I put her away shortly after Chris sold me to get out of a gambling debt. Which was a lifetime ago. I forgave Jayla for being so trusting. I for sure won't forgive Cherie if she trusts anyone. That's our understanding.

For a while I'd bring Jayla out when I thought I had a few minutes. I remembered what my life was like. I remembered school and my favorite books. I remembered Mama. My little brother and sisters. Even my dad. Then that got too hard.

To tell the truth, I might never be able to bring Jayla out again. I'm afraid I might not know how to find her. And if I did, what would I say?

I miss Denver too. Haven't been there from almost the beginning. I'm getting how this works. Grab a girl or more than likely, buy her. Then send her someplace where she probably won't run into someone she knows who might be looking for a good time, a teacher or minister or something.

One of the girls is whimpering.

Shit.

If she keeps it up we'll all be punished.

No one is making a move toward her. I stand up, find my balance in the shifting vehicle and signal the boy sitting next to her to make room for me. I put an arm around the crying girl. She's not much younger than me. She's got stringy brown hair and feels about as strong and solid as a baby bird. She continues to sob until I gently close my hand around her arm and give a soft squeeze. "This is new and scary, isn't it?"

Silence. A sniff. Then a tiny nod.

"It was for me too."

A slight stiffening.

"Yeah, really. You want to know how I survive?"

Nothing. But I know she's listening to my every breath right now.

"What's your name? Your real one. Not the one they gave you."

"Karen," she whispered. "My name is Karen."

"Your job right now is to keep Karen safe. Because one of these days Karen, and her life, will be back. You'll be able to put all this behind you." I squeeze her arm again. "Did they give you another name?"

She shakes her head.

"Okay. When anyone asks, your name is Debbie. Debbie is someone who you are not. Debbie is strong. She can handle whatever anyone wants to throw at her. Debbie will help you keep Karen safe."

Oddly, a giggle erupted.

"Did I say something funny?"

"I was thinking of that movie... *Split*? The one with multiple personalities? Am I going crazy?" Another giggle, this one higher pitched.

"Look at me." I edge her back a few inches so our eyes meet. "The difference between you and that movie is that Karen knows exactly what she's doing. And Debbie doesn't require anyone else. You won't go crazy. Trust me. Someday you'll get out of this. Someone will help. And when they do? You can let Debbie go."

I felt the girl's shoulders relax. "Are you better?"

She nodded.

"What's your name?" I asked.

"My name is Debbie."

"You go, strong Debbie. Ask for Cherie if you need me."

She snuggled into my arm. "What's your real name, Cherie?"

"Jayla," I whispered into her ear. "And I'm keeping her safe."

Human trafficking is one of the largest sources of income for organized crime.
— *Human Trafficking Facts & Stats, Force4Compassion*

CHAPTER THIRTEEN

ALEXIS

This time when I wake up I'm on a plane. I have no idea how long I've been on it. I'm sore and I'm scared. Suddenly my life sucks and I don't know how the hell it happened.

Was it only last night I was at Donny's? Or maybe the night before? How long was I out of it?

Someone bought me. Someone actually bought me.

Or, I guess I should say, someone else bought me. Goddamn you, Donny. If it's the last thing I do, you're going to pay for this.

The cabin is dark. No reading lights are on.

Maybe I can talk to a flight attendant? Tell her I'm in trouble?

But why in the world would any of the bad guys put me on a commercial flight where I could do exactly that? Get help.

This sucks.

When I reach to undo my seatbelt a weightlifter is suddenly standing at my side.

"I have to pee."

He moves aside and waits for me to stand, then follows me to the lavatory. And even though I'm scared shitless, I wonder for the umpteenth time why a john on an airplane is called a lavatory. And then, I wonder for the very first time, why it would ever be called a john.

This so sucks. Something twisted is squeezing my heart. Breathing is painful and I'm pretty sure it's for more reasons than getting punched a couple of times.

I look around the small lavatory for a weapon of any kind. There's nothing I can get to.

Macho man escorts me back to my seat, and I look back into the plane. There's no one else here.

I'm the only passenger.

This more than sucks.

I want to ask where we're going, but I don't want to sound whiney. Somehow asking any question at all feels like it would diminish me. We're going where we're going. I'll figure it out when we get there.

My seatbelt secure, I squeeze my eyes closed to keep the threatening tears from overflowing onto my cheeks. I can't fall apart. Not now. Not ever.

That's when the shaking begins. It starts in my hands and rapidly overtakes my whole body. The harder I try to make it stop the worse it gets.

"Here." Macho man thrusts a blanket in my face. I grasp it but it takes a few seconds for me to be able to put it over my shoulders.

I'm fine. I'm fine. I keep telling myself this. Eventually, whether out of the strength of my thoughts or the exhaustion of my body, the shaking subsides.

What happens next? Nothing pleasant.

Selling women and young girls happens in other countries. Not here. Not in my own backyard, my own gym. Not there. I repeat this 'not me' concept until I'm dizzy with denial.

Yet here I am.

Is anyone looking for me? Did Mom come out of her fog and notice I was gone? Did Dad come home and ask where I was?

I don't like the answers that flash in my mind.

I'm on my own.

Swallow. Try to plan.

Treat it like a game. Anticipate your opponent. Plan your move. Stick it to him. Make him pay.

But I've never played this game before. I don't know the rules.

I'm alone and out of my depth.

How the hell can I survive this? With a slam to my gut I realize that's all I want to do. Survive.

God, if you exist, help me keep my shit together. Better yet, rescue me. Now. From this plane. Teleport me or whatever. Or if that's not your plan, help me stay strong. Please, help me. Please, God.

And Donny, God? Don't strike him dead. That's too easy. Whisper in his ear that he's gonna pay. Tell him that you and I have got his number and it's only a matter of time.

There's a change in the plane's pitch. We're descending.

This is what most people imagine the Dark Web to be: an electronic black market where anything is available. And the researchers I spoke with confirm all that—and worse—is available on websites hidden within Tor.

Inside the Dark Web, by Max Eddy, February 4, 2015

CHAPTER FOURTEEN

Mex woke in the middle of the night, pillow soaked, heart pounding. He hadn't been in time. He hadn't been there to save the little boy's life.

But it wasn't young Samuel Halston he'd wanted to save.

Quietly, Mex slipped into the bathroom and dug through his Dopp kit looking for his medication. It wasn't there. He remembered Cade asking if he wanted her to pack it. Why wasn't it—

"Here it is, Cowboy." She handed him the pharmacy bag. "Do you want to talk?"

"Nothin' to talk about. You know the story." He opened the bag and dug out the bottle.

"Oh, *mon cher,* the story is never over. It's part of who you are. It's fluid. And it's never very far from the surface. When there's a trigger, like there was yesterday surrounding that sweet three-year-old boy, the story grows."

Mex filled a glass with water then shook out a pill. Depression sucked, but at least with pharmaceutical help he could function. He swallowed the helpful bit of sanity and sat the glass down on the bathroom counter. He turned toward Cade, tears once again streaming down his face.

Thirty minutes later, completely exhausted, voice hoarse, and soul laid bare yet again, he looked at the woman who graced his life. "What did I do to deserve you?"

"You did nothing to 'deserve' me. Our fates scattered and then magically coalesced. We have this moment, not deserved and not undeserved, to choose whether or not to forge another moment. For now. And maybe tomorrow. It's our choice."

"Woman, do you have to be so damned complicated?"

"Now *that*, Mex Anderson, might be something you deserve."

After a few hours of sleep, Mex and Cade made their way down to the restaurant, expecting to order coffee and have a few minutes before Darius arrived. But there he was, clicking away on a keyboard, a phone to his ear, and a stack of papers next to him.

Mex smiled. The three of them were back in action. If the reason wasn't so goddamn ugly he might feel downright giddy. Must be the meds kicking in.

Darius held up a finger for a split second to acknowledge their arrival before returning to the keyboard.

Mex and Cade slipped into the other side of the booth and waited.

When Darius ended the call he looked at them and said, "I had no fucking idea. Pardon my French."

"The word "fuck" is not French," Cade said.

"Oh, yeah. Sorry about that. No offense meant."

"None taken."

Mex watched the waitress approach. "No fucking idea about what?"

"Two coffees, please," Cade told her. "And three of your best omelets, with hash browns."

"I was thinking pancakes or waffles," Darius said.

"Can't have you sluggish," Cade replied.

"No fucking idea about what?" Mex repeated after the waitress left.

"I had no idea trafficking was such a major issue. Anywhere. I mean *anywhere* in the world. And I had no idea it was a major issue in the U.S. And I had no *fucking* idea that Colorado ranked at the top of the states where it was a problem. Here? Really?"

Darius signaled the waitress.

"Yes sir, what do you need?" The way the woman looked at Darius made Mex think she'd like to give him a telephone number. Hers.

Cade was about to interrupt but Darius cut her off with another raised finger. "A side of pancakes, please." He looked at Cade. "I promise to limit the syrup. Will that help?"

"Minimally."

Mex's phone rang. Steven Halston. Mex answered.

"Are you working on this other missing girl's case?" Steven demanded to know.

"In conjunction with your daughter's. How do you know?"

"I know people and I'm not paying you to find anyone else, Anderson."

"I understand that. But I am not your exclusive agent, and my team will be working both cases. We're on top of things, I assure you."

A cough, then some muffled sounds like someone holding a hand over the phone and talking to someone else. Mex said,

"We're making progress. It won't be overnight, but I promise you I'll do everything I can to bring your daughter home."

"You're right, of course. I apologize. I didn't mean to offend you."

"No offense taken." Mex disconnected the call and turned his attention to Cade, Darius, and the food before him.

They ate their breakfasts while Darius brought them up to date on what he'd learned from his Denver Police Department contact on the Jayla Thomas case.

"There's a mixture of old and new trafficking suspects who, for the moment, have both the DPD and the FBI scrambling to figure out the intel. It looks like a couple of them might be teaming up."

"Pimps teaming up?" Mex asked.

"It doesn't happen often, but it happens."

"Why would they go into partnership?"

"They can save on the expense side of their businesses. Probably get deals on housing and off-the-books medical care. Maybe even legal help."

"What else?" Cade asked.

"In the last six months the two agencies have managed to identify and extract, for want of a better term, four young girls who had been targeted. A lot of it was strong police work, but any one of the officers and agents involved would have also said it was pure damn luck. The grooming process had begun, and two very alert teachers had seen the signs. Three girls were from one school district and one from another."

Darius paused. "And everyone I talked to wondered what kid or kids they might have missed in between the four they saved."

"What do you mean by a teacher seeing the signs?" Cade asked.

"Teachers are being trained to spot things like suddenly nicer clothes. Cleaner hair. Polished fingernails."

"Those things are bad?" Mex asked.

"Not on their own they're not. But overnight? Suddenly? In addition to educating our children, teachers are tasked with protection, social work, law enforcement, and detection. Teachers are asked to step up to the front lines in areas other than instruction."

"That's all informative and interesting, Darius. But how the hell does that help me with my missing girls?" Mex asked.

"Have you heard of the Dark Net or Tor?"

Cade leaned into the table. "Why didn't I think of that before?"

"Think about what? I don't have a clue what Darius is talking about," Mex said.

"Tor was originally developed by the Department of Defense," Cade explained. "Specifically for the Navy, to protect government communications. It's used by other branches of the military, journalists, law enforcement, all of the good guys. It's an anonymous way to seek information on the internet. Which makes it automatically attractive to the bad guys."

"Exactly," Darius said. "And what better way to peruse the world for nefarious things than in an anonymous way? Once you land on the Dark Net through Tor, it's like Google. An electronic black market where everything is available."

"Everything?" Mex asked.

"Everything. From malware to child pornography to murder-for-hire. It's all there. The sites come and go for security reasons, but I'm pretty sure most of their customers don't have loyalty cards."

"And my missing girls?"

"My guess is they're on the internet somewhere. But the sites go up and come down, changing their name and contact information for security. Their customers will always find them. And each of them has hundreds of pictures to wade through."

"I need something faster."

"I'll see what I can do."

Due to the hidden and illegal nature of human trafficking, gathering statistics on the scale of the problem is difficult.
—*Human Trafficking Facts & Stats, Force4Compassion*

CHAPTER FIFTEEN

Mex spent what felt like hours interviewing Alexis's friends. Vapid. Self-centered. Entitled. If he weren't already subject to depression, these kids would have opened the door.

Feeling brain-dead and heavy-hearted about the future of society, at least he came away with a few places Alexis frequented. A clothing store in Boulder, a restaurant in LoHi, and her gym in Greenwood Village. All over the map. While he was tempted to head for the gym because she went there more often, he needed to eliminate the other two locations.

Boulder was out of the way, but apparently Alexis made the trip a couple of times a month. He couldn't ignore it as a possible contact point with an abductor.

He finally found a parking place, a full two blocks away from Cedar and Hyde. The exercise would do him good. That's what everyone told him.

The small shop had an inviting entrance and an atmosphere that, while laid back and casual, screamed expensive. Clothing was racked and stacked between artful and engaging displays. While someone else might have packed the tiny space to its gills with inventory, the person or persons behind Cedar and Hyde had figured out how to balance the feeling of availability with exclusivity.

"Can I help you find something?"

"You have some great items here. I'm gonna have to let my friend know."

"Are you looking for something to surprise her?"

"Well, no. Not really. At least not today. The reason I'm here is to talk to you about one of your customers."

The salesgirl looked at him closely. "You're here about Alexis Halston, aren't you? I've seen the news. It's terrible."

"She would be the one. Her dad hired me to help find her."

"Lexi hasn't been in for a few weeks. But I can tell you there wasn't anything odd about her visits. If there had been, I would've called the police."

"I figured as much."

"Do you have anything to go on? Can you find her?"

"We're doing our best." Mex handed her his card. "Call me if you think of anything, or hear of anything, that might help. Even the slightest piece of information could be important."

Next he headed to the restaurant in LoHi, about a half-hour drive back toward the Denver area. Linger was a new hotspot. Taking over the site of what was once Olinger's Mortuary, the restaurant now served water in formaldehyde bottles and offered Happy Hour specials printed on toe tags. Creative. Apparently their food was in demand too because he'd tried to make reservations for lunch and they were booked. While he would forgo food, he was going to have to crash the busy place, and throw his weight around if necessary. No way he could be subtle doing that. Not a way to win a popularity contest.

Mex drove around the congested LoHi neighborhood looking for a parking spot. Not happening. His mission inside the restaurant was short and sweet so using a valet didn't make a lot of sense, but in the end he didn't have a choice.

"I'll only be a few minutes," Mex said to the young man. "Sorry to trouble you."

"No problem, sir. A ten-minute tip is as welcome as a two-hour one. Maybe even more so."

Mex walked up the ramp to the entrance. The open restaurant was crammed with diners, laughing, eating, drinking. It was all too loud for Mex's taste. A pretty girl behind the front desk looked up. "Are you meeting someone? I'm afraid we don't have anything available right now."

"Do you know this girl?" Mex held up a picture.

"Yeah. That's Alexis. I saw she was missing on the news. She comes in a few times a month with her friends."

"Is there someone who usually waits on her I could talk to?"

"Yeah. We're busy so it might take him a minute, but she always asks for Evan's station. I'll let him know you're here and that it's about Alexis."

Mex passed the minutes waiting by checking out the photographs of the old mortuary. He guessed that in the days when this place was receiving bodies from the morgue and accommodating grieving loved ones, no one really wanted to eat. Goes to show that one weird idea can gain a following.

A young man hurried up to him and stuck out his hand. "Hi. I'm Evan. You're here about Lexi?"

"Her father has hired me to find her. What can you tell me?"

"She pays the bill. And she always adds a sweet tip."

"Anything notable about the last time she was here?"

"Do you think she was taken from here? I can't picture it, man. I just can't picture it."

"Why not?"

"First of all, it was same-old, same-old, ya know? Nothing at all different from the last time she was here. Pretty much the same people, I put the bill on the table, and she paid it."

Mex wasn't surprised the restaurant was a dead-end. His money was on the gym. It was the cop in him that had to eliminate things. Part of him wished he could "go for the gold," but he'd always have doubts if he did. Especially if the gold wasn't solid. Elimination was part of the process and it wasn't like he had a squad to check into everything. One step at a time.

He thanked the waiter for his time.

"I hope you find her. She had style."

Next up, the gym in Greenwood Village.

* * *

"I'd like to talk to the manager," Mex said as he handed the receptionist his card.

The girl didn't bother to look up. "Do you have an appointment?"

"I'd like to talk to whoever's in charge." He gave her his best cop stare. "Now."

The girl looked him in the eye and then tore her gaze away. She visibly shook, put the phone to her ear and dialed. "I think you should come down here. Like now."

"It's been a pleasure," Mex said. "And thank you."

A long twenty-three minutes later a woman approached him. Fit, devoid of makeup and apparently proud of it, she looked like someone who would run an athletic club.

"I'm looking for information regarding one of your members."

"Sorry. Our member records are confidential."

"Have you been watching the news? I've been hired by Steven Halston to look into the disappearance of his daughter, Alexis Halston, a member of this athletic club."

"Oh, yes. I've heard. Terrible, terrible. Please wait here while I contact Mr. Halston and our attorneys. You understand our need to be correct in this, don't you?"

"I know this won't sound polite, but do you understand my need to find this girl? I really don't care about your attorneys."

"Please wait. I won't be long."

Frustrated, Mex mentally punched out at least three bad guys while he once again waited. They were touch-and-go encounters and he hoped he wouldn't have to dream about them tonight.

A man, shirt straining against his muscles, walked toward him and held out his hand. "I'm Chip, one of the owners. I understand you're interested in obtaining information about one of our members?"

"A member whose life might very well be in danger, and whose father could close down this entire facility if I don't get some answers."

"I'm waiting for a callback from our counsel. They're very prompt so it should be—"

The owner's cell rang and he looked at the screen. "Ah, here they are." He accepted the call. "Yes, there's a Mr."—Chip checked the card—"Mex Anderson here who says he's been engaged by Steven Halston regarding the disappearance of his daughter, Alexis."

A pause.

"You have? Yes, I see. No, no problem. Thank you."

The man tucked his phone away and regarded Mex. "It seems that Mr. Halston contacted our attorneys an hour ago authorizing full release of any information in our records relating to him or his daughter."

Mex nodded. "That would be about when I asked him to do it."

"Why didn't you just say so?"

"Would it have made any difference?"

"Probably not."

The owner turned to the receptionist who couldn't disguise her interest in the discussion. "Give Mr. Anderson anything he requests in connection with Alexis Halston. Nothing more."

"If you require anything further, ask the girl to call me." He motioned in the direction of the front desk.

Mex watched as Mr. Tight-Ass walked away. His casual clothes belied his formal speech pattern. Mex knew the type. Insecure and a bully. Hell, sometimes he *was* that type.

He walked up to the desk. "I apologize for my earlier behavior. I tend to get focused on results that might help me keep someone alive, and I forget details like common courtesy. Forgive me?"

"I'm glad someone is trying to find Alexis."

"My name is Mex." He held out his hand. "So, can you help me?"

The young girl slipped her slim hand into his. "I'm Amanda. What do you want to know?"

"How often did Alexis visit the gym?"

"She was a regular, but let me get you her specifics." Amanda's fingers flew over the computer keys. "She doesn't usually come on weekends, but she's here at least four times during the week."

"That's important information, Amanda. Thank you. Does she have friends here that you've noticed?"

The girl blushed and looked down. "Sometimes another member would work out with her, but not very often."

"What are you saying?"

"She could be, um, demanding. Even bitchy. Oh, I'm sorry I said that. I shouldn't say—"

"Your truthfulness might help me save her. Don't be sorry."

Mex waited while Amanda processed his words.

"Did Alexis have a personal trainer?"

"Yes. Yes, she did. She always worked with Donny."

"Is Donny here now?"

A few more keystrokes. "Nope. He's off for the next three days." Amanda looked up at Mex and winked. "Would you like his home address?"

In Georgia in 2000, while children were being arrested, put in jail, and chained like the worst of criminals, the men selling them and having sex with them were rarely arrested.
—*Selling Atlanta's children: What has and hasn't changed, by Jane O. Hansen, Special to CNN*

CHAPTER SIXTEEN

Cade sat in the car in front of Jayla Thomas's apartment building and motioned Mex and Darius to listen. The men exchanged a look. They'd worked together before, so she understood their impatience.

"Here's the thing," Cade said. "Steven Halston got people to listen to him because he has money and influence. While we don't know Mary Thomas's history with her daughter, we do know Jayla has been missing for six months. Her mother has done everything within her power to get help. Maybe because of race or a lack of financial resources, her story hasn't gotten play. This woman is frantic for her daughter, and because she hasn't had any positive response from authorities, she contacted Mex."

Cade paused. "I can read you both. You have an end-game in mind and in order to get there you require certain information. You know how to soft-step, but you need a woman's touch here. We don't want to go into her home, the one place where she should have complete control, with guns blazing and an expectation to get the answers we want in a hurry. Let's walk in and be respectful. If you can't do that maybe I should take the lead."

Silence.

Then in stereo, "You should take the lead."

"You boys are smart when you're presented with the facts, I'll give you that."

"Can we go now?" Mex opened his door.

"One more thing," Cade said.

"What?"

"Don't try and take the lead away from me."

A chorus of grunts filled the air.

There wasn't anything special about the apartment complex. Spare landscaping that required minimal time and money, brick and laminate exteriors for the same reason. It was clearly public housing for people who couldn't afford the prices the rest of the city demanded. Most of the tenants who lived here paid no more than thirty percent of their adjusted gross income for their housing. Sadly, it showed. While the owners pocketed full rents thanks to the program, they were clearly putting nothing back in the property for improvement, or even maintenance. Darius had informed them that while newer, the Whittier housing complex had received a failing score by HUD.

Cade added this to her list of causes she wanted to advocate for in the next year. She'd find an owner or policy maker to hound until someone improved living conditions for the people who lived here. Damn. She needed a clone.

As they approached the unit where Jayla's family lived, Cade tried to get a sense of what it must have been like for the young girl to arrive home each day. This was her anchor in a world that must not always have been idyllic. The whole place felt worn out and sad. Like it had given up.

Had Jayla given up? Is that why she was targeted?

Cade rang the doorbell and stepped back, Mex and Darius close behind her. She heard someone come up against the door and stop.

Then nothing.

There was a peephole but the noise she heard was significantly below it.

"We're here to see Mary Thomas. She's expecting us," Cade said loud and clear to the closed door. She heard scuffling through the flimsy wood.

Finally, it opened. Three sets of eyes were on her in an instant.

"Mama! It's them. They really came," a girl called over her shoulder. She couldn't have been more than eight or ten.

A woman wearing a bandana and impossibly large hoop earrings walked up to the door. "Go, now." With those two words her children scattered.

She opened the door wider. "Please. Come in."

After quick introductions, the group settled around the kitchen table.

"Can I get you something to drink? I got water, or iced tea, or Seven Up."

Mex and Darius both shook their heads.

"I'd love iced tea," Cade said. "Is it sweet?"

"Iced tea in my house don't come any other way."

"Perfect."

Mary took a closer look at Cade. "Where you from?"

"Louisiana."

"My mama was from Slidell."

"Then your tea better hit the spot."

"It will." Mary went to the refrigerator and brought out a pitcher. She turned to look at Mex and Darius. "Are you sure you boys don't want any?"

They smiled in acquiescence. "Thank you, ma'am," Darius said. Mex merely nodded.

Teas poured, Cade took a sip and nodded her approval. "Tell me about your daughter, Mrs. Thomas."

"Call me Mary."

"Tell me about Jayla, Mary."

"For one thing, she too smart for her own good."

"What do you mean?"

"She thinks, because she got important shit going on in her brain she don't have to pay attention to the shit going on in her life. She got no street smarts."

"What do you think happened to her?"

A tear slipped down Mary's face and she angrily wiped it away. "What do you think?'

Cade slipped her hands across the table and held them out. And waited.

And waited some more.

"I called you. I want to believe you care. Up till now, no one I've called has. Why should I believe you do?"

Cade waited some more.

Finally, Mary grabbed her hands. A desperate cry escaped her lips. "She's my first baby. Can you help her?"

"We're gonna try."

"Okay. Okay." Jayla's mother collapsed like a punctured balloon.

Cade took charge. "We want to know everyone she's in contact with. I don't care if it's a best friend who knows all her secrets or a passing acquaintance. Can you get me those names?"

Silence.

"Can you get me those names?" Cade repeated.

"I can get you everyone I know."

"Thank you."

Mex cleared his throat. "Ma'am, would it be possible for us to see Jayla's room? It can help us get a clearer picture of your daughter."

Mary looked from Mex to Darius, then to Cade, who gave a nod. "Okay then. Jayla gots her own room but her younger sisters sleep in there a lot. 'Specially since she gone. It's like they gotta breathe her in." She swiped another tear from her face and straightened her back. "Go on then, room's right back there. I'll stay here and get workin' on that list of names."

* * *

Cade thought of her room as a young girl. It wasn't much different from this one. She glanced at Mex and Darius and knew they were also relating to this space.

The room was small but well organized. Posters of current musicians and actors covered the walls. Cade thought she might recognize one of them but couldn't be sure. Three stuffed animals sat on top of the twin bed. Extra bedding, presumably for the younger sisters, lay folded neatly at the foot.

A three-shelf bookcase sat next to the dresser, crammed with well-worn copies of many of the great books of literature along with equally worn copies of contemporary authors, including Octavia Butler, James Baldwin, Walter Mosley, and Michael Connelly. Cade smiled, wondering how Connelly made it into the mix.

"She probably bought the books used," Darius said. "Did she have a job?"

"Her mom told me she babysat for kids in the neighborhood once in a while, and tutored through the school," Cade said.

Mex nodded. "Make sure her mom includes those people on the list."

Cade looked at the sparsely filled closet. "You know there aren't going to be many names on that list, don't you?"

"One name will lead us to more. All it takes is one."

"Well, look what I found." Darius, crouched next to the bed, fingered a bound book from in between the box spring and mattress.

Cade and Mex looked at him, mouths open.

"What? Why are you looking at me like that? It's where my sister hid hers when we were growing up."

"You read your sister's diary?" Cade asked.

"Every chance I got." Darius laughed. "She never could figure out how I knew so much. I even remember her writing about accusing her friends of telling me stuff."

Cade held out her hand. "Give it to me."

"Are you kidding? We might find leads in here," Darius said.

"Not without Jayla's mother saying it's okay." Cade didn't retract her hand.

"Bullshit. The girl is missing. Her diary could be important," Darius said. "What if she says no?"

"Look," Cade said. "Her mama is not going to say no. But it's essential she feel part of our team."

"Cade's right," Mex said. "The woman has had enough stolen from her. My bet is she'll let us have it, but she needs to experience a sense of power right now and we're the ones who can give it to her."

"Know that this goes against every one of my journalistic instincts." Darius handed the journal to Cade.

"Check in with your father instincts and tell me this isn't the right thing to do," Cade said.

Back at the kitchen table, Mary Thomas slid a sheet of paper toward Cade. It had three names on it. "I couldn't think of anyone else. She didn't hang out that often with friends, ya know? She mostly just read." Cade knew Jayla's mother probably wasn't all that in touch with kids her daughter considered friends. Cade had seen it a lot in families where children turned to cults.

"Did you include the neighbors Jayla babysat for? The one's she tutored through the school?"

Mary added a couple more names. "These the ones she sat for. The school ones you have to get from the school."

Cade nodded and handed her Jayla's diary. "We found this Mary. It's your daughter's journal."

Mary took the bound pages and pressed them to her heart. "My baby's?"

Cade nodded.

"Did you read it? Did you find out what happened?"

"It doesn't belong to us. It could hold important information, evidence even, but it rightfully belongs to you since Jayla isn't here."

Mary pressed the diary tighter.

"We're hoping you'll lend it to us. Maybe we'll find a few more names we can add to the list."

"I could do that—"

"And we're experts at seeing other things that might not seem important to anyone else." Cade leaned forward in her chair, hands folded in front of her on the table. "Would you be willing to trust us with your daughter's journal? I promise you, we won't damage it, and we'll get it back to you as soon as we've had a chance to read it."

The wall clock ticked seconds off as they waited for Mary Thomas's answer.

Cade wondered if maybe Darius hadn't been right. To just take the damn diary and return it later. Hell, any law enforcement agency would've confiscated it as evidence. No drama.

But that'd never been the way she operated, and she wasn't going to go all official now. Not when this mother was in so much pain.

Slowly Jayla's mother inched the precious pages away from her breast. She sat the diary on the table, her hand resting protectively on top. She looked down at it and blinked, mouth fighting back the anguished cries fighting to get out. "Jayla might not be important to the people on the news. She might not be important to cops who already have too much to take care of. But she's my baby. She's important to me. And you're the first who want to help."

She extended the book toward Cade, but didn't let go.

Cade reached her hand out and Mary Thomas slapped her other hand over Cade's wrist and squeezed. Hard. "Don't mess with my baby girl. If there's shit in here that could hurt Jayla, it don't go nowhere."

The two women made eye contact. Intense brown eyes met intense green eyes, and held.

"On my word, Mary Thomas, we will not cause more harm to your daughter. And we'll do everything in our power to bring your girl home to you."

Jayla's mom released her grip on both Cade's wrist and the diary. "Do it then. Do it quick. My baby's in trouble."

The global sex slavery market generates $32 billion in profits every year, outpacing illegal drugs. Factor in the statistic that the average human is sold into slavery for less than $100 and you begin to see the scope of the problem.
— *Human Trafficking Facts & Stats, Force4Compassion*

CHAPTER SEVENTEEN

"Donald Miller?" Mex watched the young man's eyes as he tried to figure out what the two strangers at his door wanted. Tried to figure out how much trouble he might be in. Tried to figure out who... and then Mex saw the realization hit.

"I saw you on the news. You're here about Alexis. Sorry, but I'm on my way out."

"We only need a few minutes."

"Mind walking with me?"

"Yeah," Mex said. "I do. Can we talk inside?"

"I, uh... sure. Why not? Come in."

"Nice art," Mex said as he looked around.

"Thanks."

Mex walked over to more closely examine a glass sculpture.

"Um, let's go in the living room where we can sit down."

The three walked into a room with sliders at the end opening onto a small balcony.

"Great view," Darius said as he looked out the doors. "Do you use the trails much?"

90

"Almost every day."

"Donald—" Mex said.

"Donny, please. Or Don."

"Donny, my name is Mex Anderson. As you know, I've been hired by Steven and Adele Halston to find their daughter. My partner here is Darius Johnson."

Donny nodded at both men.

"We understand you're Alexis's personal trainer. Is that correct?"

"I am. I was. I mean, yeah. I am."

"How long have you worked with Alexis?"

"A couple of years I guess. Maybe a little longer."

"How long have you been a trainer?"

"About nine years."

"Have you always worked at the same place?" Darius asked.

"Uh, no."

"Where else have you trained?"

"Three or four other places. At least two of them have closed."

"Can you get us the names and locations?"

"Yeah, sure. But it'll take some digging."

Darius handed him a card. "Let me know."

"Why do you want to know about my old gyms? What do they have to do with Alexis?" He looked at Darius, then Mex. "Wait. You think I had something to do with her going missing?"

"We're just being thorough. The Halstons are paying us to find their daughter, and in order to do that we're examining everything in her life including the people around her."

"I get it."

"Was there anyone at the fitness center you might have noticed who seemed to take an unusual interest in Alexis?"

Donny shook his head.

"Think, Donny. Think."

"Alexis was... *is* a great looking girl. She always gets attention. Some of it might have been unusual, but not from me."

"Did you date her?"

"We went out once."

"It didn't work out?"

"Look around you. She's out of my league. Her daddy would never approve of his daughter hanging out with a gym rat. We both decided it was best to keep our relationship physical. In a non-intimate way."

"Where were you the day Alexis went missing?" Mex asked.

"I'm not sure when she disappeared, but the day before I heard about it we'd had a workout session. She was depressed at the beginning, but her endorphins kicked in and I'm pretty sure she left happy."

"What time was that?"

"Probably about five o'clock."

"Okay, thanks. We're trying to put together a timeline." Mex handed him his card. "Call me if you think of anything. Sorry if we made you late."

"No worries."

Back in the car, Darius's deep voice filled the space. "What was that all about?"

"He's at the top of a very short list and I don't want to make him run. I want you to find out everything you can about the other centers he's worked at as a trainer or anything else."

"What am I looking for?"

Mex put the car in gear and pulled out. "We'll know it when we see it."

Darius's phone rang and he looked at the Caller ID. "It's my contact on the Denver PD."

"Hey, Mark," Darius said. "Wow, buddy. That's terrific. Wait a minute, I need to get—"

Mex passed him a pad and pen.

"Never mind. Go." Darius scribbled. "Thanks, man. We'll be in touch."

"Why didn't Halston give you the name of the detective working his daughter's case?" Darius asked Mex after he'd ended the call.

"I didn't want it."

"Why?"

"Bureaucracy. You have no idea how much faster you and I can move without it."

"Yeah, but the bureaucracy has access to things we don't."

"Point."

"At any rate, we now have the name and number of the Greenwood Village detective assigned to the Halston disappearance.

"Okay. Keep it. We'll contact him if necessary."

"And we have an appointment with him first thing in the morning."

"Shit."

A month into her training for the mounted police, Skates called again to say she just spent a sleepless night. At two p.m. the day before, she cruised past the Motel 6. "And there they were all over again—14-,15,-16-year-old girls in five-inch heels and miniskirts, walking across the parking lot. I called my old lieutenant and asked him if he could do something.

—*Sex Trafficking of Americans: The Girls Next Door, by Amy Fine Collins*

CHAPTER EIGHTEEN

JAYLA

Sunlight flares hot-white into the interior of the dark van, causing all of us to shield our eyes before stepping out into the parking lot.

I have no idea where we are or even what city we're in. What's familiar is the cheap motel and a sports stadium within spitting distance.

"You! Cherie! Get your ass over here."

I walk over to the man everyone calls Daddy. My third night after being turned out, a customer started yelling and beating me. He'd somehow managed to lock the door. The crazed man brandished a knife and I knew for sure I was going to die. But Daddy broke into the room and saved me. I thought maybe Daddy cared about my safety. Turns out he did, but not in the way I'd hoped. He was only protecting his investment.

I stand silently in front of him, waiting to hear what he has to say. If I speak first I could get a pop in the jaw.

"Since you're so kind and nurturing with the new bitch, you can show her what's expected. I want to see money from her tonight. Not tomorrow, got it?"

"Yes, Daddy."

"What do you think we should call her?"

"I think we should call her Debbie," I offer.

He laughs. "Like the old Debbie Does Dallas pornos. Good. I like it. A dose of history won't hurt and a few of our customers are likely to get the reference."

"Daddy?"

"What? I don't have time to chit-chat."

"Since I'm training her, can I get some credit in my own account from you?"

"I should knock you to the ground right now. Did I say you'd get some credit?"

"No, sir."

"Then don't fuck with me. You will bring me your usual tonight or pay a special price tomorrow. Got it?"

"Yes, Daddy."

"Oh, and since you're training? You're both in the same room. I got double beds." He hands me a baggie with capsules in it. "You know what to do with this. Now get in your room, freshen your makeup, and get clothes on that make you vaguely hot. The big game isn't for two more nights, but fans are coming in early."

I nod and start to walk away.

"Cherie?"

I turn to look back at the man I've come to hate.

"How about a hug for Daddy?"

* * *

"Come with me." I bump against Karen, the new girl who'd been crying when the van trip began.

"Where're we going?" Karen followed me without question. I felt a rock in my gut. I'm to Karen like Ginger was to me.

"What's your name?" I asked.

"Kar—"

"No. What's your name?"

"My name is Debbie."

"Perfect." I led the girl to the unlocked room Daddy said was ours. I didn't have a key, I never did. That would give me too much control.

Once inside the room, I dump my bag on one of the sad looking beds and inspect the room. The carpet is old and crappy and probably hasn't been vacuumed in six months. I sure don't want to look too closely at the corners or the bathroom or even the sheets on the beds. It looks like every motel room I've seen since my life has turned upside down and inside out. One more battlefield. One more place to try and survive. What I know is today I will not be a victor.

But I'll be damned if I'll be a victim.

"Come on, Debbie. We gotta get cleaned up."

The new girl stands in the doorway looking at the room, eyes wide and tearing up.

"I have one last question for Karen, and then you're going to put her away someplace safe, got it?"

A nod.

"Have you ever had sex?"

An anguished cry answers the question.

I have to wonder how this girl ever got past the Virgin Police. Virgins could command special prices. Sometimes even a bidding war. I realize I can play this. Get a positive bounce with Daddy, not become Karen's Ginger, and...

Ginger hadn't asked me if I'd ever had sex. Ginger had assumed that since I was fifteen and from "that" part of town, it was a given I wasn't a virgin. That first time had been terrifying and painful.

I sit Karen down on the edge of the bed and kneel on the floor in front of her, grabbing her hands and demanding the attention of her eyes. "Are you sure you've never had sex? That you're a virgin? Don't lie to me."

Karen nods.

"What the hell does that mean?"

"I'm a vir-vir-virgin."

"Okay. I'm gonna go talk to Daddy. You should know this only buys you limited time. He could have a guy lined up for you tomorrow, or even later tonight. But for now, you can relax."

"Jayla? I mean, Cherie? What does it mean that I haven't had sex? Will it be better or worse?"

I remember my first time. The john had tried to pretend he was interested in me, but I was too scared to play along with him. When it was over, and I sprawled on the bed in tears, he didn't even acknowledge me as he zipped up his pants and left the room. Other than my humiliation, physical pain, fear and the man's lack of interest, all I can remember about my first sexual experience is the blood on the sheets.

I look at Karen. "I don't know. All I can tell you for sure is that it won't be now. Is that okay with you?"

Karen's entire body shivers. She nods. "Whatever you think is best."

My heart clenches. This is so not what I think is best. What I think is best is that we shouldn't be here. You and I should both be back where we could be regular teenage girls. I take a breath. "I'll go talk to Daddy."

The expression on Karen's face was a combination of hope and worship. Like she'd been saved from a fate worse than death. The truth was, she hadn't.

"Just in case, freshen your makeup and get dressed. I have a feeling regardless of how it ends up for you, it's going to be a long night." I set the baggie of drugs on the bed. "When I tell you to take one of these, and I will, don't hesitate. I don't care if it's in thirty minutes or sometime later this week. Take the damn pill."

"I trust you."

I want to throw something. "Don't trust me. Trust Debbie. Protect Karen. Haven't you heard a thing I've been telling you?"

"Yeah, but you're still here. You're someone I can trust."

"And what did I just say?"

"You said not to trust you. But I do. Because you're the only one who's tried to help me."

"So this is the end, *Debbie*. The last thing you will trust me about is to take a drug. Period. After that you only have yourself. You only have Debbie. Don't listen to anything anyone else tells you. Debbie has the instincts to keep you safe. Only Debbie. Jayla will be gone and there's no tellin' what Cherie might say."

"Okay. Only Debbie."

"I've done all I can do. Now it's up to you. I'm out of it. I have to be out of it."

I give Debbie one long last look before I shut the door behind me and seek out Daddy. He's standing in the parking lot, smoking a cigarette and looking stoned. *Shit, he's wasted.* If he is high he might not register a thing I'm telling him.

"Daddy?"

"What do you want, bitch?"

So it's a hate day. His tone is like a hard slap in the face and a reminder he can be violent. Tomorrow he might show me how much he loves me, protects me, counts on me.

I learned in my second week, when I tried to run away, it's all about control. His control. He'd beaten me almost to the point of death, and threatened my family as well. For the next several days, it was Daddy who nursed me back to health from the beating he inflicted. He was kind and gentle.

But today is today.

"I've learned something you should know."

He laughs. Mean and hateful. A laugh that originates from evil. "What in the world could you have to tell me?"

"Do you remember the girl who was crying in the van? The one you wanted me to train?"

He looks blank.

I try again. "Debbie does Dallas?"

Hesitation followed by a smile. "Yeah. My retro girl."

"Well, your retro girl might score you a lot more."

"How's that?"

"She's a virgin."

Daddy starts to laugh and then catches himself. "A virgin?"

"Yeah."

"You're not trying to stall are you, Cherie?"

"Nope. She said she's a virgin and I believe her."

"Well that changes shit."

"I thought it might."

"I have a fuckin' auction."

"What do you want me to do about tonight?"

"You both stay in the room. No visitors. No communication."

Since the launch of Operation Predator in 2003, HSI (Homeland Security Investigations) has arrested more than 14,000 individuals for crimes against children, including the production and distribution of online child pornography, traveling overseas for sex with minors, and sex trafficking of children.
—Evidence Technology Magazine, *from an article written in 2008*

CHAPTER NINETEEN

ALEXIS

The plane touches down and I want to barf. I have a horrible feeling I'm about to go from bad to worse. Right now I've got to seriously dig for a backbone. Planning revenge against Donny won't keep me strong for whatever comes next.

I take a breath.

The private jet hasn't stopped yet. No one cares about whether or not I have my seatbelt fastened. That my tray and seat are in the upright and locked positions. That if I had baggage in the overhead compartments, it might have shifted. No one cares about my safety because Macho Man is yanking me from my seat.

As I walk down the ramp to the tarmac, I search for a clue. Any clue.

Where am I?

It's not a major airport. Not even a minor one. This is a private airstrip. But where? I know for sure it's not Colorado.

Aside from the hours I was on the plane, the air is humid, and while there are mountains, they're definitely not the Rockies.

Macho Man drags me to a stretch limo and tosses me in. As soon as he closes the door I hear the locks engage and the car moves off. I want to talk to the driver but the privacy partition is up and I can't see a way to bring it down. I knock on the window. Nothing. Harder. Still nothing. Pounding doesn't even make the driver look in his rear-view mirror. He's like a Nazi. Just doin' his job.

It hurts to breathe. All I want to know is where the hell I am. Can it get any more basic than that?

At one point I thought I might be able to use my dad's money and influence to buy my way out of this nightmare. Now, with all the muscle, the private plane and airstrip, the limo, and the obvious determination to get me here at whatever expense, I'm thinking that even if I could contact him, Daddy couldn't get me out of this mess.

Someone went to a lot of trouble and expense to get me here, including what they paid for me. I must have value to this person. Maybe that's something I can use.

We're not on the road too long before the driver turns off onto what I assume is a private drive. It's paved, but the headlights show only a narrow strip. The plants along the roadside are generic. They could be almost anywhere.

Except Colorado.

What I want to do right now, more than anything else in the world, is curl up in the corner of this bench seat and bawl my eyes out. But I'm already smart enough to know that wanting something isn't always the thing that's gonna keep me alive. Wanting something, like taking a hot poker to Donny's balls—even if I got it this instant—would not guarantee that I won't be dead when the sun rises tomorrow. It could be my value is for a psycho who wants to torture me before his final kill.

I've seen the movies.

And then what good would Donny's skewered balls or me sobbing hysterically possibly do?

I feel like I'm losing my mind.

The car rolls to a stop and a small man in a tidy uniform opens my door. "Welcome, Miss Alexis."

I sit and don't move a muscle.

"Please, Miss Alexis. Be welcome to here."

I look at him and see the pleading in his eyes. He wants to stay buried, unnoticed, but events are conspiring against him. While I want to kick and scream, if I can't cry in a corner, I don't want to make someone else's life more miserable than it already is.

I put one leg out of the limo and the uniformed man noticeably breathes.

"Please, Miss Alexis. Follow to me." He bows and waits for me to exit. He bows again.

"Please," he repeats. "This way."

There is an armed guard on either side of the massive entry. I wonder if the small man I'm following is armed. Probably.

Everyone seems to be Hispanic, but that doesn't mean I'm in Mexico. How can I be in Mexico without my passport? Maybe this is California?

I keep my eyes directed in front of me but am acutely aware of things in my peripheral vision. I'm looking for a clue. *Where the hell am I? Is there a way out?*

The ceiling is at least two stories high, maybe three. And the walls are covered with amazing art. Not Donny's apartment quality art. Screaming-amazing-quality art. Most of it is contemporary but interspersed, in brilliant ways, I recognize works of the masters. There's a Titian, and one I swear is a Vermeer.

The Denver Art Museum docents had become my mentors over the last two years. When I couldn't stand staying in my cold house or doing something stupid with greedy friends, I'd head to the DAM and spend hours learning about great works. I wish there was someone I could tell about what I'm seeing.

Not sure where I am geographically, but damn... there's serious money involved in this place.

We move to the left and there's a sweeping staircase that begins with risers that are at least ten feet across. When we get to the top we turn left down a wide hallway and enter the first door on the right.

"Please, Miss Alexis." The man swept his arm gesturing to the expanse of the room, bright sunlight pouring into the space. "This you." He walked over to the closet and threw open the doors. "This you."

Inside the closet are three garments. One looks like something my little sister, if I had one, would wear grudgingly. A second looks like something my mother would wear. Stylish but stuffy. And the third is straight out of casting for *Xena: Warrior Princess*.

"I'm fine."

"Please, Miss Alexis."

God help me, if he doesn't stop with the "please-miss-alexis" I'm going to have to hit something.

"Here." He gestures to a door in the far corner that opens onto a luxuriously appointed bathroom. "Two hour. You be ready two hour."

This is more like it. I kick off my shoes and turn to look at the man. I am *not* going to waste this opportunity. "You can leave now."

I follow him as he scoots through the bedroom and out the door. When he leaves I lock it, surprised there even is a lock, throw the deadbolt, which is also a surprise, and for good measure, shove the chair from the desk under the knob.

Yes!

Back in the bathroom I find three separate choices for shower and bath gels. One is a bubble bath with the picture of a fairy princess on the front, another is Shalimar, something my mother or even grandmother would use, and a third is something called Carnal Flower. I unscrew the top on that one. Easy choice. A luxurious-looking bathrobe hanging on the back of the door prompts me to touch it.

I strip and lay my clothes on the bed. They're not in terrible shape and by far my first choice regarding what I'll be wearing when I walk out of this room given my options hanging in the closet. My plan is to take a quick shower to get the grunge off and wash my hair, and then go in for a long hot bath.

In two hours I'll have answers, and maybe be on my way home.

Suddenly the normalcy of the room rises up. It's not so much the smell, but the lack of smells, the odor of filthy and fear-riddled bodies from only hours ago, that takes me to my knees. I lose the strength I'm barely holding onto in the desire for something I can't have—home. I want to go home.

Please, Miss Alexis wants to go home.

* * *

I step out of the bath and wrap a huge fluffy towel around me. I spent so much time in the tub that only the tips of my hair that had dragged in the tub-water are still wet. I'm clean now. Refreshed. Ready to take on whatever situation I'm in.

Not being a complete idiot, I know what's happening to me. Bastard Donny thought he could make a few bucks by selling me to another bastard. Donny should've just held me for ransom, because once this new guy figures out he has the daughter of Steven Halston, managing partner of an international law firm, he'll be happy to add a few hundred thousand, maybe even more, to his coffers.

Daddy will pay. Daddy has always bought me out of problems. And this is a big one.

But will Daddy's money mean a thing to someone who has this much?

I dismiss the idea I might never get home and make a firm mental note to load up on Carnal Flower when I get there. It smells fabulous. It's like a promise.

I will get home.

How long was I in the bathroom? A soft gray-tinted light filters through the windows, replacing the bright sunlight from earlier. The silly soldier man told me I had two hours. Probably close. I loosen the towel from around me and drop it on the floor then turn to the bed to get my clothes.

They're gone.

The chair is still under the doorknob. Did I put them somewhere else? I spin around the room.

My clothes are gone.

A chill crawls up my spine and I grab the towel and pull it back around me. Someone got in my room.

My room? Really? Like I chose it.

After I disengage the chair I check the locks. They're exactly the way I left them. Even knowing it's apparently useless, I tuck the chair back in position, then slowly do a survey of the room. Everything looks normal. Seamless.

Then I get to the floor-to-ceiling bookcase. Tug out a couple of books at a funky angle and wait for the door to swing open like in the movies. Nothing happens. But when I put a book back into place, there seems to be some give in the wall.

I apply pressure. Yeah. Definitely. There's a give. I press harder and the bookcase splits, pushing in like a folding door. It leads to a dark hallway.

No wonder they have locks. Locks don't mean a damn thing.

I take a step into the hallway behind the bookcase and hesitate. If they've got all of these details figured out, from the costumes to the enticement of the bathroom to the useless locks on doors, what else do they have figured out? I need to think about this a bit more.

I review the clothes hanging in the closet. I have a decision to make.

In San Antonio, the Heidi Search Center often finds out that the person who is reported missing has fallen into the grasp of sex traffickers.

Dottie Laster, the Heidi Search Center's executive director, said when she looks at the victims' social media activity, "I find someone has been grooming, luring, recruiting them and now they're missing."

—Super Bowl known as 'largest human trafficking event,' by Jesse Degollado for KSAT 12, February 2, 2017

CHAPTER TWENTY

I look in the mirror and swing side to side before deciding to tuck the sheet in tighter.

Not bad.

There is a pair of sandals in the closet (probably meant for the little girl dress) and after I get over being freaked out that they are not only a perfect fit but are also used, I put them on.

The toga look. Greek goddess. I feel like I'm taking back control. Making my own decisions.

There's a light knock on the door. Right, I think, let's pretend that there isn't another way into this room.

I move the chair back behind the desk, release the deadbolt and throw the door open.

The slight uniformed man takes one look at me and visibly pales. "Oh, no. Please, Miss Alexis. Please." He rushes over to the closet. "Here. This you. This you." He thrusts his hand over and over and over again at the hanging garments. Sweat appears on his forehead.

He plucks out the little girl dress and points to the sandals I'm wearing. "Here. This you. Please!" He thrusts the dress at me. Because he looks so damn desperate I gently accept the hanger, then rehang it.

"No. *This* me." I use my own hand to waft the air in front of my sheet. Calm. In control. Ready to bargain my way out of here and get home. If Daddy doesn't have enough money, surely he knows someone who does.

The small man begins to shake. Seriously shake. I stand it for as long as I can and then I touch his shoulder. "It's okay. I'm happy with what I'm wearing. You can save the other things for someone else."

He looks at me with those sad eyes for what feels like minutes, then looks down to the floor and sighs, holding perfectly still.

At least he isn't shaking. What is with this guy?

Finally he nods. "Okay." His voice is barely above a whisper. "Follow to me."

"Hey, what's your name?"

He ignores me as he leads me out of the room.

"You know my name. What's yours?"

"*Mi nombre* does not matter. *Muerto. Finito.*"

"Dead? You're dead? Finished?" I tug on the corner of the sheet under my arm. "I don't understand. What is your name? I want to know."

The man looks at the floor. "Miguel. *Mi nombre es Miguel.*"

"Okay, Miguel, we're simpatico, right?"

He doesn't acknowledge me. He just keeps walking. A miniature military step, like in *March of the Toy Soldiers*. There is nothing casual about the steps he takes.

Something tells me not to press the issue. I mean, in the context of things, how important is knowing his name? Or knowing we're simpatico? Even though somehow that would make me feel better. Maybe even make me feel safer.

After walking a bit we descend some steps. Actually, a lot of steps. At the bottom, we emerge into a room of breathtaking beauty. The floor is shining hardwood, the boards deeply dark and wide and perfectly laid. The walls, equally shining, are of a dark reddish wood. They stretch at least two stories and feature feathered lighting both up and down in an enticing way. If simply left to the wood, this room would be special. But the added art leaves me drooling. I would swear anything that I'm looking at original Monets and Renoirs and a contemporary Jenny Saville that simply terrifies me.

We move through the gallery and emerge onto a stage. The lights are too bright for me to see what, or who, is in the audience.

"We have a problem." A deep voice speaks from the darkness beyond the stage.

"Yes, sir," said Miguel.

"Did you explain to Alexis what would happen if she didn't wear one of the three choices?"

"No, sir. That forbidden."

"Well done."

"We need to talk," I direct my words to the area the voice. "My father has a great deal of money and influence and I'm sure he would—"

"I didn't give you permission to speak," said the voice.

I'm shocked into temporary silence. First that he interrupted me and second that he said I needed permission.

"Look," I try again. "I don't want to start a fight, but if you listen to me this could all be over and we can all go away happy."

I hear a throaty chuckle. "What makes you think I'm not happy now?"

"I meant—"

"Why are you wearing bed linens, Alexis?"

"Because someone stole my clothes."

"Stole?"

"Okay, maybe not stole. But they're missing."

"Why aren't you wearing one of the outfits I personally selected for you?"

"Because I didn't *personally* like any of them. Where are my clothes?"

"You don't get to ask questions."

"Where are my clothes?"

Silence.

"I want my clothes back. I want to leave. You have no right to keep me here."

Silence.

"Miguel."

"Yes, sir."

"Explain to Miss Alexis what would have happened had you told her our rules about her clothing options earlier."

"You kill my family."

I can't believe he said that. "Kill his family? Because I won't wear a goddamn costume?"

"And what happens now because you weren't persuasive enough to get her to wear one of the options I'd so thoughtfully provided?"

"I lose."

"Lose what?"

"Finger."

A man rolls a butcher's block out onto the stage, a brick and a gleaming knife on its surface. A bucket containing towels, antiseptic, bandages and tape hangs from a hook on the side.

Miguel approaches the table and places a finger of his left hand on the brick. For the first time I notice he's already missing two fingers from that hand.

He knew this was going to happen. It has happened before.

My heart is zinging in my chest. Mouth dry. This can't be happening.

"Who must cut your finger off, Miguel?" The voice sneered at the same time it dripped with boredom. Like a tired teacher talking to a slow-learner.

The small man swallowed. "Miss Alexis." He can't look at me. Instead he looks at a spot on the table. A blood stain from another time?

"Fuck this. Fuck you. I'm not cutting anyone's finger off."

The man who'd rolled the butcher's block out reappears and lays some photographs on the table. I resist looking at them. I don't want to know.

"Please, Miss Alexis." Miguel gestures with his head toward the pictures.

I look at his sad, sad eyes. What might happen to him or his family if I don't do as I'm told? I wonder how in the world he found himself in this position? What happens when he's down to a thumb and one finger on his left hand? Does he offer up a finger on his right hand the next time?

The photographs are catching reflected glare from the lights and I can't see them from my angle. I'm going to have to pick them up.

There are three of them.

The one on top is a shot of my parents at an event. It's time-stamped and I know it must have been a press conference about me. I look at the drawn and haunted faces of my parents and my heart breaks. We might not have been the best family on earth, but I can see from this photo they love me. My father might be traveling ninety-three percent of the time and my mom might be dulling her senses an equivalent amount of time, but my going missing has obviously caused them pain. Tears pour into my vision.

The next two photos have more current time stamps. My guess is within hours. One is of my dad sitting out by our pool, phone in hand and gesturing like he always does. Was he talking to someone about me? Or was it business? Hard to say.

The other is a picture of my mom, blurry, obviously taken with a telephoto lens. Her head is nesting in her arms that are folded on top of the desk in their bedroom. I can't see her face but I can read her shoulders. Dejected. Afraid. Lost.

"I'm not a monster, Alexis. Your refusal to punish Miguel won't cause the deaths of your parents."

I feel a sense of relief.

"But it will cause the death of one of them. Which, I can't say. Do you have a preference?"

"You bastard."

"You have thirty seconds."

"Please, Miss Alexis."

"Did I happen to mention that if you don't cut off one of his fingers, he too will lose a family member."

"You son-of-a-bitch."

"Here's a tip. I've seen tentative cuts. They only prolong the agony. Hard and swift is the way to go. You have ten seconds."

I take up the knife, raise my arm, and while I want to close my eyes I can't risk not making the perfect cut. Either entirely, coming down on the butcher block itself, or slicing off his hand.

Fuck this shit.

I bring my arm down.

In general, organized crime units tend not to be involved with children younger than 9 years of age—not out of a sense of morality but because such young children are "too difficult" or "too hot" to handle. The exception to this pattern is the use of very young children as subjects of pornography.

—The Commercial Sexual Exploitation of Children, U.S. National Study, by Richard J. Estes and Neil Alan Weiner, University of Pennsylvania 2001 (revised 2002)

CHAPTER TWENTY-ONE

"What do you have for me?" Mex asked Darius. The two were meeting for an early breakfast to share information and discuss strategy. Mex wanted a clear plan before their appointment with the police detective who was working the Alexis Halston missing person case.

"Where's Cade?"

"She said she had something she had to take care of." Mex looked at the expression on Darius's face. "What? We don't babysit each other."

"Okay, which first, Donny Miller or Dark Net?"

"Dark Net."

"I didn't get a lot I'm afraid."

Mex sighed.

"Here's what I do have. There's a chance we can utilize facial recognition software. The problem is that it's unreliable. It doesn't work nearly as well as it does in the TV shows. The other problem is the sheer volume of photos to sort through could take days, weeks even, and we still might not get a definitive answer."

"I hope you have something better."

"Not better, but it's worth taking a closer look. Maybe come up with a plan."

"What is it?"

"An online site called Backpage. While mostly legitimate, the site is also the online equivalent of classified ads. A few of the FBI arrests I've turned up have a Backpage connection."

"They post photos of kids?"

"They do."

"How can they do that?"

"Attorneys for these places do their best to blur the line between freedom of speech, and pornography and pedophilia."

"That's fucked."

"You wouldn't say that if someone stopped you from exercising your right."

"Freedom of speech doesn't give anyone the right to exploit children," Mex insisted.

Darius nodded. "I agree. The laws are slowly changing, but not everywhere."

"So how does Backpage help us if we can't use the facial recognition software?"

"I'm thinking we can place a couple of ads. Be specific. Who knows, we might get a hit."

"Good idea. Better than nothing. Cade can write a couple of ads."

"Cade? I'm a writer."

"You write books. Cade lays traps."

"Point taken."

"What do you have on Miller?"

"On our young friend, I have a bit more for you."

"Go."

"Donny Miller's only discernible employment has been as a personal trainer. Three of the five previous gyms where he's worked have since closed." Darius looked at Mex. "Remind me to never get involved in the fitness business."

"Done. Keep going."

"Nothing notable about his employment, but during the time he was working at Al's Fitness in Lakewood a sixteen-year-old high school student went missing. She was a member of the gym."

"Was Donny her trainer?"

"No, she had a general membership and didn't pay for a personal trainer."

"Was she ever found?"

"Two years after she went missing, her body was found in Kansas City."

"Cause of death?"

"Asphyxiation. Her body was beaten beyond recognition. Her injuries were pre-mortem and post-mortem. They ID'd her through dental records."

"Killer?"

"It's a cold case. The LEOs liked either the pimp she was sold to initially or one particular john, but they were never able to get enough evidence."

"Damn."

"I also did some digging on Les Franklin, the Greenwood Village detective. He's got a good close rate and doesn't seem to have an ego that gets in his way."

"How do you know?"

"Lack of press. He solves cases but refrains from publicity."

"Anything else?"

"Yeah, he's black."

"Well then, we won't have to worry about Hollywood making a movie about us."

"You got that right." Darius finished off his stack of pancakes.

"Here's the plan," Mex said. "We go into this real slow. I don't care what color his skin is, unless we both okay this guy, we don't do a lot of sharing."

"I'm down with that. Is there a secret code we're supposed to use to vote him up or down?" Darius winked.

[Julie] Greiner [of Lakewood, Colorado] was arrested in October [2015] after investigators learned she was allowing her [12-year-old] daughter to have sex with a 23-year-old Australian man in exchange for gifts and money, according to authorities.

Greiner's daughter met Thomas Keski, of Australia, in an online chat in mid-2014, Jefferson County prosecutors say. The two bonded there, according to an arrest warrant, and their relationship became sexual over video chat before they eventually met in person.

Keski sent money and gifts to the girl and Greiner, including thousands of dollars that was sometimes used to pay Greiner's rent and other bills, authorities say.

—Lakewood child sex trafficking conviction is first under new Colorado laws, by Jesse Paul, for The Denver Post, *Updated May 25, 2016*

CHAPTER TWENTY-TWO

Cade waited in the parking lot at the police station for Mex and Darius. The appointment with the detective was fifteen minutes away. Mex wouldn't show up fifteen minutes early for anything if he could help it.

The trick for her was to keep her male counterparts strong and confident while she took over this interview. They required an ally in the Greenwood Village PD. And she knew it was up to her to make their meeting beneficial, even if they didn't wind up with the advantage.

Which meant it was also up to her to help the two alpha-males in her life find reason. Which, in her experience with them, could be a crapshoot.

Her phone buzzed. Louisiana area code. Bingo. Advantage, Cade. Or so she hoped. "Boudreaux, tell me you have something that makes me wish I could buy a round."

"Maybe I do. Can you be here in twenty?"

"Can I owe you?"

"For you, *mon cher*, anything."

"Talk to me."

"You were right. Your police detective, Les Franklin, has strong ties to the Big Raggedy. He was involved in the Michael Aarons case and primary on the Sheila Wilkins assault."

Cade had remembered correctly. Two cases she'd worked in Baton Rouge, a/k/a the Big Raggedy, had turned out well. A young girl, Sheila Wilkins, had been lured into a cult that professed all women to be virgins regardless of their past, creating a lifeline onto which the young girl had clung. Then there was a young man, Michael Aarons, who somehow had believed in the promise of virgins at his beck and call and that he lived above the law. He'd actually helped lead Cade to the cult. There'd been a lot of uncertainty about both the existence of the cult and the assault until Cade tied them together.

But she was certain of the detective. Les Franklin was invested in the outcome of his cases more than any other police detective she'd worked with. Now he was in Colorado. A coincidence? Cade didn't believe in coincidences any more than she believed in luck.

A few minutes later, Darius's Range Rover drove into the parking lot. Cade waited for the two men to get out and walk to the main entrance for City Hall. She opened her door as they approached.

Mex gave her a quick kiss. "I thought you had something to take care of this morning."

"I did, and it's been taken care of."

Mex looked uncomfortable.

"What? Do you have a problem if I join you?" Cade asked.

Now Darius looked uncomfortable.

"Give, guys."

"We've worked out a plan," Mex said.

"Plan? I can't wait to hear it."

"Well, it's common sense, really. We're gonna hold our cards real close to our vests, not share much. Then we both have to okay him before we share more."

"C'mon, boys. Lives are at stake here. Isn't that a teensy bit egotistical on your part?"

"You're right. Lives are at stake. And we don't want to get caught up in bureaucracy. You know as well as we do that police departments are nests of bureaucratic shit."

"It's how they function," Darius added.

"Okay. I'll let you two play your game."

"Good. Just follow our lead." Mex gave her a look, confused by how easily she'd acquiesced.

The trio walked into the building. A large open lobby filled with natural light made the space feel more like professional offices than an adjunct to a police department. A small sign directed them into a smaller lobby. Mex told the woman behind the desk they had an appointment with Les Franklin.

"Take a seat and I'll let Detective Franklin know you're here."

A wall-mounted television was on mute in one corner of the lobby, and the same rigidly plain chairs sold to doctors' offices lined the walls.

The detective came through the secured door and made immediate eye contact with Mex, who'd been standing by the wall containing brochures on alcohol, crime prevention, and about twenty other topics. Mex slipped the brochure he was reading, *College Students and Depression*, into his pocket. The detective held his hand out and introduced himself. Mex did likewise.

Darius came up and joined the introductions, while Cade stood in the background. When Mex turned to introduce her he didn't have a chance to get a word out.

"Acadia, is it you?" Franklin crossed the room to envelope Cade in a bear hug. "Are you with these two?"

"I am."

"Suddenly I'm feeling a lot better about working with them. And you."

Cade smiled as Mex and Darius each shook their heads in embarrassment and held up a thumb.

One was an engineer with a Top Secret government clearance. Another was a financial analyst.
—From an FBI article regarding the planned purchasers of kidnapped women 12/11/15

CHAPTER TWENTY-THREE

ALEXIS

After I cut off Miguel's finger I threw up. I don't know which one of us screamed the loudest, but I do know the echoes of our screams lasted longer than either of our mouths were open. The disembodied voice in the darkness instructed another man to escort me back to my room and said I was to wait until summoned. I felt a strange sense of the surreal when a woman hurried up to Miguel intent on seeing to his hand. Violence followed by concern? I don't think I'll ever be able to look at blood again without recalling the fear and pain contained in those thirty seconds.

I sit here in my nicely appointed prison cell and realize I'm forever changed. If I suddenly wake up in my old bedroom, nothing would ever be the same. These last few days have left their mark. I'm not the same Alexis I was a week ago or even twenty-four hours ago. Every day that goes by here changes me.

I walk over to the closet, hoping my clothes will be there. They're not. To be on the safe side, I select the outfit I think my mom might wear to a committee meeting. Fashionable but conservative. Not my taste, but I don't want to run the risk of anyone else losing a finger. And it sure does beat the Little Bo Peep or Dominatrix alternatives.

The light-weight knit really does look like something my mother would wear. I check the label. Yep. St. John's. It's a pale lavender with heather-gray piping. Not my colors. But I do have to admit it fits well. I only wish I had my turquoise eye makeup to make my own statement.

Blindsided. Reality. Rape. The threat of death and torture. My parents' safety. Hell, I cut a finger off a man's hand because the alternative was worse. How the fuck am I even thinking about eye makeup?

I'm in hell. This isn't a game. I'm lost here. No one knows where I am. No one can help. I'm only pretending.

And then I remember the slight resistance when the knife met Miguel's finger. My head was filled with the sound of our terror, but I distinctly remember the contact. The slice. Like it happened separately.

There's a knock on the door and yet another guard enters. I'm about to say something about his rudeness, but stop when my eyes meet his. His hate rips through me and I feel heat rise from my chest to my face. He knows about the finger. I can't help but glance at his hands. He's either new to the dance or silently persuasive because he has all of his digits. He's probably wondering if I'm going to be the one to change his luck.

He thrusts one of his fully-intact hands toward the doorway. I don't hesitate.

When I arrive in the hallway, Mr. Hate draws ahead of me. I weigh my options and don't see any escape avenues. I follow him. The house is enormous. In a far corner he stops and presses a button. An elevator door opens momentarily and we enter, not speaking. Mr. H pushes a button and the car descends.

Keep it together, Alexis. Keep it together. Don't let anyone see you sweat. I hear those words in my head and want to hit the speaker, whoever it is. How the hell am I supposed to keep it together when I'm being hand-delivered to a sadist? Maybe a sadist who kills?

When the elevator doors open we enter a room that confirms my worst fears. I stop and look around. Everywhere I look are objects of torture. I don't know what they are by name, but I'm pretty sure I'm headed for crazy.

Before I can take a breath, the guard is gone and I'm isolated in this chamber of horrors. While I'm afraid, I'm also angry. How can one human being do this to another human being?

"Stop where you are." It is the same voice from the shadows earlier.

I stop and square my shoulders. Nobody else is going to stand up for me.

"Are you vexed, Alexis? Peeved? Pissed off?"

I suck in a sharp breath and hold it.

"Don't you want to express yourself?"

Screw this. I exhale and take a deep breath. Work to find the voice I know can carry. The voice that demonstrates my strength. "At whose expense? Are there more fingers you wish me to remove?"

Laughter, deep and robust, fills the air. "Do you know why I bought you?"

"No one can buy me."

Heavier laughter. "That's where you're wrong. I purchased you. All of you. Because you aren't the typical mindless cunt just out to make a few bucks for her pimp. I purchased you because you will give me a challenge. You're beautiful and intelligent and strong-willed. It's your will I want to break. When I break your will, I can watch your beauty and intelligence crumble."

"And if you can't?"

"That won't happen."

A phone rings. He answers, voice low. I can't make out the words.

"I must leave you for a few minutes, Alexis. Please make yourself at home. Explore my collection." He chuckles. "I might even let you choose."

After his footsteps recede, I'm alone in this room filled with shadows. What is it with this guy and weird lighting? I walk around the perimeter seeking assurance there's no one else hiding. Leather straps and serious looking metal hand tools on the walls. There's a magnetized column, like a tall Lazy-Susan, that holds dozens of knives and implements. A refrigerator in the corner looks normal and out of place until I open it. Vials upon vials of drugs are laid out ready for use.

I'm grateful I didn't choose the Xena outfit as a joke. It would have been like me to do something stupid. But it might have saved Miguel a finger.

I go back to where I'd been standing when he left. Does he think he can break me with pain? With drugs? My heart thunders in my chest. He probably can. But I'll be damned if I'll make it easy.

* * *

His voice comes from behind me. I still haven't seen him.

"See that stage in the center of the room? I want you to take it. Claim it. Make it yours."

I can't seem to move or answer him.

"What have you got to lose, Alexis? Oh, right. Quite a bit as it turns out. At least *you* think so. Get on that stage. Do it now. Do it now or experience my anger. And I'm quite sure you don't want to experience my anger over something so trivial. Save your pride for later, love, when it actually matters."

I hear him light a cigarette, smell the tobacco burning.

"Go on, now. Move your stiff, useless self up onto that stage."

What is it with this guy and stages?

Thankfully, my feet are now back in my control. I move to the raised platform in the center of the room. The minute I reach the center of it, a blazing spotlight turns on, blinding me. The rest of the room drops into complete darkness.

I sense him walking around me, examining me, evaluating me. He's not trying to hide his movements, he's simply quiet as he makes the circle.

"Remove your clothes."

There's a roaring in my ears. I stop breathing.

"You heard me."

Suddenly the fog lifts. I see two ways I can play this. I can be completely humiliated, which would show he's on his way to breaking me, or I can strip and stand proud. Stay true to who I am and not let him get a win. Any kind of win.

I strip.

Music is pumped through speakers I hadn't noticed before. It's strong and suggestive. Before he orders me to dance, I will my limbs to move fluidly, with energy and purpose... and pride.

He cannot see my soul if all he's doing is looking at my body. My body is not me. I feel safer now than I've felt in days.

Screw you.

The children coming into her courtroom weren't seen as victims by law enforcement, she said. "They're seen as consenting participants."
—*Selling Atlanta's Children: What has and hasn't changed, by Jane O. Hansen,*
    Special to CNN

CHAPTER TWENTY-FOUR

JAYLA

Karen/Debbie isn't speaking to me. She's not speaking to anyone. The tiny white girl, who I'd later found out was from Lakewood, just west of Denver, was sold at auction because she was a virgin. She came back to our group even more broken than she'd left us. No telling what happened to her on her first night out. Maybe she'll talk and maybe she won't. We all keep secrets.

I'd been a virgin too. But I'm the wrong color from the wrong part of town, so no one even suspected. Even if anyone had known, there would've been no auction for me. At least that's my guess.

Now, tonight, I need to figure out a plan. To get through. To make sure Jayla survives. I've come to love Cherie, my alterego, because she can take the hits. The degradation. The shit.

Jayla, on the other hand, demands more protection than I ever could have imagined during my life back in Denver.

I smooth on the skintight clothing that covers next to nothing and check my makeup. I'm honest about the way I look. No sex-goddess here. But I've learned that for the most part, a girl can look like crap and it won't matter. Daddy, however, will do a check as I leave the motel. If I don't meet his standards I'll meet his fist. Not something I enjoy.

"Cherie," he says as I walk out. "Step over here a minute."

I follow him into a shadowed spot on the sidewalk outside of the motel and wait for him to talk.

"That was a good catch you made about the new bitch being a virgin."

"Thank you." I can't help adding, "You doubled your money."

Daddy laughed. "More like tripled it."

I hesitate but I have to ask. "So was her first time easier?" Easier than mine, I wonder?

"What the fuck do I care?"

I stand silent.

"But I gave you a break by letting you babysit the virgin. So tonight you gotta make it up. I expect double from you, Cherie." He reaches out to tilt my chin up. "You know what happens if you don't meet my expectations, right?" He presses his fingers into my jaw.

"Yeah," I force the word out.

"Then do it." He releases the painful grip.

Double? I'm not stupid, Daddy. If I get you double tonight, that'll become your expected. But I'll get you sufficiently more. Enough more to make you think I worked extra hard, but not enough to make you think I can do it every night.

As I force my feet to move across the parking lot in the direction of the arena, I can see the silhouettes of three other girls walking ahead of me. Where do they call home? Colorado, like me? Or somewhere more exotic. The Philippines? New York City?

Do they have Watchers?

About a month after Daddy put me on the street, one of the newer girls tried to run away. Two men brought her to Daddy and dumped her at his feet while a couple of us looked on. Daddy paid the men with dope and when they left he killed her in front of us. Slowly. Even though she was half-dead already.

"I have Watchers on every block you work, in every city you work. If you think you can leave me, you can't. If you try, this is what happens." Her damaged face and broken body is never far from my thoughts.

I'd also heard of other pimps recognizing a girl and either taking her for themselves or gaining favor by returning her to her trafficker.

Sometimes I think traffickers lay traps just so they can inflict pain.

Five blocks from the sports arena, a clean, new model car pulls up in front of me. Seven months ago I would have plowed right on past him, intent on my destination and oblivious. Now, I stop. Look at him. Wonder briefly about whether or not he has a wife. Kids. People who look up to him.

"Wanna party?" he asks.

"We can talk about it," I say as I look him over. First, I try to see if there's any sign of him being undercover. He's pretty out of shape for a cop. Next, is he going to get off by trying to kill me? There's nothing about him that shouts psycho-abuser, but I've learned those signs can be subtle. "What are you looking for?"

"Just an hour or so of romance."

Shit. First of all, there is no romance, and second of all, an *hour*? In whose fantasy?

"It'll cost you a hundred." That's at the high end for someone like me on the street, but I need extra cash tonight.

"No problem." A red flag shoots up. He's not even going to try and negotiate? Off of a top price? I look around trying to spot Daddy's Watchers.

"Sorry," I say. "I forgot I have a date."

"A hundred and fifty."

That could go a long way toward my extra cash for Daddy. I'm tempted. "What's your definition of romance?"

He looks at me like I'm from Mars. "Definition?"

"Yeah. If we get together, what exactly are you looking for?"

Is he blushing?

"You are blowing the whole idea of romance. Do you want my money or not?"

The combination of his blushing and a hundred and fifty dollars takes care of my concern. "Sure. Let's party."

I get into his car and discreetly check out the interior. Completely clean. No Binky's or any other sign of children. I can't stand the idea of johns with kids. This might not be so bad.

My hotel is two blocks away. He turns into a parking space and I believe I've hit my jackpot for the night. Two more dates and I can quit, make Daddy happy, and get the sleep of normal people. More or less.

Daddy moved me to a different room after Karen/Debbie experienced her first sale. Not out of any sense of compassion for Karen. Just commerce. No way a guy was gonna wind up satisfied with a weepy girl in the room.

I open the door (Daddy had disengaged the automatic locking mechanism) and walk into the room.

And I wait.

It's not like I'm suspicious, even though I am. It's more like I don't know this john and how he operates. A bruised and swollen eye a few months ago taught me to watch and listen. Let the customer tell me what he's looking for.

"You clean?"

I hate this question. Do I get to ask johns if they have an STD? Shit.

"Yeah, I'm clean." And you? I ask silently.

"As of when?"

"Last time I was checked." Which of course has never happened. Daddy has earned back whatever he paid for me ten times over. Probably more. He couldn't care less about what happens to one of his older girls—which I've become in the span of six months.

"Well get over here then." He unzips his pants and drops them to his knees and his dirty underwear follows.

The ignorant fool didn't even consider that the john before him might have given me something.

I refrain from asking him about the romance part.

[Denver is a convenient hub for the comings and goings of kids indentured to magazine sales crews or migrant farm workers in bondage to debt...]The surprise is the backyard nature of it all. The Colorado Project revealed that trafficking is thriving statewide—in Denver, Lakewood, Aurora, Colorado Springs and rural Colorado—and is as likely to involve a white middle-schooler at odds with her parents as it is an undocumented worker fearing deportation.
—Moving in the Right Direction, by Leslie Petrovski, January 30, 2014

CHAPTER TWENTY-FIVE

Mex sat at an outdoor table at Tamayo, a restaurant in Larimer Square, about seven blocks from The Ritz-Carlton in downtown Denver. He slowly sipped a three-year old Patron and nibbled at a plate of chicken tinga tacos. Earlier he'd told Cade and Darius he needed space, and he figured they could use a break from him as well.

He focused on the throngs of young people who walked past him on the sidewalk, a lot of them with their heads bent as they chose electronics over people occupying their space. A digital interaction that didn't require eye contact.

Every culture and economic status was represented on this Denver street corner. While the cultures were evident in Aspen Falls, he missed the diversity of economies. The sheer energy and optimism that can come from people who don't have much to lose. Who have more faith than fear.

Who didn't know how vulnerable they were.

Alexis. Jayla. Those names never left his thoughts. He needed to do right by them. While he could identify with the anguish their parents felt, it was the girls themselves who filled his daily mind map. It was his awareness of what they were facing every day—every night—they were apart from their families that sawed into his heart. He wanted to find them yesterday, sweep in with sword flaying and cape flying.

But the real world sucked.

He took another sip of tequila.

Mex watched as a man in his twenties began gesticulating to a girl who was fifteen at the most. He grabbed her arm and she tried to twist away but he was too strong. Mex left his table and jogged toward the pair.

Forcing through with his shoulder Mex butted the young man away from the girl, breaking the threatening hold and powering the instigator to the ground. A small crowd gathered, unsure of who the bad guy was, the old guy or the young one. A woman put her arms around the girl.

Mex yanked the man's wrists together and hauled him to his feet.

"What the fuck are you doing, man? Get your hands off me!"

Mex squared their faces. "What the fuck are *you* trying to do to that girl?"

"She's my sister!"

"Your sister?"

"She lied about where she was going today."

Mex relaxed his grip but didn't let go. He looked at the young girl in the woman's embrace. "Is he telling the truth?"

When the girl nodded he could see the physical resemblance between brother and sister. He released his hold. "I'm sorry. I misread the interaction. I was only trying to protect her."

"Screw you." The young man brushed himself off as if Mex had left him filthy.

The woman who had moved to protect the girl stepped forward, inserting herself into the brother's space. "You should thank this man. If someone had been trying to take your sister and do her harm, what would have happened to her? You would have lost her. He was the only one here to step in."

The young man stared at the woman, obviously digesting her words. Finally he reached out, grabbed his sister's arm, and gave Mex a quick nod before heading down the sidewalk, his sister walking slightly behind him, head bowed.

Mex wondered how many siblings sold their siblings? It had to happen. He hoped it wasn't happening with those two.

After the crowd dispersed, the woman approached Mex. "That was brave of you. Thank you."

"I saw you hug the girl. You got involved as well."

"I don't see as I had a choice."

"You always have a choice."

The woman made a sad face. "Not always."

Mex found his manners and reached out his hand. "I'm Mex Anderson."

She did a double-take, hesitated, then put hers into his. "My name is Rachel. Rachel Hanson."

Mex motioned toward his table at Tamayo where the wait staff and customers were standing, looking in his direction. "Would you join me? I'm enjoying some tequila and tacos."

Rachel looked into his face and seemed to arrive at a decision. "Sure. I'd like that."

The victim enters into the sex industry where [s]he experiences constant violence and severe trauma. Victims undergo a process of being recruited, groomed, abused, controlled, and being turned out by violent pimps. The result of this step is a "trauma bond" between victim and pimp or trafficker that can be equated to Stockholm Syndrome.

— Pimp-Prostitute Relationship, by Anna Engel, November 2012

CHAPTER TWENTY-SIX

Settled, an order of a pepito steak wrap in front of her at the outdoor table, Rachel looked up at Mex. "I recognize you from the news the other day. You're the guy trying to find the missing rich girl."

"Yeah, her and another one."

Rachel raised an eyebrow.

"Not so rich. Not so high profile. Just as important." Mex evaluated the woman in front of him. No makeup. Plain clothes. It was like she was trying to disappear. But she couldn't quite keep her eyes from challenging her surroundings.

Mex knew she had a story and he had a hunch she might be able to add something to his dedicated band of rescuers. He also knew she wasn't likely to confide in him. "Do you mind if I ask someone to join us?"

Rachel's face relaxed. She almost smiled. "No, not at all."

After another Patron and a glass of chardonnay for Rachel, Cade finally approached the table and placed her bag over a chair. "Hi. I came as soon as I could." She looked at Rachel and held out her hand. "Cade LeBlanc."

"You're his partner," Rachel said, shaking Cade's hand.

"On our better days," Cade answered.

"Rachel Hanson."

Mex described the event that occurred earlier and how he and Rachel got involved. He didn't embellish. He didn't get emotional. But he did paint a picture.

Mex nudged his Patron away from him. He looked first at Rachel and then at Cade.

Cade took a bite of Mex's taco while Rachel sat back in her seat, color fading from her face, almost like she knew what was coming.

"Ms. Hanson," Mex said, "I've been reading people for almost longer than I can remember. My ability to decipher motivation, to appraise a situation, has almost always been to my advantage." Except for one momentous occasion, he thought. He reached for the glass and sipped his drink. "Can you tell us why you were so willing to become involved in an altercation that could've turned violent?"

Rachel licked her lips and whispered, "The girl looked as if she needed help."

Mex settled deeper into his chair and closed his eyes.

Cade focused on the young woman, then watched as Mex emotionally pulled away from the conversation. She understood this was now her show. Cade had also seen the same haunted presence Rachel was exhibiting in people she'd removed from cults.

"Do you have enough to eat?" Cade asked nodding toward her plate. "Would you like something else?"

"No, I'm fine." The young woman shifted in her seat and swallowed. Cade noticed Rachel's Adidas-clad foot pumping under the table.

Cade signaled the waiter and asked for a zin and another order of chicken tinga tacos. She waited quietly, giving Rachel a chance to find her center and relax.

Placing her hand next to Rachel's, close but not touching, Cade said, "Ninety-nine times out of a hundred, your reaction would have been spot on. You had no idea that the forceful-sounding young man was her brother trying to keep her safe."

Rachel nodded. Her hand twitched.

"You've had experience with this." It was a statement, not a question. Cade covered the anxious hand with hers. She knew she couldn't force anything from this young woman, or everything she might share would be lost.

Rachel nodded again. She gave a slight cough. "It's been a long time since I've stood in the moment. That place of control. Or rather, lack of control. My reaction was instinctive."

Her voice got stronger with each sentence. She made eye contact with Cade and pulled her hand away. "I was forced into prostitution when I was fourteen. I lived the life until I was twenty-three. Nine years. Nine years in a prison without bars."

"Do you want to talk about it?" Cade asked.

"Not today. Not after what just happened."

When the food and wine were delivered, Cade thanked the server and waited for him to leave. "What do you do now?"

Rachel forced a laugh. "I'm an advocate. I'm on call with all of the local law enforcement agencies, shelters, churches, GOs and NGOs. You name the agency or organization or group, if someone comes in who's been trafficked, I'm on the resource list."

Cade was impressed. Government organizations and non-government organizations didn't always share their help lists. "You must know your stuff."

"I don't know about that. I only know that the victim assistance positions are filled by women who can pass a background check. It doesn't mean they aren't helpful, but the girls who come into the system have a hard time relating to a college educated woman who's been able to direct her own life, make her own choices. That's where I come in."

"You're a bridge."

Rachel's face brightened with the tiniest of smiles. "Yeah. I guess that's exactly what I am."

"Are you aware we're trying to find a couple of girls who've gone missing?"

"I saw the news interview."

"When we bring these girls in—and we will—would you be willing to work with them? Get personal? I'm not talking about an advocate. I'm talking about a sister." Cade leaned forward and took Rachel's hand. "I'm talking about being there with us from the beginning."

"I'd like that, yeah."

Cade sipped her wine. "Tell me a little about yourself."

Rachel hesitated, then nodded once and looked Cade in the eye. "My parents divorced when I was twelve, and my dad moved away. Mom, well... all I can remember about my mom after the divorce was her anger and bitterness toward my dad. Those emotions consumed her and she had nothing left for me. And to be honest? She was so angry I was afraid that anger would boil over given the opportunity. I didn't want my mom to lash out at me like she lashed out at my dad."

"What happened?"

"I ran away. Hitchhiked from Denver to LA if you can believe it. I think back on it now and can't believe I survived that trip. It was when I hit LA that my vulnerability lit up like a neon sign. It didn't take long for a cute guy to offer to save me from hunger and sleeping on the streets."

"Did you try to leave him?"

Rachel hiked up her shirt a few inches to reveal several scars slashing across her abdomen. "Only once."

"How did you finally get out?"

"He was killed. Ironically, he was stabbed to death." Rachel ghosted a bitter smile. "About six months before, I'd heard about a place where girls could find refuge. I hadn't dared until that night."

"Tell me more."

"If you're sure you want to hear it."

"I'm sure."

After they'd cried, ordered more wine, and finally begun to eat, Cade reflected on how much emotion can be packed into a few minutes of discussion. While Rachel's story was uniquely her own, it sadly blended with dozens Cade had heard. A young girl's moment of weakness or desperation, or simply trusting the wrong person, catapulted her into a world she couldn't escape. A world she began to believe was all she was worthy of. A world girls often begin to believe they've chosen. Those were the girls for whom Cade's particular area of expertise was most valuable.

"We're going to get these girls back. In the meantime, I'd like you to get to know the parents. It will help you get an understanding of them before they were taken."

"The parents? But I don't have any experience with that."

Rachel's own story included the not-so-pretty picture of her family wanting nothing to do with her when she finally escaped life on the streets.

"Because of your experience, you might also be able to begin to counsel these parents as to how their daughters might feel when they're reunited. You might be able to help them find empathy." And, Cade thought, you might also find a measure of acceptance from them for yourself.

Rachel was quiet. A tear slipped down her cheek. Her foot quit shaking. "Tell me how to begin."

"I'll take you to meet Jayla's mother first," Cade said.

That's when both women looked up and seemed to register Mex was still with them. He'd sat silently for the last forty-five minutes. Eyes closed. Drink unfinished. A small smile now spread across his face.

The majority of children associated with organized criminal units have liberal access to drugs and other substances that increase their dependency on the crime unit. Not infrequently, the babies of girls who become pregnant are removed and raised either by members of the organizer's extended family or by others within the criminal network. Once taken away from their mothers, these babies are used to exert even greater control over the prostituted youth.
—The Commercial Sexual Exploitation of Children, U.S. National Study, by Richard J. Estes and Neil Alan Weiner, University of Pennsylvania 2001 (revised 2002)

CHAPTER TWENTY-SEVEN

JAYLA

"Amber, listen to me. You've gotta stay tough." I reach for her hand. We're standing on a sidewalk littered with cigarette butts and used condoms. The shadows cast by the streetlights are either dwarfed or elongated. All eerie, none looking the way it is in reality. Amber's real name is LaTisha, but right now she needs her hard name. The name that can help get her through this.

"I can't do this again."

"You can if it's what you have to do to survive. To one day be able to claim your babies when this is over and lead a normal life."

Amber laughs. "What the hell is normal? I forget."

"It'll come back to you. You have to believe that."

"This baby isn't healthy. I've been doing lots of heroin and I don't think I can stop. If I had this baby, it'd be addicted. It'd be sick."

"You can't know for sure."

"Even if the baby would be born fine, they'd take it away from me. Like they did my Krystina. Make me go over quota just to see my own kid." Amber backs to the wall and slides her bottom to the ground.

"I can't do this again," she repeats.

"You see any old hookers in our crew?" I ask her as I sink down next to her.

Silence. "No."

"So where do you think they've gone?"

More silence. Then, "I think they were sold off to another pimp or they're dead."

"Or?"

"Or what?"

"Don't you think they might have found their way back to their lives?"

Silence. "How long you think this been goin' on?" she asks.

"You mean girls leaving?"

Amber nods.

"A while."

"Do you seriously think that many girls got back to their old lives? Their real lives?"

I can't answer her.

"Do you?"

I begin the lie, but it's the lie that's helped keep me alive. "Here's what I think. I think that you and me have choices to make. Even when it doesn't feel like we do. And the choice we make every day is the choice that gives us the best chance of getting back to those old lives of ours."

That's the lie—believing there's a chance. I hang on to it anyway, knowing it for the deception it is.

I keep talking. "It might feel like we're giving in at the time, but the longer we can stay alive, the longer we can remember who we are, the better shot we have to have a life after this one. To tell these assholes to piss off."

"I wish I had your strength."

"You do. You've misplaced it for a bit, that's all."

Amber shakes her head. "I don't think so. If I ever had it, it's gone now." A tear slides down her cheek.

I reach over and wipe it away with my thumb. "Then borrow some of mine until you find it again."

"You know what, Cherie, I don't think I want any. I think maybe this is easier."

"What do you mean? What's easier?"

"Let 'em do what they're gonna do. My life is done. My daughter's caught in this hell and it's because of me she's caught. I can't do that again."

I hate doing this. I do. "You never know, Amber. Tomorrow could be the day you're free. Maybe one of your johns will be one of those guys who will take you someplace safe." I hate the lies coming out of my mouth but she has to find something to hang on to. "And if not tomorrow, maybe next week. Maybe before your baby is born."

She closes her eyes.

"You've gotta believe, LaTisha. You've gotta believe."

Amber shakes her head. "LaTisha's gone." She stares ahead at nothing. "Amber too."

I try to figure out a way to take Amber and me off the track for tonight. I'm afraid to leave her alone. I think about telling Daddy that we're sick and throwing up. Must've eaten something bad. To have him buy that though, we'd have to puke in front of him. Maybe I can find something that'll make us sick.

"I know what you're trying to do," Amber says.

"What's that?"

"Get us a night off."

"We're due."

"We're never due and you know it. Besides, it's too late."

"What do you mean?"

"I've done it."

"What are you talking about?"

"Just sit here with me, will you? I don't want to die alone."

I realize what Amber/LaTisha has done. I want to call out for help but I know that won't save her.

In the end, I can only hold her and try to respect the decision she made.

And be grateful I can still cry.

Afterward, I do one of the hardest things I've ever done. I wipe away the wetness on my cheeks, kiss my friend, and then get up and walk away. There's nothing I can do for her now. Someone will discover her body. Daddy will find out he's lost a revenue stream, but not from me. Any involvement on my part and I risk his particular brand of discipline.

Tears stream down my face as I move toward the shadows down the street. I'm not sure if I'm crying because LaTisha has died or because I'm still alive.

Colorado is known for its mountainous regions and reclusive landscape... Areas which are hidden away from the general population are attractive to traffickers looking for a place to hide potential victims. Many people who are exploited for their labor are often taken to farms that are hidden from roads and cities where other people may report trafficking. ... This state brings in people from all over the country for its tourist attractions and destination resorts... which makes it possible to transport trafficking victims to and throughout Colorado without being questioned.

—Observing Vulnerability to Human Trafficking within Regional Districts in the State of Colorado,

by Charlotte Anderson, To Fulfill the Requirements of the Senior Honors Thesis, Metropolitan State University

CHAPTER TWENTY-EIGHT

"Come on in, then." Mary Thomas opened the door wide for Cade and Rachel.

"Thanks for taking the time to meet with us, Mary," Cade said.

She eyed Rachel as she spoke. "You the best hope I have for getting my Jayla home. Course I'd meet with you."

"Mary, this is Rachel Hanson. Her experience might be very similar to what Jayla is experiencing. She's here to support you, and more importantly Jayla, when she comes home."

Mary let loose a sob. "Is she coming home?"

"You know I can't promise you. You know that, right?" Cade asked.

Mary crumpled in a chair and closed her eyes. Her entire body quivered. A moment passed. "I know."

"But that doesn't mean we aren't without resources. It doesn't mean we aren't without hope," Cade said.

Jayla's mom flexed her shoulders. Her hands gripped the arms of the chair as she straightened her back. Her eyes opened. "I want my baby home."

"That's where we're headed. That's what I want you to prepare for. And that's why I've asked Rachel to meet you. To prepare you."

"Prepare me?" The mother's voice lost all the strength it had held.

Cade positioned a chair to face the woman. Knee to knee she reached out to grab Mary's hands. "Look at me."

Mary ignored her.

"Mary, look at me."

Cade waited.

Mary's gaze slid over Cade's shoulder. They held there for a moment before finally making that electric contact. The point where everything was honest. The point where pain was a promise. The point where Cade understood any mother would rather die than acknowledge as truth.

"You understand the daughter you lost won't be the same girl we find, right?"

Mary squeezed her eyes closed and held still. Finally she opened them and looked at Cade. She positioned her mouth but nothing came out. Instead of speaking, she nodded.

"But Jayla, for all that's happened to her, will still be your daughter." Cade paused. "Do you believe that, Mary? She will still be your little girl. She'll still be your baby."

Tears streamed down Mary's face. "How do I—"

"That's why Rachel's here. She can help you understand what your daughter has been through. That's important. You've never needed to know anything more than you need to know this. But even more importantly, she can help you understand what Jayla is going to require from you when she gets home. The space. The time. The unwavering belief that while your daughter has been forced to take part in acts many would consider sinful, your daughter is not a sinner. That while she survived because she could be sexual, it wasn't her choice. It was only a matter of survival. Her survival. Your baby's survival."

Mary looked at Rachel for the first time. *Really* looked at her. "You did this? You lived it?"

Rachel's eyes were downcast. She shuffled in her chair. Finally she lifted her face and looked Mary in the eye. "Yes, ma'am. I lived it, and I survived."

Mary closed her eyes, but the tears slipped out and slid down her face anyway. Her jaw clenched and her lips worked to hold in her pain. Finally, she opened her eyes and held out her arms. "Come to me, baby. Come to me."

Rachel twitched and hesitated, then skidded to her knees in front of the woman she'd just met. The two embraced and all other sounds were washed away by sobs. Cade knew that for Mary, the tears represented a need to nurture her absent daughter, and Rachel was releasing years of self-punishment and doubt.

Cade gave them a few minutes. "I should get back. Are you two set for now?"

Mary had already moved to the kitchen to prepare a light snack for her and Rachel to share. They would probably talk for hours. In the end, Rachel would not only know more about Jayla, she would feel the acceptance of Jayla's mom.

"We're set," Mary said. "Just bring me back my daughter."

Much later that night Cade and Rachel sat in the suite at the Ritz-Carlton, searching for all of the answers and not finding many.

"Mary made me feel special," Rachel said.

"You understand that while it's mostly based on positive emotion, part of it is based on guilt, don't you?"

"Guilt?"

"Regardless of whether or not Mary Thomas's actions played a role in her daughter's abduction, she's bound to feel guilt. After all, keeping her daughter safe was her responsibility."

"She had something to do with Jayla being taken?"

"We can't know that. But think about this, even if she was negligent, is her anguish any less? Not at all. If anything, it's more. There might be a part of her that will transfer the feelings she has for her daughter on to you. You're going to have to deal with that if it happens."

"So what do I do?"

"Right now, nothing."

"Okay. But I can't just sit and wait."

"I was hoping you'd say that. Tomorrow I want you to talk to the parents of Alexis Halston, the same way you talked to Mary Thomas."

"Oh, no. I can't possibly speak to them."

"Why not? In truth, they're no different from Mary Thomas. They've lost a daughter. You can be their bridge, too."

"Bridge? They own the bridges. They own everything."

"That's where you're wrong."

"What are you talking about? I can't bring them anything they can't already access."

"You might be surprised, Rachel. My gut tells me that the information you can provide will be far beyond what Steven and Adele Halston might have access to. Let's play it by ear, shall we?"

Anonymity Newsletter

By signing up to the Anonymity Newsletter you will receive invaluable information about how to remain anonymous online to hide your Deep Web activities. You will also receive the latest news on what is happening on the Darknet Marketplaces and Deep Web as well as great resources to use on your journey through the Darknet.

—A popup on an article about Silk Road Online that says Silk Road 3.0 is "back online and open for business. The team did a massive security overhaul on the site to try and make it more secure and anonymous." A link to the Silk Road 3.0 Guide is offered.

CHAPTER TWENTY-NINE

"Mrs. Halston, thank you for agreeing to see us today." Cade said after introducing Rachel.

"Do you have information regarding my daughter?" Adele Halston, anorexically thin before the ordeal, looked cadaverous. The smell of booze drifted from her body like something sick or dead.

"No, I'm sorry we don't. But we are working on a few things we believe will provide leads. We should have something in a couple of days."

"Who is she?" Adele nodded toward Rachel. "Why is she here?"

"Rachel is uniquely qualified to help Alexis when she returns home."

"How?"

"That's Rachel's story to tell you, but because of her experience, I think you should talk. Is your husband home?"

"He's not here. I want you to tell me how this girl can help Alexis."

Cade looked at Rachel and nodded.

Rachel took a breath. "I was forced into prostitution when I was fourteen. I know how—"

Adele Halston physically shrank away. A guttural, animal-like sound came from deep inside the tiny woman. "No."

"Mrs. Halston, Adele," Cade reached forward and placed a hand on the thin shoulder. "This is important. You want to give Alexis everything she'll need when she gets home, don't you?" Cade didn't wait for an answer. "Rachel could be part of that."

"No. Get away. Leave."

"We'll go. But you should seriously think about what Alexis will require, not what you're afraid of."

"How do you know what I'm afraid of?" Adele Halston sat taller.

"I know about Samuel. I know how devastated you must have been to lose your little boy. How frightening and suspicious the world became to you. How you've lived in different levels of fear and pain for all these years, moving through life like a ghost."

"How dare you—"

"Now you have a chance to make sure Alexis gets what she needs. You have a chance to be the mother you can be, and the one she deserves."

"Get out of here. Get out of my house. Get out!"

As Cade and Rachel got in Cade's SUV Rachel said, "I'm sorry. I've messed things up. I—"

"You didn't mess anything up." Cade started the engine and drove out of the circular drive. At the street she turned right and then pulled over.

They sat.

And sat.

Rachel fidgeted. "I did something wrong. Please tell me what I did wrong."

"You didn't do anything wrong."

"Why are we here?"

"Because if I'm right, and I usually am, it would be a waste of time and gas to return to the hotel." Cade put her phone on the dash.

"What did you think of Adele Halston?" Cade asked.

Rachel closed her eyes and then looked out the windshield, like the trees and manicured lawns and flowerbeds on both sides of the road would provide either answers or security.

She shifted in her seat, but stared ahead. "I think she's troubled. I wasn't aware of the other loss she experienced."

"We all experience losses, Rachel. You know that as well as anyone. The quality of the next part of our lives, or the entirety of our lives, depends on how we respond to them. We make choices. We can dwell in the loss, giving power to who or what caused it, or we can take it and turn it into something positive."

"What was yours, Cade?"

"I've had a few. You can't get to be my age, done what I've done, and not feel sadness. But my first one, my big one, was a sister I loved who took her own life. She'd gotten involved in a cult, regretted her decision but felt stuck, and ended her life."

"You found her. You found the body."

"I did."

"And that loss made you help others trapped in religious cults."

Cade nodded. "And now I'm working on a twist."

"What's that?"

"Trafficking cults."

Rachel processed those words then chuckled. "Yeah, I get that. False gods come in all kinds of disguises."

Cade's phone rang and she looked at the ID and winked at Rachel. "Like I said."

"Hi, Adele."

"I've thought about what you said. About doing the right thing for Alexis."

"Yes?"

"Can you come back? And bring that girl? That prostitute?"

"I can come back. I'll ask Rachel if she's willing to join me. But Adele?"

Silence.

"She's not a prostitute. She's an advocate for your daughter. If you're not willing to accord her the respect she deserves, I can't guarantee that she'll be willing to help."

Silence.

"I understand. I was wrong. Please tell her I was wrong."

"You can tell her yourself when you see her."

The document goes into incredible detail about Greiner's alleged decision to allow her pre-teen child to have sex with Thomas Keske, a 23-year-old man from Australia, with references to vibrators, lube and articles such as "8 Things Every Woman Should Try in Bed."

Julie Greiner Accused of Pimping 12-Year-Old Daughter: Orgasm Tip, 50 Shades of Lube

—By Michael Roberts

CHAPTER THIRTY

"Hi, Amanda. I don't know if you remember me." Mex smiled at the receptionist at the fitness center as he handed her his card. "This is Darius Johnson, my partner."

People in various workout clothes, most of which would buy a week's worth of groceries, arrived to achieve the perfect bodies to go with their perfect lives. Tone meant everything, along with the trendiest workout gear.

"Of course I do. To tell you the truth, Mr. Anderson, most of the people who come in here every day of every week don't know my name. I pay attention when someone considers me worthy of one."

"Why do you work here?"

"Paying my way through school. Plus I have access to all of the equipment after hours."

"Do you have the time to actually use any of it?"

Amanda laughed. "No, not really. It sounded super when they offered me the job though." She smiled brightly. "You looking for Donny?"

"Yeah, as a matter of fact. Is he working today?"

"Your timing is perfect. Not only is he here, but he doesn't have a client on the books for another thirty minutes."

Mex looked up at the catwalk. The administrative offices and employee lounge were within easy view. If Donny saw him standing down her he was likely to bolt.

"You want to surprise him, don't you?" Amanda asked.

"Are you asking because you want to warn him?"

"No way. He's a prick. If you can put the screws to him, I'm more than happy to help."

"Okay. How do I do that?"

"We have a VIP Lounge. It's on the third floor and requires a code to enter." Amanda stripped a piece of paper from a pad and jotted down some numbers. "Is he gonna be able to bring blowback down on me?" she asked as she handed the paper to Mex. "Could I lose my job?"

Mex looked at the young girl who continued to hand him the code. He couldn't lie. "You might lose your job, Amanda. But if what I think will happen actually does, you'll be one of the heroes. If you're fired and don't get a better offer right away, contact me. I promise you I'll find you something."

"It doesn't matter. If Donny had something to do with this, he has to be caught. I'm cool with a hiccup in my cash flow."

Mex wanted to hug her.

"Go up to the lounge. I'll page Donny and tell him he has a potential client there. I can't guarantee nobody will walk in, but you'll probably have the lounge to yourself."

Mex and Darius entered the elevator and selected the button for the third floor. A keypad appeared and Mex entered the numbers Amanda had given him. When the elevator doors opened it was clear they were at the VIP Lounge.

Two men, in what Mex called penguin suits, rushed into the main room. One moved toward them. "What can we get for you?"

Mex eyed him and took a breath. What the hell, he thought. "Two Macallan 18s. And leave the bottle."

When left to themselves, Mex and Darius looked around the opulent room. Mex had a hard time tying what he was seeing to a fitness joint. It looked more like a place for bankers or lawyers. Polished wainscoting, thick carpet on top of thicker padding, perfectly placed lighting next to butter-leather seating. Tables arranged to take in the views, linens in place. Every table held fresh flowers and a candle, and there were at least three enormous flower arrangements spread throughout the room.

"Shit," Darius said. "I'm changing my mind about investing in a gym."

One of the penguins returned with a tray, two glasses filled with an amber liquid, a capped bottle next to them. "I hope this meets your expectations, sir."

Mex took the tray and sat it on a table. "I'm sure it will be fine. Now leave us. We have business to discuss."

"Yes, sir. Should you require service, simply press the star key on any of the phones in the room."

"Thank you, we'll be fine."

They were alone. Each took a full glass, sipped, and moved away. Instinctively, Mex and Darius found themselves in a corner that would be behind Donny when he entered the room. No reason to give him an easy escape. Keep it simple.

They sat their drinks down on a table and waited.

The elevator doors opened and Donny walked into the VIP area, optimistically looking around for someone with enough swag to score the third floor.

Then he saw Mex.

Donny spun back to the elevator but Darius stood in the way.

"Aw, shit. What are you trying to do to me? I told you what I know."

"Nope, Donny. I don't think you did. We have a lot to talk about."

"What do you mean?"

"Alexis Halston wasn't the first girl you sold, was she?"

"I don't know what you're talking about."

"Of course you don't." Mex waited. "Do you want me to spell it out to you or do you want to gain a few points with early cooperation?"

"Like I said, you have the wrong dude."

"Well, Donny, why don't you have a seat and tell us why?"

"I don't have to do anything. You have no authority."

Darius moved to stand directly in front of the personal trainer. "Look, you can help us or we can upend your life so bad you'll never figure out which way is up."

"You think because you're a tough, black bad-ass you can scare me?"

"I think I just did. Sit down punk."

Donny flung an arm in the air and turned his back. "I don't need this shit."

Darius grabbed Donny's arm and yanked it behind the trainer's back. "My partner asked you nicely to sit down and talk to us. Trust me, it's in your best interest to cooperate." Darius walked Donny to a chair and thrust him into it.

"I could have you arrested."

"Really? Really? Are you going to play that card? You're even dumber than you look."

Mex lifted his glass. "Would you like a drink?"

"Yeah, I would."

"Darius, will you ask our friends for another glass?"

While Darius went to a phone to call the waiters, Mex leaned over the table to watch Donny's face. "You know, people make terrible decisions for what they think are the right reasons all the time. I've experienced that in my own family. Making a bad choice doesn't necessarily make you a bad person." He peered into the eyes of the young man in front of him. "Do you agree, Donny?"

Donny's eyes flew to a far corner of the lounge, then he met Mex's gaze. "I guess."

"You ever make a bad choice, Donny?"

"I'm pretty sure everybody has."

"You ever make a terrible choice?"

"Probably."

One of the penguins emerged with a glass.

Mex thanked the man then poured Donny some of the Macallan. Darius took his seat at the table.

"Well, Donny," Mex said, "this is the best chance you'll have to talk about it, and by 'it' I mean Alexis."

"Do you find Alexis attractive?" Darius asked.

"Sure man, who wouldn't? The chick was hot."

"Was?" Mex asked.

"She's gone. That's the only reason I said 'was.' Don't be reading shit into what I say."

"How much money did you owe before Alexis went missing?" Darius asked.

"None of your business."

"We can find out."

"And today? How much money do you owe today?"

Donny sniffed and squirmed in his chair.

"Donny, look at me." Mex waited. "We know what you did. And we know what you did out of at least one other fitness center." Mex took a sip of his drink. "I'll be honest with you. We can't prove everything right this minute, but we will. It won't take long. Mr. Johnson and I are that good."

Donny began to lift the glass to his mouth but had to use both hands to minimize the shaking.

"Here's my idea. Are you interested?"

A blank stare was Donny's answer.

"My thinking is that if Alexis's life is in danger, helping us now might make things look better for you. If she's killed, you'll be looking at a whole other scenario. And you'll have no edge."

Donny drained the glass.

"Are you ready to talk?"

A nod.

Here in this country, people are being bought, sold, and smuggled like modern-day slaves, often beaten, starved, and forced to work as prostitutes or to take jobs as migrant, domestic, restaurant, or factory workers with little or no pay.
-FBI

CHAPTER THIRTY-ONE

OLIVIA

Dear Diary,

I wish I was grown and a vet already. You can count on animals. Not so much people.

Being twelve sucks. Being twelve in *my* family sucks more.

Tonight all my parents can talk about is the great cut Ethan made in his football game. How many times do I have to hear them describe his terrific moves? Dad especially. All he really seems to care about outside of work is Ethan. If I had been a boy I doubt there'd ever been a third kid. I probably disappointed my dad so they had to try again.

And get this, tomorrow Mom is taking Sarah to get on birth control pills. Are you kidding me? After months of shouting and threats, they cave? I'm sick of Sarah's drama. And sick of my parents paying attention to it.

I don't understand how Sarah and Ethan can each be so special to my parents while I sit here waiting for someone to notice me. Thank goodness for Madison, and my online friends. I'd be totally alone otherwise.

Totally.

* * *

Dear Diary,

I'm in love!!!!!!!!!

Maddy knows everything. I was on the phone with her forever. Maddy asked a lot of questions and doesn't seem to get everything, but she will. In the end she'll come around and not be jealous. Yeah, that's what she is. Jealous.

His name is Ian. Isn't that a great name?

He loves me. And he hasn't even met me! We've been talking on Facebook for over a month from Maddy's house. He knows everything about me and I know everything about him.

He's older. But not creepy older. Like 20s or 30s or something. He's 16. And cute!!!

Ian and Olivia. Ian and Livvy. Doesn't that sound perfect?

* * *

"I know, Maddy, right? It's like a miracle." We're at a table by ourselves in the school cafeteria. As usual, no one is paying any attention to us, but still I keep my voice low. "We're perfect for each other."

Maddy takes a spoonful of her fruit cup. She swallows. "No. Listen to me. Have you watched those TV movies where the people they met online are psychos? I'm not saying this isn't a miracle. I'm only saying you don't know enough about him. I mean *really* know stuff about him. You might be rushing things. It's kind of early in the relationship, don't you think?"

"A psycho? Are you kidding me? You're just jealous." I feel a tingle of doubt.

She puts her spoon in the cup and we both watch as it tilts to the side. Maddy adjusts the spoon and the cup stays level. "I'm not jealous, I'm worried. You can't just go meet this guy somewhere. You know there are bad people on the internet."

"I get that. It's been drilled into us. But Ian is different. We have a relationship. We have a connection. People get matched up on the internet too, don't forget. Once we meet in person, you'll see. He'll be everything I think he is. And I'm not going to meet him, he's coming to meet me."

"Have you stopped to think how a sixteen-year-old boy is coming to meet you?"

"He has an uncle who lives twenty minutes from me. It's like destiny." Why do I feel like I'm arguing my point?

"Where are you supposed to meet?"

"Utah Park."

"You're joking. How come you're not meeting at either his uncle's house or your house? And how are you going to get there?"

"Ian wants our first meeting to be private. Personal. Romantic."

"Why Utah Park? It's big. Why not one of the smaller parks by your house?"

"Did you hear me say private?" I'm tired of Maddy's attitude. "Besides, Utah is halfway. We're meeting by the parking lot."

"So he isn't coming to meet you, you are going to meet him."

"What's the difference? We're in love."

"How are you getting there?"

I feel my face get warm. "I told my mom I'm going swimming."

160

"What time?"

"Four o'clock. After school today."

"Can I come?"

I hesitate. While I would love to share this moment with my BFF, Ian has his own ideas. And they don't include Maddy. I remember an online conversation he and I had a week or so ago. He didn't want me sharing our relationship with anyone. *What we have is special. Between the two of us. It's our secret. I'm not going to tell anyone yet, and I don't want you to either.* Would he be upset that I'd already talked to Maddy about him? Hopefully he'll never find out. But even if he does he'll know it's because I love him.

"Don't be mad, but no. You can't come. This is between Ian and me." Once I say those words I feel so grown up. I'm convinced I'm doing the right thing. I don't have to think about it any more. Cool.

She looks straight into my eyes, her voice cracking slightly, as she tells me the number she wants me to remember—43,200. ... When she was 12 she was targeted by a trafficker who lured her away using kind words and a fast car. ... By her own estimate, 43,200 is the number of times she was raped after falling into the hands of human traffickers.

She says up to 30 men a day, seven days a week, for the best part of four years.

Human trafficking survivor: I was raped 43,200 times, by Rafael Romo, for The CNN Freedom Project

CHAPTER THIRTY-TWO

Maddy sat on the wide bumper of a pickup truck in the last row of the parking lot. She held her phone in her hands, praying she wouldn't have to use it. She knew Livvy would be pissed off at her for even being in the area. But someone needed to keep a lookout. All Livvy could see was love.

A lookout who would decide whether the appropriate call would be to 911 or parents. Parents who might or might not be available.

911 was looking stronger every minute. She hoped desperately she wouldn't have to choose either one.

Livvy's mom's minivan rolled up and Maddy watched as her friend hopped out, a gym bag over one shoulder. She had to give her friend points for production. Livvy was playing the role.

She watched Mrs. Campbell drive away. As the minivan disappeared into traffic, Livvy emerged from the building, phone in her hands, thumbs flying. She barreled around the corner and headed into the park.

Maddy scooted off the bumper and followed her friend, keeping a safe distance between them even though Livvy was intent on her texts and unlikely to notice her surroundings.

Utah Park was large with lots of grass and small lakes, ponds and a waterfall. The only problem with the park was that when it rained heavily it flooded, turning into one gigantic water feature. This afternoon was warm and sunny. The couple could be meeting anywhere.

Maddy kept Livvy's pace, staying about thirty feet behind, while also trying to see who might be lurking off to the sides or waiting expectantly ahead. She wiped her sweaty palms on her pants. The protection racket was obviously not something she was cut out for. Good thing she wanted to go into IT. Livvy's veterinary practice was going to be her first client. Maddy wanted to protect not only her friend but her future income.

Livvy made her way to a bridge and halted in the middle of the span. Maddy moved in the other direction and found a place to sit under a stand of trees where she could observe. The bridge must be the meet-up point.

She looked around. People walked their dogs, jogged, clustered in after-school groups. No one looked threatening. No one looked remotely interested in Livvy.

Until someone did.

* * *

"Livvy?"

I spin around to the voice and run into his arms. "Ian!" I inhale his cologne. A rich, musky scent. I think I'll love that smell forever.

His shoulders are broad and his strength is amazing. Finally I tweak out of his hug to look into his eyes.

"Livvy? Is something wrong?"

My heart is hammering so hard it's hard to breathe. If Ian is sixteen, he's seriously sick.

"You're old!" I blurt out before I can stop the words.

"Not old, Livvy. I'm only a couple of years older than I told you."

"Why did you lie?"

"Because by the time we discussed our ages, I'd already fallen in love. I didn't want to lose you. Can you forgive me?"

He'd already fallen in love with me?

"How old are you?" *Please don't say you're thirty. Please, please, please.*

"How old do you think I am?"

"Twenty-four? Twenty-five?"

Ian laughs. "I've always looked old for my age. I'm actually nineteen. Like I said, only a few years older than what I told you."

"Yeah, but that would be like me telling you I'm fifteen."

He takes my face in his hands. "In the last month we've spoken our hearts. We know our souls. You have the ideas and thoughts of a woman twice your age. Besides, age is only a number." He leans over and whispers in my ear, "And even more important, I love you, Olivia."

My knees tremble and I feel Ian's strong arms hold me up.

"Please tell me you forgive me." His eyes search mine. It's like his whole world hinges on my answer.

"Promise me you'll never lie to me again."

Ian smiles. He has a gorgeous smile. "I promise."

"In that case, you're forgiven."

That's when he kisses me. Sweet and tender. More like a boy than a man, but I couldn't say for sure.

* * *

Maddy watched from her place under the trees, 9-1 entered into her phone. When she saw Livvy stiffen and back away she was ready to press the last 1 and jump into action. But Ian didn't grab her friend and Livvy didn't try to run away. The two figures stood in the middle of the bridge and appeared to be talking. Maddy didn't want to create drama where drama wasn't necessary.

She curled her thumb into her palm and continued to watch.

If someone asked Maddy why she was tailing her best friend, she couldn't have answered. An uncomfortable knot in her gut was all she had to go on. Livvy didn't want to hear any words of caution so those were the words blasting Maddy's thoughts. Loud and bold and red.

Then she saw them draw together and kiss.

Maddy drew in a deep breath and held it. Maybe she'd been wrong about Ian. Maybe the knot in her gut was because she'd never actually talked to him. Didn't know him. Couldn't possibly know how he felt about Livvy.

Maybe she'd been wrong all along. She exhaled. Livvy and Ian stood at the rail and talked for another thirty minutes.

Maddy watched as the couple, arm in arm, moved off the bridge in her direction. She turned her back to the path, waiting for them to walk past.

Livvy's not in danger. At least not now.

Maddy wondered why she couldn't get rid of the worry... couldn't get rid of the knot.

She followed her friend.

At the parking lot, there was one last, long embrace. Ian took off and Livvy began texting almost immediately.

Maddy's phone buzzed.

It was wonderful. RU home? I want to come over and tell u everything.

Maddy thought quickly. Not home now.

Want to come to dinner?

If OK with ur mom.

She loves u. Come as soon as u can.

K.

Maddy tucked her phone in her backpack and watched Livvy pile into a minivan that belonged to one of the Campbell's neighbors. After the van drove away, she unlocked her bike and straddled it while she called her mom to tell her she was going to Livvy's for dinner. Maddy decided to ride straight there, wishing her friend lived closer to Utah Park.

He began selling T for sex across the West Coast. It turned out that her youthful "tween" body (she was 10), was a major selling point, and he demanded that she meet a quota of a thousand dollars a night.

—Stockholm Syndrome in the Pimp-Victim Relationship, by Natalie Kitroeff for the New York Times May 3, 2012

CHAPTER THIRTY-THREE

I watch Ian load the bags into his car. We almost bought out TJ Maxx. "You're spoiling me."

"Nothing's too good for the girl I love."

"Really? You love me?"

"I will do anything to keep you safe. To give you everything you want. To make you believe you're the most important person in my life." He comes over to me and tilts my head up for a kiss. "And I believe you feel the same way about me."

I wonder how I'm going to explain these new clothes to my mom. There are too many to slip into my wardrobe without her noticing.

"Do you?" Ian asks.

"Do I what?"

"Feel the same way about me?"

Suddenly I feel lightheaded. The idea of love was one thing. Movies and music and my imagination made me believe I was ready. But now here's Ian. Older than I thought Ian. Expecting me to be mature about all of this Ian. Waiting for me to say something Ian. "What do you mean?" I stall.

"I mean, am I as important to you as you are to me?"

I'm relieved. He's not talking about love right now. "Sure, but I don't have money to buy you clothes." I nod to the packages in the backseat.

"That's not important. The clothes are my way of showing you how much you mean to me. How much I want to make you happy. Do you want to make me happy, Livvy?"

* * *

Maddy's phone rang. She looked at the Caller ID and wondered why Mrs. Campbell would be calling her and felt the knot in her gut that had never left give a twist.

"Maddy, is Livvy with you?"

The knot threatened to explode into her heart.

"No. I haven't seen her since before lunch. She said she had a dentist appointment."

"Oh-god-oh-god-oh-god-oh-god."

"Did you try calling your dentist?" Maddy already knew the answer.

"Livvy didn't have a dentist appointment."

Maddy couldn't help it, she started to cry. "I'm so sorry. I'm sorry."

"What, Maddy? What are you sorry about? What do you know?"

"I think I ought to come over," she managed to say through her sobs.

"Come. Now. I'm calling the police."

Maddy left a note saying where she was going. She didn't feel like getting into details with her mom. Not before she got into them with Livvy's mom. She'd have to tell Mrs. Campbell about Ian.

Maddy knew where Livvy hid her diary.

Ten minutes later Maddy stowed her bike in the courtyard of Livvy's house and shouldered her backpack. Mrs. Campbell stood in the doorway looking scared. Maddy took a couple of steps toward her unsure of who needed a hug the most. They fell into each other's arms and Maddy didn't want to let go, but a police car appeared and Mrs. Campbell stiffened.

"Can I go up to Livvy's room? There's something there that might help."

"Yes, go."

Livvy's older sister, Sarah, and younger brother, Ethan, were both sitting in the living room. They weren't talking. They weren't moving. "Hey," Maddy said.

"Hey," Sarah responded. Maddy barely heard her. Ethan kicked out a leg.

"Where's your dad?"

"On his way home from Atlanta."

"Oh."

"Why are you here?" Sarah asked. Ethan kicked out his leg again.

"I, um... I need to go to Livvy's room."

Silence.

"Your mom said it was okay."

Silence.

Maddy ran upstairs, careful not to pound her feet inside the quiet house.

She threw open the door to her friend's room and stopped. Someone, probably Mrs. Campbell, had turned on all the lights. Livvy was everywhere. The two friends had spent as much time in each other's bedrooms as they'd spent in their own. Maddy's feet were glued to the floor while images and sounds of shared secrets flooded her brain.

"Forgive me, Liv." Maddy closed the door then went to the bookcase next to Livvy's desk and drug out five classic novels.

"*No one will ever find my diary behind these,*" Livvy said. "*Who reads these unless they have to?*"

"*What about under your mattress?*"

"*That's the first place Sarah or my mom would look.*"

Maddy reached her hand to the back wall of the case and grabbed the small book that contained the life of her BFF. A tear slid down her cheek. "I want you to write in this again, Liv." She slid to the floor, shoulders shaking as she began to truly believe the worst had happened.

Hold it together. For Livvy. You might be her only hope.

When Maddy scrubbed the tears off her face, she also scrubbed away her fears. Then she scooted back against the bed to go through her friend's journal, intent on finding only the pertinent entries and keeping the rest of Livvy's secrets secret.

A few minutes later, Maddy wondered how she was going to share this information without being forced to turn the diary over. She knew she didn't have much time, but she wanted to think. She stuffed her friend's words into her backpack and stood up.

As she turned to the door, it opened.

"What are you doing in here?" Sarah asked. She stepped into the room like she wanted to pick a fight.

"I, uh... I needed to be here for a few minutes."

Sarah held Maddy's eyes for a short count and then nodded. "Me too."

* * *

"You told me you wanted to make me happy. The way you're acting does not make me happy." Ian is pouring himself a drink. He pours a second glass.

I curl deeper into the corner of the only chair in the hotel room. It's hard and scratchy but feels like my best safe place.

"Were you lying to me?"

The camera is sitting on the corner of the dresser crushed up against the television.

"You know I bought all of those clothes to make you happy, right?"

The camera is pointed in my direction.

Ian sees me looking at it and turns it away.

"I want to see you in your new clothes. Hasn't anyone ever taken pictures of you in new clothes? For school? Easter?"

I can't find my voice.

"Answer me, Olivia."

"Uh-huh."

"Uh-huh, what?"

I swallow. I do want to make Ian happy. I do. He's the one who makes me feel special. Nobody else makes me feel the way he does. Why am I behaving like a baby? "Yeah, I've had pictures taken of me in new clothes."

"Well, that's all I want too."

"But you want more." My voice is soft and sounds like a whiney baby.

"The other pictures are only for me. I promise. I want to see you go from the old things you're wearing to the new things I bought for you. Because I want you to be happy."

He takes a drink and gives me a disappointed look. "Do you want to make *me* happy, Olivia?"

My throat sticks so I nod.

"Good. Let's go then." He hands me the other glass. "Here. Take a sip. Loosen up."

Almost an hour later, Ian sets the camera aside and holds his arms out to me. "You were wonderful."

I'm tired, what my mom calls "punchy." I've had so many clothes on and off I'm not even sure what I was wearing last. But still I walk into Ian's arms.

"You're beautiful and you mean everything to me. You make me so happy." Ian smooths the hair on my forehead.

"I'm glad."

"Now that you're here with me and we're together, I'm going to need more money to take care of us." He tilts my face to his. "You understand that, don't you?"

"Of course."

"There's a way you can help."

"Sure, but I can't get a job."

"You can understand something instead."

"Understand? Understand what?"

"I'm going to sell these pictures of you on the internet."

"What?"

"Don't worry. I can blur your face and we won't use your real name. But Livvy, these are gorgeous pictures. You look like a model. People will pay, and that will help me. That will help us."

I'm confused. I didn't like the idea of the pictures to begin with. But now they've been taken. And if they can bring in money because Ian has to pay for me too, maybe that's a good thing. "No one will know it's me?"

"No one, I promise."

"And this is what you want?"

"Yeah, this is what I want. It's what *we* want."

I suddenly realize he hadn't asked me if I was okay with this. He'd just announced he was going to sell the pictures. "Did you plan this all along?"

"What I'd planned was a way for us to be together. That's how much you mean to me. How much the two of us mean to me." He kissed her lightly on her cheek. "Do we mean as much to you?"

"I guess."

"You guess?"

"I mean yes. Yes, we're important."

"That's good. I think we're ready to take the next step."

"Next step?"

Ian hands me a pill and a glass of water. "Here. Take this."

I look at him.

"Would I have you take anything that would hurt you?"

I think about what he said and pop the pill in my mouth. I can't imagine Ian ever hurting me.

Ian turned his favorite music on. "Take your clothes off."

"I thought we were finished."

"No cameras now. It's just you and me."

I strip off clothing. "What for?"

"I want to make us both happy."

It's called TraffickCam. People can upload photos of their hotel rooms to the app, along with the hotel they were taken at. The pictures are fed to a national database of photos from escort advertisements, many of which show images of workers in hotel rooms.

—*Here's A Really Simple Way You Can Help Catch Sex Traffickers, by Ben Lawson*

for Newsy

CHAPTER THIRTY-FOUR

Donny logged into the chat site just as he'd done before and left the same message. "This is how I've always done it."

"Print that page for me," Mex said to Donny.

"So then what happens?" Darius asked as his fingers flew over his keyboard making notes.

The sound of the printer kicked in.

"He calls me," Donny said.

"And then?"

"I send him photos and we negotiate a price."

"What did you get for Alexis?" Mex asked.

"Twenty-five k."

Mex and Darius exchanged a look.

"This poor excuse for a human being paid you twenty-five thousand dollars?" Mex asked.

"That's what I said."

"What did he do with her?"

"How the hell should I know?"

"What do you *think* he did with her?"

"Probably sold her to a private party."

"For how much?"

"I've heard of girls going for as much as half a million." When Mex and Darius looked at him with incredulous expressions, Donny shook his head. "Damn, dudes, there's a lot of people with money out there."

"And apparently a lot of them are sick-ass," Mex said.

"How can we find out who bought Alexis?" Darius asked.

"Shit, man. Someone pays that much money for a piece has enough money to stay hidden," Donny said.

Mex clenched his jaw. *A piece?* Are you kidding me? Mex took a deep breath and prepared to unleash a few choice words.

Mex felt Darius grab his arm.

"I get that," Darius said before Mex could express his outrage. "But there must be a way to follow the trail."

"Good luck with that," Donny said. "You don't think I tried to figure it out so I could cut out the middleman?"

"I wouldn't doubt it," Mex said.

"You don't need to be so sanctimonious."

"Contact him," Mex said. "Do it now. I'll tell you what you're going to say."

"I can't man, he contacts me. That's how it works."

Mex stood and paced the room, thinking out loud how the conversation would go down. He wanted to spur this thing forward, to be in control.

Donny interrupted him. "He's going to want pictures of the product. You got any porn shots on you?"

Donny's phone rang as Mex was about to clock him one.

Timing.

Donny answered and put the call on speaker. Mex hit the record button on his high-tech recorder. "Hi. Yeah. I've got another girl."

"Too soon. Too dangerous."

"Well, it's not me exactly."

Silence.

"Who've you been talking to?"

"No one."

"How do you know 'No One' is looking for a handoff if you didn't talk to him?"

"He came to me. We, uh... sort of worked together before."

Silence.

"Who the fuck do you think you're dealing with? Why did he come to you?"

"Because his buyer is out of the business."

"Prison?"

"Dead."

Mex nodded. Apparently Donny had been paying attention while he'd paced.

"I don't need any of this shit. Why are you dragging me into this? Jeopardizing our relationship?"

"Because I need the money."

A harsh laugh. "Now that I can believe." A loud sniff. The guy was snorting. "What's your cut?"

"Ten percent."

"That's pretty steep."

"Hey, he needs the money too."

"What's he asking?"

"Twenty-five."

"You got photos?"

Mex scribbled something on a piece of paper and shoved it toward Donny.

"Did you hear me, kid? You got photos?"

"No. She's not my girl to hand off. But I know this guy. He's one of those personal trainers who has a client list of girls with their own gyms at home. She's probably worth twice what you paid me for Alexis."

"Who?"

"The last girl."

Silence.

"Who's the guy?"

"He doesn't want me to say. He said if this works this time, then you can know more." Donny rubbed his chin. "You know, just like you don't like me talking about you, he doesn't like me talking about him."

"I'll need right of refusal."

"Does that mean we've got a deal?"

"No deal until I see the merchandise. But if she's as special as the last one, yeah. We've got a deal."

"When and where?"

After the call ended, Donny turned to Mex. "Okay. I helped you. Now you help me."

Mex gave Darius a nod and watched as his partner pressed the button to call the elevator. "How's that, Donny?" Mex asked.

"Keep my name out of it with the police."

Mex shook his head and turned to leave.

"You'll do that for me, right? Right?" Donny called after him.

Mex walked out of the meet feeling better than he had in days. It wasn't perfect, but this new guy was one more link in the chain. He'd be a harder sweat, but there was no doubt in his mind he could figure out the scumbag's weakness. He'd always had an intuition.

"Why aren't we having Donny arrested now?" Darius asked once they were outside.

"Because we might need him. If Franklin and the Greenwood Village PD get their hands on him we're SOL. He'll lawyer up and then we're done."

"So when?"

"Right after we meet with the buyer."

"There's a big demand for boys," she said. *"We just don't talk about it as a community. We just don't want to talk about it."* —Officials say sex trafficking cases with male victims highlight issue, an article from The Denver Post, *10/05/2015,* by Jesse Paul

CHAPTER THIRTY-FIVE

JAYLA

Someone gulping for air wakes me. I look at the digital clock in the room where five of us are sleeping. Four-thirty. The summer sun will be up pretty soon. The light from the bathroom spills out onto the crowded floor. There aren't any beds, only mats with blankets that have seen better days.

At least when there are five people sleeping in a small room, the rats tend to stay away.

The gulping is coming from the mat next to mine. I'd come in late and hadn't really taken note of who I was sleeping next to. Hadn't really cared. I turn to see a small figure lying in a tangle of torn fabric. "Hey, it's okay."

The noise stops completely and I worry that whoever it is has stopped breathing.

"Breathe. Nice and easy. There's plenty of air."

I'm rewarded by steady breathing. A bit fast, but at least it doesn't sound desperate.

"What's your name?"

"Da-Da-Da-David."

I reach out and rub his shoulder. "Is that what people call you? David?"

"Davie."

"Okay, Davie. You can call me Cherie." He's way too young to get the name game. And if he were ever to call me Jayla while Daddy was around, we'd both pay a price.

"How old are you?" I ask.

He's shaking so hard I'm afraid he might get sick. "Se-se-seven."

I rub his arms.

LaTisha is gone, with the baby inside her, and now there's this *boy*? Seven is too damn young. Oh, please God. Why? You and me are gonna have a serious sit-down when I get out of this. I take a flash-second to remember the Sundays at church back home in Denver and don't for a minute believe any of those ministers could give me answers to the questions I'm coming up with lately. God better be ready.

Davie's shaking lessened.

"Where're you from?"

"Golden."

I stifle a gasp. I'm starving for any news. "Colorado?" It would be cool if he was from my home state, but I've learned there are Goldens and Lakewoods and Englewoods and Auroras all over the country. I try not to get my hopes up, and quickly remind myself, even if he is from Colorado, what can a seven-year-old kid tell me?

"Yeah. By Denver."

A million questions pile into my mind. I want to know about everything. Has my disappearance made the local news? Is my mom doing anything to try and find me? Has anyone questioned Chris? And then I look into this boy's sweet face and realize he won't have any answers.

I'm learning. I can't expect answers from seven-year-old kids or ministers.

Rather than him saving me, he needs me to save him.

And I'm pretty sure I can't.

"Has Daddy put you on a track?"

"Track? Like a race track?"

I shake my head. "Never mind." While I'm relieved Davie doesn't know the street slang, I wonder how long it will take before he knows a track is the section of street assigned to him. "When did they take you?"

He starts to cry but screws his face into a determined mask. "I was home two nights ago. Now I'm not."

Tonight's the third night. Most kids are turned out the first night—there are customers who get off on the fear. I've never heard of anyone lasting three nights.

The investors want to get their money back.

Maybe his age will help save him. Maybe all he'll have to do are some naked photos for online pervs. Maybe, at least for a while, he won't have to personally engage.

I don't really believe any of this shit I'm thinking. But it's what I've got at the moment.

And moments are all I've got.

"I get asthma sometimes when I'm scared," Davie says.

Oh, great. No telling what'll happen if Daddy finds out he's got a kid with a health issue on his hands. "Do you need an inhaler?"

"No. I just need to get unscared."

"Listen to me, Davie. Don't tell anyone else about your asthma, okay?"

"Okay. But—"

"Promise me."

"Okay. But I'm not scared now."

"That's good. But you need to promise me you won't say anything. Promise?"

"I promise."

"What made you stop being scared?"

"You remind me of my mama."

I almost laugh out loud. First, I'm only fifteen, and second, there's no way I look like the mother of this paler than pale, thinner than thin, little white boy with hair sticking out in sprouts on his head. But I guess if I remind him of his mama, and that helps him breathe, it's a good thing. Anything to keep his mind off where he is now. And where he'll be tomorrow.

"Tell me about your family."

He starts talking about his mama. The friends in his neighborhood who he'd play with until dusk. Normal memories of childhood. I want to cry. It doesn't take long for Davie to fall asleep. Hopefully with dreams where he's surrounded by people who care about him.

I wonder if he made it on the news even if I didn't, and immediately regret the comparison. If I ever get out of this, I promise to speak up for the people of color who are forced into whatever kind of slavery—while not discounting the terror of everyone else. We're all victims. Every person counts.

God, I want out of here.

During the three-day operation, undercover Agents posted ads on <u>Backpage.com</u>. During that time, more than 300 contacts were made to those ads.
—32 Arrested in Knoxville Human Trafficking Operation, from the TBI Newsroom, May 23, 2016

CHAPTER THIRTY-SIX

Cade looked at the list of names she'd made from mentions in Jayla's diary. Like most who keep personal journals, Jayla hadn't bothered to use last names when it came to her friends. They'd gotten one last name from Jayla's mom and the rest fell like dominoes. Still, it had taken a while to track them down, especially when there was more than one possible surname to work with.

There were three names left. Caroline Jones and either Chris Williams or Chris Stevens, maybe both.

It wouldn't be unheard of for a woman to be involved with an abduction, but those events were usually between strangers or enemies. The Caroline mentioned in Jayla's diary felt more like a friend. Christine Stevens was described as a girl who'd moved to Denver recently.

If one of the remaining people in Jayla's circle was responsible, Cade's money was on Christopher Williams.

Mex and Darius were running the last three down now.

In the meantime, they'd come up with a plan to use Backpage in their favor. Cade was working on a couple of things that might pay off. She'd created ads from both Mex and Darius looking for a particular type of girl. Both were looking for Jayla and it was a challenge to make the ads unique.

Cade wasn't sure how she felt about Mex trying to get in with the group of traffickers involved in Alexis's abduction. Sure, she thought, it was smart using two different angles, but she just hoped the Backpage ads would pay off first. Going into a nest of scorpions and expecting not to get stung was stupid. Never mind that she'd done the same more than once when extricating a kid. The difference was that most people involved in cults have a modicum of respect for human life.

Her phone rang. Darius.

"We've got another one. Well actually two."

"Shit. Talk to me."

"A contact at the Aurora Police Department knew I was looking into the other two girls. He tells me that while girls go missing all the time, there might be links to a young girl from Aurora. We've hit the perfect storm. The trifecta."

"Tell me about her."

"She's twelve."

Cade held the phone against one ear while she rubbed the opposite temple. "Twelve? Even if we could get her back tomorrow she's been robbed of any normal youth."

"The girl kept a diary, so we know some of the behavioral aspects of her abductor. And a name, clearly an alias, but still it's someplace to start."

"How long has the Aurora PD been involved?"

"Almost from the beginning."

"Someone we can work with?"

"I think so. She wants results and she doesn't much care how she gets them as long as it's legal and can hold up in court."

"When can we meet and compare notes?"

"She can be available whenever we are."

"Damn. I like her already." Cade paused. "Have you tracked down the last three from Jayla's list?"

"Caroline and Christine are both cool. Not involved in any way. We're heading over to Chris Williams's place of employment now."

"My money's on him."

"Why?"

"Process of elimination. Plus, we need a break."

"Good to know. I'll pay special attention."

"You're an ass."

"Another specialty."

"Did you set a time to meet with the APD detective?"

"Yep. Her office. Tomorrow at nine."

"How did it get kicked from a missing to a trafficking case?"

"There are always a few flags. No reason to run away, no reason to be kidnapped for ransom. No reason, right? There are things law enforcement can tell in the beginning, and they'd always rather be safe than sorry. In this case, the kid's never done anything like this before. Had a cell phone she was attached to that went silent."

"And? It was kicked fast."

"She had a friend who witnessed the girl and her probable abductor together."

"What about the other one?"

"A young boy from Golden. Seven years old. Law enforcement initially thought it was a custody thing but now it's officially an abduction. Mom and Dad are adamant they want to leave it to the authorities with no outside involvement."

Cade felt a heaviness on her chest. "That poor boy." She shook her head. "Okay. Let me get these ads written and placed before someone tells us we can't."

"Mex says to order room service. It could be a long night."

"Ah. *My* specialty." She smiled.

After hanging up, Cade sat back and stared at her computer screen. Then deleted everything. She decided she needed to do more research and went to the Backpage site.

It wasn't as straightforward as she'd thought. They'd have to post under the Men Seeking Women category. And then make the title clear and ambiguous at the same time. Her hopes that this would be successful took a dive. None of them were actually offering money. Well, except maybe for the ad whose header read: Looking for $ome Good Head.

Shit.

A couple of the ads looked like they were bait. Like law enforcement bait. She'd have to be careful. If she could spot them there was no doubt in her mind someone adept at staying outside of the loop could as well.

An image of her sister, dead in the isolated cabin in the swamps of Louisiana, floated into her consciousness. Deep in the throes of cult worship, cut-off from all of her family except Cade, Delphine had killed herself. The day Cade found her was both explosive and paralyzing.

Almost from that moment, Cade had dedicated her life to extricating people from cults as an exit counselor. She'd had more successes than failures, but it was the failures that were the easiest to remember. It was the failures that haunted her.

Cade and Mex met when he was tracking down a young girl who'd been targeted as a sacrifice through a fanatical sect with ties to a drug cartel. Now, as she looked at the ads in front of her, the concept she'd shared with Rachel became clearer. She could see a cult of a different kind. Pandering in sexual gratification was a religion of sorts, and while most of the young women and men found themselves there against their will initially, many would begin to believe that's where they belonged.

Going through Tor to hide her ISP, Cade started with the easiest one for her—Mex. While she hit lightly, and vaguely, on his emotional needs, she drilled down to a physical type. With a picture of Jayla at her side she described the young African-American girl ambiguous enough not to be specific, but detailed enough that Jayla was a fit. She ended the ad with MONEY IS NOT AN ISSUE IF THE GIRL IS RIGHT AND IN THE DENVER AREA.

Next, she played with Darius's ad. She decided to go hardcore to make it significantly different from Mex's. While Mex wanted someone who could at least fleetingly meet an emotional need, all Darius wanted was someone with a certain amount of sexual skill. Cade smiled to think about how this was a complete reversal for her sensitive, romantic, and committed friend. Again, she ended the ad with the concept that he had all the money in the world if the hookup met his specifications. And the girl was in Denver.

Then Cade wrote two more ads, with Olivia Campbell and Alexis Halston in mind. She worried that someone might try and trace her IP address even though she'd gone through TOR, and get suspicious of all the requests originating from one source. She decided that if these guys checked every IP address they'd never get any business done. Even so, she concocted the story that third parties paid her to place the ads to protect their privacy.

"I ain't gotta give 'em much, they happy with Mickey D's."
Lloyd Banks in a remix of 50 Cent's platinum-selling song,
"P.I.M.P."
Girls Like Us, *by Rachel Lloyd*

CHAPTER THIRTY-SEVEN

John, the owner of Bugz-B-Gone Computer Repair, nodded to Mex and Darius as he moved a laptop from the drop-off desk to the work desk. "That Chris is a computer genius." He put the machine down and turned back to them. "Good thing too because he's been taking a lot of time off work the last few months. I would've canned anyone else a long time ago."

"How long has Christopher Williams worked for you?" Darius asked.

"On and off since he was in junior high. What's that? About five years?"

"What do you mean on and off?"

"School always came first. Now he's here full-time and attending Metro State at night."

"Good kid?" Mex asked.

"Like I said, a computer genius."

"Other than sick days, is there anything else that concerns you?"

John rubbed his forehead.

Mex raised an eyebrow at Darius.

"Look, the kid knows his way around a computer. I might have seen him once or twice on websites he shouldn't have been on."

Mex thought maybe they'd get a direct link to the reason why Jayla was taken. "Porn?"

"No, no. Nothing like that."

"Like what then?"

"Gambling."

Mex jabbed the button next to C WILLIAMS #306 on the apartment directory list, and waited.

Darius looked through his notes. "Jayla made it sound in her journal like this guy was one of her best friends. How would he have anything to do with her abduction?"

"Won't know until we talk to him." Mex's finger hovered over the button. "If he had gambling debt, it could be how someone got to him."

"Okay, you know I'm all about the beauty of African-American women. But there's nothing special about Jayla. Why would someone target her? And through a nerdy kid who's taking night classes?"

"Water flows downhill."

"What the hell does that mean?"

"There are people, like water, who want to take the easiest road, the low road. You get someone who wants a few bucks, tied to someone who has money and would like to make more, and what's special or not special about a living, breathing, human being is no longer relative. It's a transaction. Nothing more. No judgment. Just dollars for product."

Mex was about to hit the button again when the speaker buzzed to life. "Yeah?"

"Hey, man. You worked on my boss's computer and he wants to pay you something extra," Mex said.

"Just leave it."

"Don't want to just leave this, man. It'll be ripped off before you get down here. Come on, I made the trip. It's a lot of cash. Don't make me have to tell my boss you declined his appreciation."

There was a long silence during which Mex started trying to come up with another plan.

Finally, the obnoxious buzz popped open the door.

Mex and Darius walked into an elevator that was barely large enough to hold the two of them. Mex punched the third floor, and with a jerk, the elevator cranked upward. The grinding and whining of the cables was disconcerting.

Darius looked at Mex. "We're taking the stairs down."

"Yep."

The elevator lurched to a stop. An uncomfortable amount of time later, the doors shuddered open. Mex and Darius wasted no time exiting to the hallway.

The cooking smells of a diverse community battled the air for superiority. Garlic, cumin, and curry fought for dominance, resulting in an intriguing aroma that made Mex make a mental note to combine these cultures into one dish the next time he felt an urge to create culinary art. He thought maybe cinnamon would tie them all together. Or maybe not.

Mex and Darius approached apartment 306. They'd worked together enough that they didn't need to go into detail.

"If we go there, I'm bad," Mex said.

"Makes sense that I'd be good."

Mex knocked on the door, not bothering to stand back for the occupant to get a full picture through the peephole in the door. Getting into character Mex thought, *Screw him. I'm bad.*

As the door opened, Mex felt Darius tug him backward. He whispered in Mex's ear, "I've got this."

* * *

"Are you Christopher Williams?" Darius asked.

The young man nodded.

"You're the computer wizard? Mind if we come in?" Darius walked into the apartment. Mex followed and moved Chris aside to close the door.

"Do you have cash for me?"

"Well, Chris, we do have something for you, but it isn't cash."

"I don't understand."

"Let's sit down, shall we?"

Darius and Mex moved into the tiny living room, shrinking the space.

"Who are you?" Chris stood by the door, eyes darting between the two men. "What do you want? I don't have anything."

"Like I said, we have something for you." Darius gestured to the spot on the couch next to Mex. "Please. Sit."

Chris sat as far away from Mex as possible. The boy-barely-man looked like he was about to throw up.

"Relax, son. Our intent here isn't to harm you," Mex said. "Unless it comes to that."

Darius popped out of his chair and placed a hand on Chris's shoulder. "Trust me. My partner isn't going to do anything violent. Or stupid. We only want to talk."

"You said you had something for me. What is it?"

Darius sat back down. "What we have for you, Chris, is advice."

Eyes squinting, Chris sat back in his tight corner and hitched a breath. "About what?"

"About being forthcoming with us. About getting past your shame."

"What are you talking about?"

"Tell us everything you know."

"About what?"

Darius silently counted to a slow ten. He figured it must have felt like minutes for the scared young man in front of him. "It's more of a who, Chris, and less of a what." Darius folded his hands in front of him and leaned forward. "We need to know everything you can tell us about what's happened to Jayla Thomas."

Watching Christopher Williams, it was like time stopped. Darius had seen this before when he'd interviewed people whose guilt had yet to come to light. They'd lived in such deep denial that when suddenly, unexpectedly, confronted with their wrongdoings they froze, unable to correlate the fiction they've constructed with reality.

Mex turned to Chris and reached out to touch him. "Son, tell us what you know. It's the only way you'll ever be free."

"Tell us about Jayla," Darius prompted.

"She's my friend."

"We know that. Have you seen her lately? In the last six months?"

Chris looked down at the worn carpet. "I've been busy. You know... work and school."

"But isn't that a long time not to talk to a friend?" Darius asked. "Surely you've at least texted."

"Maybe."

"So you've texted back and forth?"

"Probably, yeah."

"Can we see your phone, Chris?"

"Um, sure, but I wipe it clean every couple of months."

"Let's check it, shall we? We really want to find out what's happened to Jayla. Her mom is worried sick."

Chris's shoulders began to shake.

"You'll feel better if you talk to us, son," Mex said.

An anguished sob raked the air in the tiny living room. "I didn't know. I didn't know. I didn't know."

"What happened, Chris?"

"It was... oh, God. Oh, God." He had trouble catching a breath.

Mex moved over and put an arm around the young man. "Take your time. Breathe. We're not going anywhere. We're here to help."

Chris's voice dropped to a whisper. "It was supposed to be a joke. Just a joke."

"What was supposed to be a joke?" Darius asked. He leaned in closer.

"A prank. We were supposed to laugh about it later." Chris shook his head. "Only, I think I knew it wasn't. I knew all along. I even convinced myself she was just pissed at me for right now. That's why I hadn't heard from her." Sobs wracked his body. "Oh, God. What have I done?"

Fifteen minutes later, exhausted and quiet, Chris looked at the two men through red and swollen eyes. "I screwed up."

"Do you have something to drink?" Mex asked.

"Water?"

"Stronger." Mex and Darius said.

"In the cupboard above the fridge."

Dishes were piled in the sink. Dirty or clean, hard to tell. A trashcan with empty takeout containers overflowed onto the floor. He looked in the refrigerator. Empty except for a covered plastic bowl that looked like a science experiment and two unopened Bud Lights. Mex checked the cupboard and brought out a bottle. He was lucky to find three clean glasses. He took the bottle and the glasses back to the living room.

Drinks poured, they each took a swallow.

Darius produced his phone, swiped it and selected an app. "We're gonna record this from now on so we can keep things straight. Okay with you, Chris?"

A nod.

"I need you to say you know it's being recorded and you're okay with that."

"Yeah, fine."

"Good enough."

"Tell us what happened that night."

If you want to understand why girls who are sex-trafficked don't run straight to the police, Withelma Ortiz, known as T, could tell you a thing or two. The 22-year-old has a pretty good grasp on the issue—having been first sold for sex at age 10.

—*Stockholm Syndrome in the Pimp-Victim Relationship, by Natalie Kitroeff,*
for The New York Times

CHAPTER THIRTY-EIGHT

Maddy had the diary in front of her and was making notes on a separate pad. The television was on in the family room. Livvy had been gone for what felt like a million years and Maddy had thought of nothing else.

What if she missed something important in Livvy's diary? What if, in her desire to protect Livvy's privacy, she neglected to make a note of the one thing that could save her?

"Twelve-year old Olivia Campbell has been missing for over twenty-four hours," the news reporter said.

Maddy didn't even bother to put down her pen as she rushed to sit in front of the television.

"Here is her picture. She was last seen at Utah Park in Aurora. If you have any information that might be relative to her disappearance, you're urged to contact the Aurora Police Department at 303-555-6050 or, if you prefer, you can contact Mex Anderson, a private investigator who is working to help find Olivia, at 970-555-9786. Again, that's 970-555-9786."

Maddy inked the number on her arm. A few months ago she'd written the number of a boy on her palm and when she went to read it, it had been impossible. She'd cried for hours imagining the great romance she'd lost. Tonight she was happy she'd learned that lesson.

Does a private investigator have to report everything he finds out to the police? Can they keep things secret? She thought about googling her questions but decided the best way to know was to ask him directly. She punched the numbers into her phone.

Voicemail.

Impatient, she tried again.

Straight to voicemail.

"Livvy is a friend of mine and I think I have something that might help. But I have a few questions to ask you first." She left her number and hung up.

How many people might be calling that number? How many concerned citizens who thought they'd seen something important?

Maddy poured herself a glass of orange juice, took a sip, and couldn't stand it any longer. She went back to her phone to call again when her vintage Frank Sinatra ringtone went off. She looked at the number on the screen and then the number on her arm, took a deep breath, and answered.

"Hullo? Mr. Anderson?"

"It is." Maddy couldn't quite decide if she liked the sound of his voice or if it scared her. "Who am I speaking to?"

"Um, my name is Madison. Madison Magnolia Montgomery. My friends call me Maddy. Is that more information than you wanted?"

"You said that Livvy is a friend of yours?"

Definitely scary.

"Um, th-that's not quite right."

"Look, young lady—"

"Liv and I are BFFs. Best friends forever?"

Silence.

"What is it you have that might be helpful?" Nicer but still on the scary side.

"I have some questions first."

"I'm listening."

"Do you have to turn over all of your information to the police?"

"That's usually how I operate."

"But is there a law that says you have to? Couldn't you keep some things secret?"

"Not if it pertains to the case. Several heads are better than one."

"But how do you know something pertains to the case?"

"Do you want to help your friend or not?"

"This was a mistake. I'm sorry," she choked. Maddy disconnected the call, tears streaming down her face.

Less than a minute later her phone rang. She checked the number.

Him again.

She let it ring and a war dropped into her head. Scary people. Scary people who told the police everything. Scary people who could help find Liv. And then there was Liv. Just Liv.

She answered. "I'm here." She waited for the mean voice.

"Hello, Maddy. My name is Acadia LeBlanc. I'm a partner of Mr. Anderson's. Can we talk for a few minutes?"

Definitely not scary.

"Yes, Ms. LeBlanc."

"My friends call me Cade."

"Okay." Maddy was feeling better.

"Our main goal is to get Livvy home. Do you agree?"

"Totally."

"And it doesn't matter who does it or how it's done. She should be home with her family. Yes?"

"Yes."

"The police have to operate a certain way. They want Livvy back home, but they also want to arrest whoever took her, and anyone else involved, and make sure they go to jail. In order to do that their actions must remain unimpeachable under the law. Do you understand what that means?"

Maddy's heart sank. "We had it in civics. They have to do everything by the book?"

"Exactly. But Maddy?"

"Yes?"

"Mex and I are not the police. While we work very closely with them, we don't work under the same constraints. Sometimes the police can do their jobs on one side of the problem while we work the other. We don't do anything wrong, but we don't have the same responsibility they have. Are you with me?"

"You're saying you're not required to tell the police everything."

"That's right." Cade paused. "Now, do you have something you want to tell us?"

"Liv met someone online. She wrote about him in her diary. And I have it."

"Online? The police checked the family computer. There wasn't anything there."

"She used mine."

Maddy heard Cade suck in air.

"Are you home right now? Do you have your computer?" Cade asked.

"Yeah."

"Would it be okay if me and one of my other partners, Darius Johnson, came by to see you? You and I could talk about the diary and Darius could take a look at your computer. It could mean bringing Livvy home sooner."

"Okay, sure. But can I ask one more thing?"

"Shoot."

"Can you bring Mr. Anderson too? Right now I don't think I like him very much. He scares me. But if you're his partner, I'd like to change my mind, and I'd feel better about everything."

"We'll be there in thirty minutes."

Branding, whether by tattoo or intentional scarring, has become a disturbing characteristic of one particular subset of this thriving criminal operation. Pimp-led prostitution is widely considered one of the most brutal and violent of all forms of human trafficking found in the States.

—I carried his name on my body for nine years': the tattooed trafficking survivors reclaiming their past,

The Guardian

CHAPTER THIRTY-NINE

Mex, Cade and Darius drove up in front of the Montgomery home in Aurora. The homes were on the expensive side, well-maintained with professional-looking landscaping. A quiet, middle-class enclave of families who were trying to carve out the good life.

Only it's a family just like this one getting carved, Cade thought.

Mex reached for the door handle.

"Did you two listen to me while we drove here? Tell me you did," Cade said. "Mex scared this young girl on the phone. We should go in soft. We're going to have an easier time if Maddy is comfortable with us, not terrified or even leery. I need to lead us in."

"Seems like we're following your lead a lot on this one," Mex said. "Are you sure you even need us?"

"I need Darius for the technical stuff."

"And me?" Mex asked.

"She asked for you."

"Were you going to tell me?"

"Not unless you asked."

Mex did his best to hide a smile. "Since she's a juvenile I know you talked to her mom," he said. "Will she be here?"

"She's on her way home." Cade hadn't made the call until the three of them were almost to the Montgomery home. While Mex and Darius constantly battled over the fastest route and who was driving, Cade waited patiently in the backseat to call Livvy's mom.

"Should we wait here until she arrives?" Darius asked.

"No," Cade said. "Let's go in now and do our best to reduce Maddy's anxiety. When Mom gets here we'll have an entirely new dynamic to work around. A few minutes of bonding will save us hours of trying to get through a protective parent."

"Let's go then," Mex said.

Mex and Darius followed Cade up to the front door and stood behind her as she rang the bell. Before the chimes finished sounding, Cade was face-to-face with an adorable twelve-year old girl who looked frantic.

"Help has arrived," Cade announced softly.

Maddy's face pinched up like a raisin before she expelled a cry and fell into Cade's open arms.

Cade took a few seconds to calm the young girl while Mex and Darius stood uncomfortably in the doorway. The two men shuffled awkwardly.

A final tight hug and Cade reached to smooth Maddy's hair out of her eyes. "Are you ready for us to get to work?"

Maddy sniffed. "Yeah. I don't know what came over me." She looked at Cade. "Thank you."

"I understand, sweet girl. It's a stressful and overwhelming time. There's a lot at stake." Cade reached out and lifted Maddy's chin. "And we're here to help." She made the introductions.

Mex grunted.

"Now, is there a place where we can all sit down and talk?" Cade asked.

Maddy led them into the kitchen. "Will this be okay?"

"Maybe the dining room would be better. That way if we're still working and someone wants to use the kitchen we won't be in the way," Cade suggested. It also meant they'd have more privacy.

Mex and Darius took seats at the long table and Cade looked at Maddy. "Can you bring Mr. Johnson the laptop Livvy used? And then let's you and I take a look at her diary."

Mex grunted again.

"Maddy, would you mind if Mr. Anderson also helped us with the diary? He's absolutely no good with computers."

Maddy took a long hard look at the man sitting at the head of the table. "I suppose that would be okay."

Cade nodded. "Good. You're a great BFF to Livvy, Maddy."

The young girl blushed and left the room.

"Be gentle, Mex. She's very fragile right now."

"I know how to be gentle. And when."

Maddy hurried back into the dining room. "Here's my laptop, Mr. Johnson. If you need a password for anything it's Travis. Not very safe, I know. Travis is our dog."

"Thank you, Maddy. And call me Darius."

Darius moved to the far end of the table, opened the lid and got to work.

"This is Livvy's diary. I want to make sure that anything personal that doesn't apply to what's happened to her stays between us."

Cade reached out and took Maddy's hand. "I promise you all we want to do is bring Livvy home. We respect her privacy, but if there's something on your computer or in her journal that will help, we need to know about it."

Mex cleared his throat. "We're under no obligation to share anything we learn with law enforcement. We won't betray you or Livvy."

"Thank you, Mr. Anderson."

He coughed. "Call me Mex."

Police are calling the teen's disappearance suspicious, noting they get runaway reports all the time but this case is different. Aurora Police Chief Nick Metz said police received information that's cause for greater concern, but they have not released what that information is.

—#FindLashaya, posted by the Aurora Police Department

(Author note: LaShaya Nae Stine went missing from my city on July 15, 2016 while I was writing this story. There's been very little news since the first of August.)

CHAPTER FORTY

Darius connected a firewire cable between Maddy's laptop and his computer.

"What are you doing?" Maddy asked.

"Making a copy."

"Of what?"

"Pretty much everything."

The young girl paled then turned beet red. "Everything?"

"Yep."

"But some of that's—"

"Personal. Yeah, I get it. We're only interested in the stuff Livvy was doing."

Maddy swallowed and shifted in her chair. "Really? Just Livvy?"

Darius gave her a wink. "Yeah, really."

"Why are you copying everything then?"

"Sometimes when we search for answers we can mess up the original data. It's always best to perform forensics from a copy."

"Forensics? Isn't that like when you have a body?"

"Forensics is a science that can be applied to anything after the fact."

Maddy's eyes widened. "So you can do this forensics thing with computers?"

"Yep."

"And you can find out things?"

"Yep."

"Like everything people have done on their computer? Emails they've sent, sites they've visited, stuff they've downloaded?"

"That'd also be a yep."

"Cool! I've heard of this but never actually seen it. How long does it take?"

"Sometimes a few minutes, sometimes several hours. It depends on how much data there is."

"Maddy," Cade said, "let Darius work his computer magic. Come sit down here with Mex and me. I want you to tell us what you know about Ian, and explain a few of the entries Livvy made in her diary."

Cade gently and deftly walked Maddy through things she knew she knew, and things she didn't know she knew.

"Did Livvy ever mention where Ian lived?" Cade asked the young girl.

"Um, no. I don't think so."

"But you got the idea he didn't live around here, right?"

Maddy nodded.

"Why? Why do you think he lived somewhere else?"

Livvy's friend lowered her eyes, clearly thinking. Her eyes flew open and she looked at Cade. "Ian told her once that he was thirteen hours away. Thirteen hours. That's not Colorado, right?"

"No honey, not Colorado. But thirteen hours? Driving or flying?"

Again Maddy searched her memories. "Driving," she said firmly.

"How do you know?"

"Because they always talked or emailed during normal hours."

"How do you know he wasn't up at three o'clock in the morning?"

"I guess I don't. He could've lied. But more than once on a Saturday morning, after a sleepover with me, Livvy told me they'd had breakfast together while they were emailing each other."

"Did they ever Skype?"

"You mean while they were alone or something?" Maddy looked worried.

"Any time."

Maddy blinked. "Yeah. Yeah, they did. Once, anyway. It was a couple of weekends ago. A breakfast thing. She told me she had to make him move the computer screen because the sun was too bright. Does that help?"

"It does, Maddy. It really does."

* * *

Darius listened to Cade and Maddy while he copied the computer data. Mex sat quietly by like a silent protector. He watched as Maddy gave a small smile even while a tear slipped down her cheek. Cade was entering something into her computer. Darius assumed it was a thirteen-hour drive-time circle from the girl's home.

While he waited for the data transfer, he brought out his phone to call Pammy. He missed her. He missed his kids. To make sure he wasn't a distraction he moved around to the living room and spoke softly.

"Hey, PJ."

"Hey, DJ."

"How was your day?" he asked. The routine of his family's daily events had a calming effect. He longed to be with them, but he knew his place was here. When he finally hung up he was surprised they'd been on the phone for over thirty minutes. They'd talked about things most people would find stupid but that he knew couldn't be more important, at least to him.

They'd talked about their life.

Finally! The transfer of data was complete. Darius disconnected the two computers and settled in to find what he could find.

He started with the trash. With any luck he'd find that youngsters, at least *these* youngsters, were as bad about cleaning their computers as he'd been about cleaning his room.

Bingo!

There were hundreds of emails between Ian and Livvy. He skimmed them. While on the surface they appeared mundane and even juvenile, Darius recognized the fact that Ian, or whatever his name really was, had been grooming twelve-year-old Livvy for months. Images of his daughters punched into his consciousness. Either of them could be Livvy in a few years. The intensity he'd been feeling about these young girls grew to an almost unmanageable level. Sweat popped out on his forehead and his breathing became labored.

He needed fresh air.

Darius hauled himself up from the dining room table, walked through the kitchen and onto the back deck without having much awareness of his movements or even where he was. He placed his hands on the rail and pressed up and down a few times.

Damn.

Slowly he became aware of someone standing quietly behind him. He straightened but didn't turn around.

"This is hard, ya know?" Darius said.

"I know," Mex said, his voice like smoke.

"Why couldn't we be going after stolen cars, jewelry, art, something else?"

"Because that's not what we do."

Darius's head sagged. His heart slowed and his breathing steadied. Then he asked the question he and his partner had asked each other over and over in the past. "And why's that?"

"We don't care as much about stolen cars, jewelry, or art. That is, unless it can lead us to innocents."

Suddenly Darius sobbed and Mex was behind him. Holding him up.

Holding him together.

"Sorry, man. Thinkin' about my kids," Darius said.

"You don't have to explain anything to me."

Ten minutes later Darius clicked onto software designed to help identify ISP information and location. He and Mex would nail this son of a bitch, and if the man lived beyond their initial encounter, Darius would testify at his trial.

In the meantime, Olivia Emma Campbell, who was twelve-years old and wanted to be a veterinarian, would have a shot at finding that dream again. Damn everything and everyone else, this little girl would have a life.

The emails were coming from two primary ISPs and a slew of others. Darius suspected that the random ones were public computers. Maybe a coffee house or library. Both primaries were registered in Phoenix.

About a thirteen-hour drive from Aurora.

If the trafficker wasn't smart enough to manipulate his ISP location, they had him.

Maddy's mom rushed into the dining room, ripping her coat from her shoulders and throwing it, her bag and her keys on the table. "Why are you talking to my daughter without me?"

"Mrs. Montgomery, I'm Acadia LeBlanc. We spoke earlier."

"Did you call me from my living room? I should have been here. Who gave you the right to talk to her without my permission?"

Cade hesitated.

Maddy stood. "Mom—"

"Be quiet, Maddy."

"But Mom—"

"I said be quiet. Sit down or go to your room." Maddy's mom pointed toward the stairs.

Mex had moved behind Cade. "Thanks to your daughter, we have a direction. We can formulate a plan to rescue Olivia. You should be proud of Madison. You're raising an intelligent, responsible young woman."

"Mrs. Montgomery, you're right. We should have waited for you. I apologize," Cade said.

"Mom, please. They made me feel better."

Darius watched as the tension flattened.

A few minutes later they were driving back to their hotel.

"We should rest if we can," Mex said to Darius. "You and I are with Donny in a few hours."

"Sure wish we could enjoy this small victory," Darius said.

"We'll celebrate when the girls are home where they belong."

... the pimp in question expresses this concern after more self-servedly claiming that most people are not forced into sex work: "I watched an MSNBC show, and some of the things the girls say on there is so disturbing to me, it makes my blood bubble. No girl is forced to prostitute. I am telling you guys the truth."

Other interview subjects echoed this view: "If you want to get away, you always can."

—Six Things Real Pimps Want You to Know, by Michelle Dean for Gawker

CHAPTER FORTY-ONE

LIVVY

Even though I'm sore, I'm happy because I think I made Ian happy. I just have to get used to adult love instead of puppy love. It's what Ian expects and it's what I want to give him.

He's sitting on the couch in his living room eating McDonald's breakfast sandwiches. I find a bottle of orange juice in the fridge and pour each of us a glass.

While I'm pouring the juice, I'm surprised when memories of my family fall into my head. I see Sarah, and while she can be a drama queen, I remember her taking the time to fix a scarf I wanted to wear and couldn't get to look right. And Ethan telling me once that I was okay for a girl. Mom and Dad, tucking me in at night and saying they loved me. The memories flash together and then settle into one big feeling.

I stick the orange juice container back in the fridge, gulp mine down, and take Ian his glass of juice.

I sit next to him. "Ian, I want to call my mom and let her know I'm okay."

Before I know what's happening he turns to me and brings his hand across my face. Hard. Tears fill my eyes and my hand touches the tender spot he's hit. I'm confused but I can't find any words.

"Listen to me, Little Bitch, you don't get to want. At least not for yourself. What you *want* is to make me happy. What you *want* is to make money for us. Get this straight, I tell you what you want."

Little Bitch? He's never called me anything like that before. His words smother the sting on my face. I'm pretty sure the tears falling onto my shirt are from his words and not his slap.

"That fuck we had? That's the last one you'll ever have without collecting cash unless it's with me. Understand?"

Little Bitch? Fuck?

He slaps me again. "Do you understand?"

My ears ring. I see Ian's mouth moving but can't hear what he's saying. All I can do is look at his face.

It's twisted.

Ian slams his orange juice glass down on the coffee table and storms out of the room. I stare at the sticky mess and know I should clean it up before it becomes a problem.

I can't get my feet to move. It's like I'm glued to this terrible couch in this terrible apartment. I can't even get my brain to move.

Mom!

A minute or so later Ian comes back into the room and kneels in front of me. He grabs my hands. "You know I'm here to protect you, don't you?"

I can't meet his eyes. "You hit me."

"I hit you because I love you. I'm the only one who truly loves you, who protects you, and who makes sure you have everything you need."

"Why did you hit me?"

"To make sure you know these things. I know what's best for you and for us."

"Best for us?"

"You have to learn to never doubt me. To never doubt our love for each other."

"So you hit me?"

"Haven't you been paying attention? The only reason I hit you, the *only* reason, is because I love you."

I don't know what to do. Or say.

"You know I love you, don't you?" Ian asked.

The best I can do is shrug.

"And I believe deep in my heart you love me. That's why we're together now. It's meant to be. You and I are a team."

When Ian mentions the word "team" I get a memory flash of Ethan. Maybe Ian's right. Ian's my team. After all, he's older. He knows things I don't.

"Are you with me? Are you with *us*?"

"Of course I am."

"Good."

Ian nudges a pill toward me.

"What is this?"

"It's new. Special."

"But what is it?"

"Take it and I'll tell you."

The other pills Ian gives me make me feel good, so why not? I swallow the pill. "What am I taking?"

"Some people call it horse. For you? It's a pony."

"Team Ian."

"Exactly."

"Are you happy?"

"Sure, baby, sure. But you're going to have to do something for me."

"Okay."

"I've set you up on a couple of dates this afternoon."

"Dates? Will you be there?"

"Nope. These dates are where you prove to me how much you love me. These are where you make a contribution to our love, our lives."

"Don't you love me?"

"Of course I do. But I want you to go on these dates for me. For us."

"What if I don't want to?"

Ian grabs me by the shoulders and squeezes hard. "You will do what I fucking tell you to do, when I tell you to do it, and you will never tell me no."

While law enforcement is important, so is providing adequate support for trafficking victims' recovery. And, in that regard, we are failing. We are failing because we have not identified human trafficking as the public health issue it is. You see, trafficking is not a short-term affliction—it affects a survivor's whole life, families and even entire communities.

—*Why Human Trafficking is a Public Health Problem, by Margeaux Gray,*
for The CNN Freedom Project, July 2016

CHAPTER FORTY-TWO

Mex and Darius sat in Mex's SUV, their eyes glued to the street fifty yards in front of them. They'd parked deep in the shadows of a parking lot of a bar that had closed hours ago. The yellow light outside their shadowland slimed and filtered like an alien presence over the block.

They were there to meet Donny's buyer. The man Donny had convinced to show up to evaluate a potential acquisition, even though she was originating from an unknown source.

Mex was convinced that every source starts out as unknown, so maybe this guy would be willing to take a risk, especially after securing an asset like Alexis. Now, after waiting for fifteen minutes, he wasn't so sure.

Donny was leaning against his car smoking a cigarette, in precisely the same location where he'd traded Alexis for cash. Mex watched as Donny bumped away from the car and crushed out the spent cigarette.

Mex dialed Donny's number. When the young man picked up, Mex said, "Call him."

"Won't do any good, man. He's not showing."

"Call him."

Darius looked at Mex. "This isn't gonna happen."

"I hate wasting time," Mex said.

"We had to take a shot."

"But it sure as hell didn't help Alexis, did it?"

They sat in silence for the next twenty minutes.

Mex's phone rang.

"He didn't call me back," Donny said.

"Let's wait another fifteen minutes."

Mex entered the Greenwood Village detective's cell phone number. "Hey, Les. Darius and I are in Denver, buddy. It's time for you to put together a joint posse with the Denver PD and round up one Donald Miller for human trafficking. He sold Alexis, and she wasn't the first." Mex gave him the cross streets under I-70. "He'll be at this location for the next fifteen minutes unless he rabbits. After that, I don't have time to bother with him."

"You coming in now to give a statement?"

"Cut me some slack. I have to figure out what our next move is gonna be. While Miller will fit into the system, we're no closer to finding Alexis."

"He didn't give you a name?"

"Pretty sure he never had a name. Just a contact number. And the minute you pick him up that number will be history."

"Give it to me now."

Mex gave the number to the detective. "Don't count on much."

"While our hopes are high, our expectations are low."

"Welcome to my world."

We're still in the Dark Ages with trafficking because, unlike incest, rape, and domestic battering, trafficking generates massive revenues—$32 billion a year worldwide.
—Sex Trafficking of Americans: The Girls Next Door, by Amy Fine Collins

CHAPTER FORTY-THREE

ALEXIS

I dream I'm walking through a town filled with people who've had various parts of their bodies amputated. Fingers and hands, arms, legs, ears. They stare at me because I'm different from them. As it goes with dreams, I'm suddenly no longer walking, I'm dancing down the street with nothing on. People continue to gawk. Then I'm dancing without arms. I'm still naked but people quit looking at me.

I wake in a sweat and throw off the bedding. The sun is barely up.

When I look at my body I expect to see bruises and there aren't any. Apparently my captor knows how to inflict pain without leaving outward signs.

I crave a shower even though I know there's not enough scrubbing in the world that will ever make me feel clean again. But maybe with fifteen minutes of gentle water washing over me I can find renewed strength.

Twenty minutes later I step out and reach for a towel. Nothing. I swear there'd been at least two big fluffy towels waiting on the shelf. I shiver to think that once again my faux privacy has been violated. The only thing available is one facecloth.

I dry what I can and move back to the bedroom. The bed has been stripped.

"What the hell?" And then I remember my toga. I finally figure out this fight might not be fair.

I walk over to the closet and picture what my options might be. Little Bo Peep? Porn star Belladonna Black? More Xena or Mary Poppins? Maybe I can mix and match. I throw open the closet door.

Empty, except for a pair of five-inch spikes.

I fly to tear open the dresser drawers.

Empty.

The fabric window coverings are also missing, leaving only the shutters and blinds.

An envelope lies on the floor by the door. Yeah, right, I think. Like someone slipped it under because he or she couldn't friggin' just walk in.

I'm pissed. Maybe scared, but mostly pissed. I snatch up the envelope and retrieve the note inside.

You will join me for breakfast in the main dining room.

Eight o'clock.

Wear something nice.

I throw the note on the floor. It's seven-thirty.

Part of me wants to crawl into a corner and die, but a bigger part of me wants to strike out and cause him physical harm. It dawns on me that I don't even know his name. And he knows a lot about me.

Fine. I'll suck it up and continue with what I started last night. Show no fear. Show nothing. Be bold and proud.

I use the makeup provided and work to put on the best face I've ever drawn. He wants a challenge, I'll give him a challenge.

There's something new in the makeup basket— my signature teal eyeshadow. I apply it carefully. While I put it on I wonder how they knew about it and then I realize someone had to have provided pictures at some point and my Facebook page is full of photos of me wearing this exact shade.

Shit. Except for that one pair of sandals, and the rest of the makeup, everything here is new. The linens, the clothes, the shower gels. But the torture room didn't feel new at all. And I get the feeling I'm the only female guest.

But not the first.

So what happened to them?

I close my eyes and feel tears roll down my face, then move quickly to the toilet to throw up. Shaking, I sit on the cold tile floor.

Hold yourself together Alexis.

I stand up, brush my teeth, repair my makeup and slide my feet inside the stilettos.

Who might be in that room? I mentally prepare for a roomful of fully-dressed people or leering men. What if there are children present? I prepare for the worst.

My hair is long and loose. If I need to take a break, I can let it fall in my face for a second or two. It's eight. Time to go.

A quick check in the mirror reflects my absurd Emperor's New Clothes situation. It proves I'm only pretending to have any control.

When I leave the room, another guard is there to escort me to the dining room. He tries hard not to look at me.

I stand before the closed double-doors, gathering as much strength as I can, and wait. The guard swings the doors open and the breath I'd been holding rushes out of my body.

The dining room is empty.

There's one place-setting. A dress box and note are nearby. A wide selection of breakfast items is laid out on a sideboard, and I can see at least two camera lenses pointed toward me.

As much as I want to rip open the box and remove whatever it might hold—and put it on—I help myself to a cup of coffee.

In general, pimp "culture" among sexually exploited children and youth, is organized along the following lines: a) most pimps manage only 1-3 girls at a time; b) at least 50% of the pimps we encountered operate strictly at the local level— they are not part of larger criminal networks; c) approximately 25% of the pimps we encountered were tied into city-wide crime rings; d) about 15% of the pimps we encountered were tied into regional or nationwide networks; and e) approximately 10% of pimps in the U.S. are tied into international sex crime networks. This latter group of pimps participate actively in the international trafficking of children—including American children and children who are nationals of other countries. Typically, these pimps are connected in some way—directly or indirectly, peripherally or centrally—to international drug networks and frequently use children as "mules" in moving drugs into and across the U.S.

—The Commercial Sexual Exploitation of Children, Executive Summary, *by Richard J. Estes and Neal Alan Weiner, University of Pennsylvania 2001 (revised 2002)*

CHAPTER FORTY-FOUR

The waiter rolled in the room service cart and proceeded to set up the table for three. The only remarkable thing about it was that there were three pots of coffee.

Darius looked at the spread. "This is it? Eggs?"

The night before, Mex asked Cade to order room service for breakfast. He wanted it delivered to their suite at six.

"Any special requests?" Cade had asked.

"Definitely nothing special. I don't want us focused on food. We have a lot to talk about and we're against the clock."

"Do you sense a threat?"

"Not directly, but it's there. Physical and emotional. Every day and every night we don't have those children back where they belong is another day and another night where their lives are hell."

Mex poured three coffees while he looked at his friend. "Yep, this is it. What we need is brain food, not great food."

"I guess I should be glad you didn't order tuna for breakfast."

"I was tempted."

"Here's what we know about what happened to Jayla Thomas." Mex started. "She was sold about six months ago by someone she considered a friend, Chris Williams."

"Who," Darius added, "had convinced himself it was a prank." He plowed a fork under his scrambled eggs.

"You can give him credit if you want," Mex said. "I think he's an opportunistic screw-up."

"He's a kid." Darius put a forkful into his mouth.

"Okay, he's a kid with a gambling problem who took the opportunistic way out of his jam and pretended to himself, for enough cash, that he was playing a joke on his friend. Yeah, right." Mex stirred cream into his coffee. Took a sip. "He admitted he knew what was really going on. He's a screw-up."

"Have you been able to locate his contact?"

"Haven't tried. If we're going to catch this worm, we come at him sideways. That's something the kid can actually help us with. He'll vouch for me. Let his buyer know I have something to offer."

"Or maybe you're in the market to expand your stable." Darius said.

"Will he do it?" Cade asked.

"At this point his guilt is so intense he'd do anything."

"You didn't need to remind him of the sale of humans in our history," Darius said.

"Yeah, I did. Clearly he'd forgotten."

Cade cleared her throat. "On a different note, we're getting quite a few hits on our Backpage ads. Let's go through them and respond to the most likely leads."

"How many hits are we talking about?" Darius asked.

Cade handed them each a printout that was several pages.

"There must be a couple of hundred hits here," Mex said as he flipped through the pages.

"Three hundred and fifty-seven."

"Shit."

"I've never been more clean," Mex said.

"What are you talking about?" Cade asked.

"This case has me wanting to shower hourly."

"If each of us goes through the list and highlights the responses we feel the strongest about," Cade said, "I'll put those we all highlight on a short list. We can start there."

"These ads are probably our fastest and best options to find the girls, but Darius, get Chris to arrange an intro to whoever took Jayla," Mex said.

"Will do. Even if we figure out how to bring the girls home without him, his ass belongs in prison."

"My feelings exactly."

Later, they finished their selections. Cade took the pages and retreated to the bedroom. When she closed the doors, Mex retrieved his medication. He shook a dose into his hand and swallowed it with a glass of water.

"You keeping this from Cade?" Darius asked.

"Don't want her to worry."

"She should know if you're exhibiting signs of depression."

"I've got this." Mex thrust dishes out of the way. "Let's talk about our meeting with the APD."

Darius checked his watch. "Give me a minute," Darius said. He moved away from the table.

"Why?"

"I should check in with Pamela."

"Does she have a problem with you being here?"

"We have three kids at home. Yes, she has a problem with me being here. But honestly? I think she'd have a problem with me being home. Besides, her mom is there to help with the kids. They can trash me together. A bonding thing, ya know?"

While Darius stepped into his room to call his wife, Mex closed his eyes and willed his mind to go blank.

In the last six years, the academic response team [at Metropolitan State University Denver] has helped 51 survivors learn about their educational options. Some have graduated; others have put their educations on hold. Seventy-five percent were born in the Denver metro area.

—Moving in the Right Direction, by Leslie Petrovski, January 30, 2014

CHAPTER FORTY-FIVE

"You're not old bosom buddies with this cop too, are you?" Mex asked Cade. He steered the SUV into a parking space in front of the Aurora City Hall and the District 2 police station. More imposing than architecturally attractive, the lawn and trees did their best to soften the buildings.

"I told you already, no."

"Thank goodness. Because if you were, I could get a complex."

Darius shook his head. "No way you could ever get a complex, *kemo sabe*. Your ego is too big."

"Only on my best days."

The trio walked into a long narrow room. Framed collages of shoulder patch insignia from police departments all over the country covered the walls. Wood benches, attractive only to those in dire need of rest, split the length of the space. The requisite public notice brochures were the only reading material available. In short, the space was depressing.

Mex trekked up to the front desk and handed the desk officer his card. "We have an appointment with Detective Elizabeth Rider."

"I'll let her know you're here."

A Hispanic woman and her young son sat uncomfortably on a bench near the front desk. The young boy fidgeted then jumped to the floor, energized and bored. A dangerous combination for a four-year old.

Darius and Cade had wandered off to look at the insignia display. Mex moved against the wall opposite the mother and son and observed them without making direct eye contact.

The mother sat texting and swinging the foot of her crossed leg. While in this moment the mother looked distracted and disengaged, her child was clean, wore clean clothes and was the picture of health. Mex knew a lot of people wouldn't bother with all the information but would instantly judge the situation based on race and the fact they were at a police station. He'd seen it time and time again.

The door opened and a young woman who didn't look old enough to have any job let alone the job of a detective, greeted them. "Hello, I'm Detective Rider. Please, follow me.

"We'll meet in this conference room." She ushered them into a room right inside the entrance.

Mex made the introductions and decided immediately he liked this cop. Detective Rider was wearing red jeans, a blue and white striped t-shirt and sparkly slip-on canvas shoes. Her eyes were clear and direct. His kind of law enforcement officer.

Plus, it was clear she didn't know Cade.

They settled down around one end of the conference table.

"You know why we're here," Mex began.

"I do," Detective Rider said. "You're trying to track down two missing girls."

"Three," Darius said.

"The Aurora girl?" Detective Rider asked Darius.

"Yes."

"Okay then. That puts us on the same page. How can we help?"

Cade leaned forward. "We've placed a couple of personals on Backpage, but we could really use your help if you have a way to filter through the photos to see if these three girls are listed there."

Detective Rider nodded. "We've tried to lure people in through Backpage, but we haven't had a lot of success."

"I can understand why," Cade said.

Detective Rider shot her a glance.

Cade smiled. "When this is over, I'd be happy to work with you on your ads."

"But you do have newer facial recognition software?" Darius asked.

"Homeland Security has the next gen software—"

Mex held up a hand and looked at Darius.

"Next generation," Darius explained.

"We don't have access to it as a matter of routine. It's not perfect," Detective Rider continued, "but it's light-years ahead of what everyone else has."

"Can you use it to find our three girls?" Mex asked.

"No way. Not unless one of them is a threat to national security. The technology is available, but we don't have enough of it, nor the manpower to run it."

Mex understood. Lack of funding was the lamentation of law enforcement agencies everywhere.

"In the meantime," Cade said, "can we share the list of responses to our ads? We've narrowed them down but I'd hate to miss the important one because it didn't make our cut."

"How many responses did you have?"

"Three hundred and fifty-seven," Cade said.

"For three girls? That's amazing. Do you have the contact information?"

"I can email them to you." Cade got out her phone, held Detective Rider's business card in front of her and hit a few keys. "I'm sending you the complete lists of responses, two each for the girls as placed by the alter-egos of Mex and Darius. Those highlighted are ones the three of us identified independently as being prime. Of course, that was before we thought we might have help from the APD." Cade watched as Detective Rider thumbed through the information now on her phone. "Can we count on your help?"

Detective Rider fingered a few keys on her phone. "I've sent this to two of our staff members to investigate and collate. I'll meet with my supervisor this afternoon after they've had a chance to do the initial research." She looked into Cade's eyes. "You have our help."

Cade huffed out a breath that Mex felt she'd been holding for ages. Her eyes filled with tears.

God, he loved this woman.

He'd thought of his wife, Maria, as his soulmate. His Only. They'd had two children together, a son who he loved beyond reason, and a daughter with Down syndrome who'd gifted them with her uncompromising, judgment-free love. A third baby had been on the way.

Then in one horrendous afternoon, they were all gone. Thanks to his idea of honor. His refusal to corrupt his name as a law enforcement officer in Mexico. His pride.

Now, many years later, he could see it was also his failure as a professional. He should have been suspicious of the call saying there'd been a break-in. At the very least, he should've sent someone else to investigate.

His sister Sedona had survived, supposedly by hiding in a barn. Instead, as it turned out, she had helped orchestrate the murder of his family. He hadn't seen it coming. And didn't know about it for years.

One more failure.

Tonya spent night after night in different hotel rooms, with different men, all at the command of someone she once trusted. She was held against her will, beaten and made to feel like she had no other option at the time, all by the man she thought she loved.

She felt she deserved it. Tonya felt she couldn't escape. Afraid and confused, she thought the emotional and physical abuse she endured was her own doing.

—Human trafficking victim shares story, Official Website of the Department of Homeland Security, ICE

CHAPTER FORTY-SIX

LIVVY

It's late afternoon and the bleak room has a gray quiet to it. I'm stretched out on the bed next to Ian, afraid to move. I don't know which Ian he'll be when he wakes up.

I want to go home. And if I can't go home I want to die. Most of me is dead already. Shouldn't be too hard to take the rest.

Forget that. I don't want to go home. I can't go home. Not ever. What would I say? How could I live with my family? How could my family live with me?

Dying is my best option.

How could I have been so stupid? I should've listened to Maddy.

My private parts are so sore. Why do people lie? They say sex feels good. They say it's natural.

It's neither.

After the first man, Ian held me for a long, long time. Told me he loved me. Told me he would always protect me. Be there for me. Make sure I was happy because I made him happy. He gave me a cute stuffed bear and told me it was a symbol of his love for me. Told me I should never forget the bear.

The next time, afterward, Ian grabbed me by my hair and threw me to the ground. Told me if I didn't smile more he would make sure I never smiled again.

That was two days ago. I don't even know how many men there've been since. I smile and take the pills he gives me.

Today he hasn't touched me. It's like I'm a piece of furniture. I'm afraid to say anything. I'm afraid to move. Maybe, if he stays asleep, I can quietly leave.

But where will I go?

For a minute I think of my family. I picture Sarah dramatically throwing a hissy-fit and Ethan hoisted on Dad's shoulders because of something he achieved athletically. I think of Madison and the dreams we shared. I was sure I'd be a veterinarian, and she knew she'd be an IT expert. We used to giggle and plan. Talk about boys. Talk about love.

I can never go back home.

There's a quick knock. Two short raps.

Ian gets up off his bed and opens the door. A man rams a girl, hands bound and mouth gagged, into the room. She's even younger than me. Darker. Maybe Mexican? Her frightened eyes find mine and our gazes lock. She receives another shove, this one takes her to the floor.

My fear freezes me. I'm weak and pitiful for not going to her.

"Hey, man! Damages!" Ian shouts.

"Shut the fuck up. I don't want any attention."

"Then stop with the physical shit," Ian says.

Inexplicably, I rise and go to the girl. I kneel down and put an arm around her.

The man laughs. "See? You've got a caretaker. No problems."

Ian looks at us like we're garbage.

"You got my money?" The man asks.

Ian sniffs and walks over to where the girl and I are sitting on the floor. "Move." He shoves me out of the way.

"Get up," he says to the girl.

She doesn't move.

"*Parar*," the man says.

The girl stands on shaking legs.

Ian walks around her. He pats her butt, lifts an arm to smell her pit. Then he moves her hair around on her head, pries her lips back to look at her teeth, and finally cups her tiny breasts. "She doesn't speak English?"

"No, but that can be a good thing," the man says. "She probably won't talk much."

"She a virgin?"

"Don't know."

"Where'd you get her?"

"She came to me. Wanted to get out of Guatemala."

"Medical exam?"

"Didn't have time."

Ian stepped back from the girl.

"Look, I had other offers. But if you fuck with me, we're done."

"No problems. I have your money."

The girl begins to cry and before I know it, Ian backhands her and she twists around before falling back to the floor.

"Hey," the man says, "you bruise her now and it's on you."

"Like I said, no problems." Ian reaches into his back pocket, removes a small wad of cash and counts off a few bills with the man watching.

The man leaves saying he'll be in touch.

Ian glares at Livvy. "Get her ready."

"Ian, she's exhausted."

"What the fuck do I care about that?"

"Can't you give her a night to rest?"

"Did you just see me give money to that guy?"

I nod.

"Unless you can cover what I paid for her, on top of your quota, she has to go out."

"Do you have clothes for her?"

"Do I look like I have clothes? Just fix her fuckin' face. What she's wearing will have to do for tonight."

I stay where I am.

"Did you hear me? Get her ready."

"Have you set me up with someone?"

"Not tonight. I'm thinking you can make me happy without me getting involved. Can you do that? Can you take, crap... what's her name? Shit. Can you take this one with you?"

I don't move.

"Well? I'm counting on you, Livvy."

I ignore Ian. "Qué es su nombre?" I ask for her name, using one of the few phrases I know in Spanish.

The girl brightens and begins to rapid-fire words at my face. I shake my head. "I'm sorry. I don't know what you're saying. I'm sorry. Qué es su nombre?"

The girl looks between me and Ian. Back and forth like a ticking clock. Finally she settles on me. She touches her chest. "Isabella."

"Great," Ian says. "You can handle her. I want eight hundred tonight from each of you. Don't come back here until you have it."

I'd seen Ian count out five twenty dollar bills to the man who sold him Isabella. One hundred dollars.

Suddenly she's my sister. And I can't save her any more than I can save myself.

A three-day operation by Special Agents with the Tennessee Bureau of Investigation and partner agencies to combat human trafficking in Nashville has resulted in the arrest of 41 individuals on prostitution-related charges; 34 men, six women and one juvenile. More than half of the men responding to ads tried to buy sex from a minor.... Those arrested include a high school teacher, a college football player, a truck driver, a student, and a state IT Specialist.

—41 Arrested in Nashville Human Trafficking Operation, August 5, 2016, The Chattanoogan.com

CHAPTER FORTY-SEVEN

Cade absently placed her coffee mug on the room service tray and stared at her monitor. Did she so badly want to see a familiar face she was imagining things? She printed out the Backpage ad using the printer the hotel had provided. Maybe looking at the photo on paper rather than her monitor would clarify her vision.

There were hundreds of ads for the Denver area. Hundreds. How many were doing this against their will? How many were doing this because they didn't think they could do anything else? How many families had given up the search?

With the help of the Aurora PD, they'd gone through all of the responses to her ads and come up with zilch. A lot of perverts, but no one who could lead them to their missing girls. Still, Cade sensed that Backpage could be their answer. It's why she checked regularly. It's why she saw the ad she felt sure was one of their girls.

My name is Cherie and I know how to be sweet to you. I'll be in Denver in a week and would love to book an appointment. When you're with me there is no one else. I will make your world spin.

Cade grabbed the sheet out of the printer and looked at it.

Damn, she thought, if that wasn't Jayla Thomas she'd stop what she was doing and find another vocation. Maybe her dream of writing a novel could find its way to the top. She checked the ad's date. It was current. Jayla would be here in seven days. Cade pulled the ad up on her cell and sent it to Mex who was at a doctor's appointment.

Could be coincidence. Could be our ad. Could be Jayla's pimp has forgotten people know her here. But it sure as hell looks like our girl (one of them anyway) is coming home. Tell me I'm wrong.

Cade sent the text and then held the phone to her chest.

What if I'm wrong? What if focusing on this girl who calls herself Cherie takes away from us finding Jayla?

She would never be able to forgive herself.

Make an appt. You're not wrong. After you make the appt let DPD know.

The person Cade really wanted to tell was Mary. Jayla's mom was in a lot of pain. But it wouldn't do any good to get the woman's hopes up only to punch her in the gut. She took a closer look at Cherie's ad. There were symbols Cade had learned meant she had a pimp. She was protected. It didn't matter that the ad said she was independent.

Cade called Rachel Hanson. Cade wanted her to be ready.

"Don't make an appointment for her first day in Denver," Rachel said.

"Why not?"

"It's a Savior Signal."

"A what?"

"People who want to save a particular girl from being victimized want to make contact with her as soon as possible. And it could tip off her pimp. I know it sucks, but set up an appointment for the second or even third day she's in town."

"Can you be available for her?"

"I'll make it happen."

"Anything else I should know?"

"Yeah, there is. Are you ready to hear?"

"Rachel, you should know by now. I'm always ready to hear."

"You've extracted people from cults, but there are a couple of huge differences between your previous experience and what you're doing now."

"Go on."

"The cult victims you rescued made the decision to leave their homes and families and lives and commit to something else. The people you saved wanted to be exactly where they were. You had a fight on your hands from the time they were extracted." Rachel paused. "Jayla didn't have a choice. She might be confused and wary, but she's unlikely to be resistant, at least for very long. That's what's in your favor with the current situation."

"I have the feeling the second huge difference is not in my favor."

"Your feeling is right. Whoever has Jayla bought her. He or she considers Jayla property. Jayla not only has a price on her forehead representing the upfront investment, she has a price on her ass representing cash flow. You are seriously going to piss off at least one person, and you'd best have a plan in place."

"I'm thinking that's where the press and the law will come in handy."

"One more thing," Rachel said.

"What?"

"These girls will require an even longer deprogramming time. You should be prepared. They may not be better in a few weeks or months. It could take years. Decades even. For some, they're simply broken and all we can do is love them."

Cade hung up and called the Denver Police Department detective assigned to Jayla's case. Her call went to voicemail and she explained the situation. "I'm making an appointment for two days after she gets in town. If it's Jayla we'll grab her and bring her to Denver Health for evaluation and hopefully meet you there. I've got an advocate on board who will be with us. If it *is* Jayla, we'll also contact her mother."

The Backpage ad had a phone number but specified no texts. Cade called Darius and brought him up to speed. "Call and book the appointment for nine days from now. That's like what? The fifteenth? Make it for late afternoon, four or four-thirty. The ad says she's on in-call or outcall, so make her come to you. Get a room. Nice but not too nice. By her coming to you she's less likely to have more than one observer. It could get tense. Remember, you're a guy who can knock off work early and likes what he sees."

"Do you really think it's her?"

"I really do. Make the call."

The child had goals. "Simple goals," [Detective Elli] Reid said, referring to the ability to make her own decisions, have her own career, and pick out her own wardrobe.

"I want to dress nicely," the child said. "I don't want to wear lingerie."

—Colorado Springs detective describes realities of human trafficking in region, by Chun Sun, April 2016

CHAPTER FORTY-EIGHT

"Hi, yeah. I'd like to make an appointment to see Cherie." Darius squeezed his left hand into a fist.

"What's your name?"

"My name? Why do you need to know my name?"

The man chuffed out a grunt. "Well my friend, it's helpful if your name matches the credit card number you're going to give me."

"Really? A credit card? I can't pay cash?"

"For a street whore, if you're lucky. For a confirmed date? Not gonna happen."

"How much?"

"You are bustin' my balls, friend. Didn't you read? It's $150 for a half hour and $275 for an hour."

"Uh, okay. A half hour should do it."

"My bet is you need less than fifteen minutes."

Darius felt challenged. "You want to make this sale or not?"

"Hey, no skin off my back. You want to book this appointment or not?"

"Fine. If I get there and pay cash, will you delete my information?" Darius made a mental note to cancel the card when this was over.

"We are all about customer satisfaction."

"And privacy?"

"That too."

In a bathroom, the predator has placed a child on the counter to photograph his evil acts.

—How child predator was caught by tiny clue in photo he posted online, Posted April 21, 2016, by CNN Wire

CHAPTER FORTY-NINE

Mex looked at the caller ID on his phone and dismissed the call. Sedona.

Shit.

He had to psych himself up to even speak to her. And now he had priorities that made it easy to relegate her to a far corner of his world.

Mex tossed his phone on the table.

"Sedona again?" Cade asked.

Mex grunted.

Cade took a sip of her drink and eyed Mex. "Before the last week or so, how many times has your sister called you in the last six months?"

"Maybe once."

"Only once? Why is that, do you think?"

"She knows I don't want to talk to her."

"And how many times has she called you in the last two days?"

"Seven? Eight?"

"And why is that, do you think?"

"Maybe she's dying?"

"Or maybe she knows what you're working on and has something important to contribute."

Mex sat for a moment and then rocked his head right and left, hoping the popping in his neck would help him relax. It didn't work.

"You have to find out why she's calling, Mex. If she's dying, you should know. If it's something else, you should know. You can always blow her off later."

"Why would Sedona have something that could help us?"

"I wouldn't know. I haven't talked to her."

"Why would she know what we're working on?"

Cade tucked her head down and raised her eyes to meet his. "Are you kidding? How many times have the local news programs played your interview?"

Mex matched her shrug. "Okay, yeah. So?"

"So call her back. Shit, Mex. At least find out why she's calling."

Mex picked up his phone and pressed the voicemail icon. "Teo, please call me."

That was all, but Mex considered what wasn't said more important than what was. It had been that way his entire career in law enforcement. He could hear the anxiety in her voice. The electrical charge he'd come to rely on buzzed his neck hairs to attention.

Holding the phone in his hands, his eyes met Cade's.

"Call her, Cowboy."

Mex made the call and put it on speaker.

"Teo!" Sedona launched into rapid Spanish, thankful he'd called her back, expressing her sorrow over what she'd done, angry he hadn't called sooner—

"Sedona. You're on speaker. Cade is with me. English, please."

"Hello, Sedona," Cade said.

"Why are you calling?" Mex asked. Let's get this over with, Mex thought.

"I wish to help."

A harsh laugh escaped Mex's throat. "Help? Help who? Me? You've got to be—"

Cade reached across the table and wrapped her hand around his wrist, silently demanding he look at her. When he did, she simply shook her head.

Mex fell silent.

"How do you wish to help?" Cade asked.

"I think I might know where the girl you're looking for is being held."

"Which girl?" Cade asked. "We're looking for three."

"The first one. The one Mex was interviewed about. The one with the family who has money. Alexandra? Something like that?"

"Alexis."

"Yes, yes. That one."

"Why do you think you have information about her?"

"I've heard things."

UNICEF has written that at any time there are two million children being trafficked in the global sex trade....People trafficking is the fastest growing means by which people are enslaved, the fastest growing international crime, and one of the largest sources of income for organized crime (The UN Office on Drugs and Crime). — Force4Compassion

CHAPTER FIFTY

"Where are you?" Mex barked.

"Monterrey," Sedona answered.

"If you're there, how do you even know what I'm doing."

"Google."

"What?"

"Since you won't talk to me, I google you. Once a week. I do have access to the internet here."

"Of all the places you could have run to, you chose Monterrey. I bought you a place in Aspen Falls and you walk away." Mex swallowed and took a deep breath. "Have you fallen back into your old habits?" Mex tasted bile in his throat and swallowed again.

"Teo, please. Let me help you."

"Both of you, settle down. You can get into all of that later." Cade took the phone from Mex's hands and turned the speaker toward her. "What have you heard?"

"There's a man in Monterrey. Quite wealthy. He has a connection to the cartel but he's not a member. He has a reputation for having, um, unique tastes when it comes to women."

"A lot of men have what might be called 'unique tastes.' What exactly are you talking about?" Mex asked.

"He likes them young. American. Entitled."

"Entitled?"

"An attitude that says they're *All It*. Rich bitches."

Mex looked at Cade. Together they said, "Alexis."

"Why do you think he might have our girl?" Cade asked.

"Because the word is he has a new one. That she only arrived a few days ago and is now at his estate."

"Wait, wait, wait," Mex said. "So what? Guys get girls every day. There are thousands of girls, even a few rich bitches. What makes you think she's Alexis Halston?"

"Rumor has it she's from Colorado."

Mex took a breath. "I'll be in Monterrey tomorrow. At the Safi. I'll call you when I arrive."

"Good. That's good," Sedona said.

"What's the man's name?"

"Sergio Montonaldo."

"What do you know about him?"

"Only that he's untouchable by the police and even the drug lords want to impress him."

Mex pushed away from the phone.

"Teo? Are you there?"

Mex shook his head.

"It's been good to talk to you."

He got up and walked away.

"Teo?"

"Thanks for your help, Sedona," Cade said. "Mex and I both appreciate what it took for you to reach out."

Mex's next call was to Darius who'd gone home to make sure his family remembered him.

"I have a question I've got to ask," Darius said after Mex filled him in, including the fact that Mex had been unable to find squat about the man named Montonaldo.

"Shoot."

"This is information you received from Sedona, right?"

"That's right."

"Could it be another setup?"

Mex was silent.

"Mex, dude. I've got to ask."

"Tell me what you're thinking."

"You don't know what they might have promised her. She's back in Monterrey. She's apparently moving around in the same old crowd. And even though you reunited one cartel family, you still have a lot of enemies in Mexico."

Mex felt the familiar stab in his gut. Sometimes moving ahead meant looking at ghosts. "Get me everything you can on this guy. Like I said, I couldn't find shit. You're going to have to go deep and use your contacts. I want to know what I'm walking into in Monterrey."

"I will. But book a suite," Darius said. "I'm coming. You're not doing this without me."

"Pamela won't be happy."

"You don't know my Pammy."

"My friend, I'm afraid that two small children and a new baby might bring out a side of your Pammy you've not seen before."

"You're worried about nothing. We're solid. What about weapons?"

"I've contacted my source."

"Is Cade coming?"

"She's got her hands full with Jayla's mom and Olivia's parents." Mex paused. "And Darius?"

"Yeah?"

"See if you can find out what Sedona is up to as well."

"I was going to anyway."

According to the Weld [County, Colorado] District Attorney affidavit, from October 2012 to April 2014, Burman, who went by the name of Haylo, induced several victims, both adults and teenagers, to engage in prostitution with numerous men. He would provide them with alcohol and drugs, and threaten them to force them to stay in his prostitution ring, always keeping the money for himself. Once, he even raped one of the girls, the release stated.

—Jury convicts Greeley man of 32 counts in human sex trafficking case, Greeley Tribune, *August 12, 2016*

CHAPTER FIFTY-ONE

Cade had the airlines text boarding passes to both Mex and Darius. The hotel confirmation was sent as well.

The logistics out of the way, she tried to figure out why she didn't feel optimistic about this venture. Part of her reluctance was surely to do with Mex's sister. At least they weren't trusting her completely. Mex and Darius weren't walking into the situation blind.

Then, assuming the information from Sedona was accurate, the fact that this Sergio Montonaldo was someone who even the drug lords looked up to unnerved her. Drug lords were deadly. The cartels had tentacles that spread money far and wide, buying a sick loyalty from those whose pockets they lined. If the cartels bowed to this man, how much power did he wield?

What level of protection would he have at his disposal?

Cade checked Mex's meds to make sure he had enough, then set the bottle out where he'd be certain to see it when he packed.

She knew better than to try and talk Mex out of heading to Monterrey. Confrontations were not unfamiliar to him. When he was after the truth, when he was after what he felt was right, nothing could stop him. Add to that the prospect of saving a young woman and there was nothing Cade could say that would dissuade him.

And frankly, she wouldn't love him as much if she could.

But she now knew why she didn't feel good about this venture. Sedona couldn't be trusted. Sergio Montonaldo had resources and money and power to put them all into the dirt. And Mex battled depression. Usually he won, but in circumstances like this? Where his sister was involved and stirring up his memories? The very events that began his illness?

What the hell was there to like about this operation?

Mex walked into the room. "Are you missing your morning hikes?"

"Ah, *mon cher*, you know I am. But they'll be waiting for me when we finally get home. What we're doing is important and I'm a big enough girl to set what I might want aside."

Mex drew her up and looked into her eyes. "You know what you mean to me."

"Tell me."

"You give me a reason to wake up. You inspire me. You make me a better man. I love you, Acadia LeBlanc."

"Sure, get all romantic when you're about to board a plane to confront a man even the cartel leaders fear. Make me get all tingly just before you go get your ass killed. Thanks a lot, Mex Anderson."

"Tell me what I mean to you."

Cade looked into his eyes, pulled his head to hers, and kissed him long and deep. "Let me show you instead." She took his hand in hers and led the way to the suite's bedroom.

Sussex County, Del.- Authorities say an eight-month investigation into a human trafficking ring operation in Sussex County has led to the arrests of two men....Police said the female victims involved were only provided with minimal amounts of heroin, and basic items like fast food and clothing.

—Pair Charged With Human Trafficking in Sussex County, by Kye Parsons

CHAPTER FIFTY-TWO

Mex and Darius watched as their driver maneuvered elegantly through the most recent criminal activity on Monterrey's streets. While other cars had been stopped in a long search line, their driver and the logo of the hotel emblazoned on the side of the limousine seemed to magically open pathways for them to travel.

The cartels and their rivalries only seemed to be strengthening. Mex was glad Cade hadn't joined them. He'd only worry.

"Tell me what you learned about my sister," Mex said. He hadn't been ready to hear about her until he had no choice.

Darius opened his tablet and pressed a few keys. "Sedona is working as a governess for three children in San Pedro, outside Monterrey. She comes into the city frequently—field trips for her charges, errands, personal time, whatever."

"Is she using?"

"None of my intel pointed to any drug use whatsoever. Nor is she dating anyone on a consistent basis."

Mex grunted. His sister was unusually beautiful. Long, wavy dark hair, on the tall side, with the same gray-green eyes as his. He seriously doubted she lacked of relationships.

"Tell me about the family she's working for."

"They are Americans. Sedona cares for twin girls who are ten, and a boy, seven. The father is an executive at Carson, a manufacturing company that makes air conditioning equipment with a plant in Monterrey. The family has been in San Pedro for almost six years."

"And the mother?"

"She died four years ago. I don't know how. All I've been able to find is an obituary."

"Keep looking. Do you have a photo of the father?"

Darius swiped his screen a couple of times. "Here. This is Kenneth Maxwell." He turned his tablet to face Mex.

A handsome man. Haunted eyes. Sallow complexion. Emotionally flat.

"Where was this taken?"

"The funeral service for his wife."

Mex figured that any picture taken of him at the funeral service of his family would have had the same result. He couldn't judge the man based on this depiction. "Anything more recent?"

Darius depressed a few keys. "This was taken a few months ago. It's blurry, but it's definitely Maxwell."

Even unfocused, Mex saw engaged eyes and a brilliant smile. He'd bet anything that Sedona was behind both. No wonder she wasn't dating anyone publicly.

Mex brought out his phone and began scrolling through his contacts.

"We're in Monterrey. Can you join us for dinner?"

"Where?"

"We're staying at the Safi and exhausted from traveling. I don't know if they still have the no visitation policy in place, so let's plan on meeting in the lobby at seven. I'll have reservations at the restaurant."

Because of the drug violence in the city, the Safi had increased its security measures to the extent that no unregistered people could visit their guest's rooms. Other hotels would accept the registration of IDs at the front desk, but not the Safi. It was both a comfort and a hassle.

"I'll be there," Sedona said. "Mex?"

"Yes?"

"I hope I can help. I hope my information might help you save that girl."

Mex dared not respond.

"I know nothing I can ever do will make up for the things I did in Agua Prieta. I was a different person then."

Sedona stopped talking but still Mex didn't respond.

Her voice dropped, almost to a whisper. "I hope my information—working with you—might be a step in building a connection between us."

"I will accept your information, Sedona, with healthy skepticism. But as far as a connection between us? Don't kid yourself. I'm here for a girl and her family. To me you're a tool, nothing more."

Mex waited so long he thought something might have happened to their connection. He was about to hang up.

"I understand. I'm grateful to be a tool."

Mex could sense the tears rolling down Sedona's face.

"I'll be at the Safi by seven," Sedona said.

"Fine. See you then."

A Greenwood Village [Colorado] man has been sentenced to four years in prison in a child pornography case involving the most images and videos ever prosecuted in the 18th Judicial District.... In all, investigators recovered more than 100,000 pictures and 300 videos depicting child pornography.
—*Arapahoe County Media Release, Sept. 1, 2016*

CHAPTER FIFTY-THREE

Mex sat at a secluded table inside the restaurant and swirled a drink in front of him. Darius was stationed in the lobby to greet Sedona. Mex had no desire to wait for her. To greet her.

To see her.

Thank goodness Cade had made sure to pack his medication. Memories of the worst time in his life were falling into his head and turning his world dark. His life ended that day as much as it would have ended had someone slit his throat. It took Cade to bring him back to the living.

He signaled the waiter to bring him another drink. He knew he shouldn't indulge in alcohol on top of his meds, but this next hour or two required it. He preferred a bit of numbness in order to deal with Sedona.

Speaking of which.

Sedona wound her way to his table, Darius behind her. She looked normal. No horns. No sign of the evil she'd helped produce.

Suddenly Mex was transported to another memory. Sedona was about four years old. She'd lost a balloon from a local street fair and cried as if the world had come to an end. Mex had taken her by the hand and gone back to the fair to buy another balloon. His sister's tears dried, her joy apparent, Mex had understood for the first time how small things mattered.

He'd have given his life for Sedona in those days.

The waiter approached with the new drink as Sedona and Darius reached the table. He waited expectantly.

"Water for me, thank you," Sedona said in Spanish.

"I'll have whatever he's having," Darius pointed to Mex's drink.

The waiter nodded and moved off.

The pair seated themselves and waited for Mex to say something.

Uncomfortable, Darius shifted in his chair. "Thank you for being willing to help, Sedona."

"It's a small way for me to begin to make amends."

"Very small," Mex said.

Darius cleared his throat. "Thank you nonetheless." He glared at Mex. "Our goal here, our purpose here, is to find a young woman who is more than likely going through hell even while we sit in the restaurant of this luxury hotel." He kicked Mex's foot. "Are we in agreement?"

Mex expelled his breath like Vesuvius venting. "I suppose."

"What do you know, Sedona, that could help your brother and me find this girl?"

"Did you research Sergio Montonaldo?"

"I tried. It's a more common name than I would have guessed," Darius said.

Sedona nodded. "It is. And this particular Sergio Montonaldo would have the means to keep his secrets secret."

"How do you know about him?" Mex asked.

"I have friends in Monterrey who surprisingly enough don't wish to drag me back into my old life. And yet they still want to spend time with me. Talk to me. And that includes gossip."

Mex slapped his glass to the table. "We're here because of gossip?"

Sedona straightened her back. "You're here because I have credible information that will lead you to a missing American girl who happens to be rich and blonde. A girl whose parents have hired you to find and bring home."

"Then prove it."

She looked at Darius. "Did you bring the map I asked you to bring?"

Darius produced a map of the surrounding Monterrey area and spread it on the table.

Sedona studied it for a few seconds and then planted a finger. "Here. This is where Montonaldo's estate is located."

"You know this how?" Mex asked.

"I've been to parties."

A [whore]monger who uses the online handle "ohiosensi" posted his two-star review of the Powell Amsun on Oct. 7, mere weeks after the spa opened. His review covers the cost of services and the ages of the women working at the parlor, as well as their hair and eye color, hair length and breast size. He checks off the various services one could expect to receive there. Ohiosensi writes he didn't get the name of the girl who gave him his "nice" and "light" massage, then went into more graphic detail about where his roaming hands were allowed (or not) and how the massage ended. The entire review is written as if he's talking about the latest Short North steakhouse.

— *The Stubborn Cycle of Massage Parlor Trafficking, by Justin McIntosh in* Columbus Monthly, *May 2015*

CHAPTER FIFTY-FOUR

After the waiter left with their orders, Mex carefully unfolded his napkin and placed it in his lap. "Tell us about Montonaldo," he said quietly.

"Sergio Montonaldo is powerful. More powerful than any drug lord. His wealth seems limitless."

"How old is he?"

"Mid-forties. He's in excellent physical shape. Drugs were never an issue for him."

"How do you know he has an affinity for young, blonde, American women?"

"Because your Alexis is not his first. And it's more than women who are young and blonde and American. They must have an attitude of entitlement. Spoiled. Opinionated. Borderline narcissistic."

Mex bit his tongue.

"Where does he get his money?" Darius asked.

"The best I can tell, all over the place. I don't know where he got his money initially, but now he has investments all over the world, from real estate to oil to pharmaceuticals to entertainment."

"How many girls has he gone through?" Mex asked.

Sedona hesitated.

"How many?" Mex asked again.

Sedona looked away and then met her brother's eyes. "In the last year I've heard of at least six, maybe more."

"And those are the ones you've heard of," Mex said in a whisper.

"How many people live on his estate?" Darius asked, anxious to bring the subject back to something they could control.

"His staff is enormous. He has household staff as well as people for the stable, garages and grounds. Probably around thirty full-time, plus people who would be brought in for special projects."

"What about security?"

"At the parties security is pretty low key, but they still stand out. Men who are obviously armed are at the front gate where they clear people to enter, but once you're at the party area, they're simply the ones who aren't drinking or dancing or laughing. They wear suits and you can see an occasional bulge from a weapon."

"Do you think he hires additional security for parties?"

"Probably."

Mex looked at Darius. "Maybe that's our way in."

"I doubt it," Sedona said. "If he does hire additional men, he would do it through a trusted source who would fully vet their employees."

"Can you ask around? Find out who he uses?" Mex asked.

"I don't see how that could help," Sedona said.

"Find out and let us decide if it helps," Mex said.

"Is there someone you can call?" Darius asked.

"Now?"

"Yes, please," Darius said before Mex ruined her helpful attitude with a snarky remark. He looked at his friend.

Mex caught Darius's glance, shook his head and closed his eyes.

"What do I tell them about why I'm asking the question?"

Again, Darius answered before Mex could say something about her deceitful past. "Tell whoever you're asking you have a friend who is going to vacation in Monterrey and wants to throw a lavish party. Get the name of Montonaldo's caterer, valet service, and security firm."

Sedona reached for her phone and walked to the lobby.

"Thanks," Mex said to Darius.

"I know you too well. And Sedona's an easy target."

Mex called their waitress over and ordered another round of drinks.

"Maybe you should be the one to interact with my sister," Mex said. "I seem to have too many unresolved issues with her."

"I agree, that's probably best for right now," Darius said. "But Mex, she's reaching out. I don't know if she's changed or not and I don't know if it matters. What she did to you and your family was epic. Something not too many people would ever get past. But she's trying. And she's your sister. After this is over consider confronting her with those unresolved issues."

Mex nodded, and sipped his drink. "Probably best if you and Cade were there with me. Keep me from killing her."

Darius shook his head. "Nope. That would be a gang confrontation. Completely ineffective for the results you're both looking for."

Mex shook his head.

"This prosecution shows that human trafficking is not simply a big city problem, but unfortunately is a plague which is permeating all of our communities," said Weld District Attorney Michael Rourke in a news release.... According to a Greeley [Colorado] police affidavit, Burman would find girls on Facebook and offer them chances to make money, then turn them into his prostitutes.... Police learned of his activities after one girl, who had been in a rehab program, shared her story with authorities. Police also talked to one girl who was pregnant with his child.

—*Jury convicts Greeley man of 32 counts in human sex trafficking case, Swift Communications, Inc.*

CHAPTER FIFTY-FIVE

Sedona walked quickly back into the restaurant and looked at Mex, energy pouring from her. "I have a contact."

Mex nodded toward Darius. "Darius will take it from here. He speaks fluent Spanish and I have other things to attend to."

Sedona's expectant face fell. She looked at the floor and slowly lifted her eyes to meet Darius's. "Okay, then. It's you and me." She swallowed and forced a smile.

Darius hoped they'd made the right decision. He sensed they had. Mex's emotions where Sedona was concerned were too volatile right now.

They needed Sedona if they were to have a half-ass chance of rescuing Alexis Halston.

Mex excused himself from the table. "I trust the two of you to make the necessary arrangements."

Sedona sat silently and watched her brother leave the restaurant. "I've lost him forever, haven't I?"

Darius sat silently.

"You agree, don't you?" Sedona asked.

"I don't agree or disagree," Darius said. "Our entire focus right now is on rescuing a young girl being held by a man you know. Everything else is secondary."

Sedona blushed and hung her head. "You're right." She looked off, unfocused. "Teo used to be such a large part of my life and I resented him. He paid for my roof, he paid for my food. I hated him for taking care of me. Even though I'd done the most despicable thing imaginable. I suppose maybe my guilt merged with my shame. I wouldn't blame him if he never forgave me."

"That's for another discussion. One between you and your brother."

Sedona straightened her back and folded her hands on the table. "You're right. Let's get on with this."

Darius reached out and held her hand. "For what it's worth, your brother, your Teo, doesn't want to hate you forever. He may not know that's how he feels, but it is. Some day—some day soon—the two of you will yell at each other. You'll both cry. You'll both feel like killing each other and want to die at the same time."

A tear welled out of Sedona's eye and trailed down her cheek.

"But for now, right this minute, let's think about a young girl who's being held against her will. Let's focus on saving her from nightmares and worse. If Sergio Montonaldo has gone through six women, or more, in the last year, there's no telling when he'll tire of Alexis Halston. As far as we know, he could become bored with her tomorrow and she'll never see her family again."

Darius dug out a handkerchief and handed it to Sedona. "Are we on the same page?"

Sedona accepted his offering, dabbed her eyes and returned it. "Yes. Let's get this done."

"Good. What's the name of your contact?"

She looked at the note she'd made. "Sanchez Security. Apparently Pablo Sanchez and Montonaldo go back years."

Darius tugged his laptop out of its case and placed it on the table. He keyed in "Sanchez Security Monterrey" and brought up their website. "Call them. You're interested in hiring additional security personnel and want to know their vetting process."

"Now?"

"Now. Aren't you paying attention? The young girl we're trying to save is in trouble. Her life could depend on us getting to her in time."

Sedona gave him a quick look, like she'd just been clued in to the importance of her role. "Yes, okay. Now."

Darius reached in a pocket and gave her a phone. "It's untraceable."

Sedona put her phone aside and took the one he offered.

"You are particularly interested in hiring black security guards," Darius said. "They will blend in better with your guests."

He pushed a slip of paper across the table and pointed. "This is the number for the cell, and this is the burner email address you'll give them if we need to use one."

Her head bobbed. "Let me think of a scenario." She stared at her drink, nodded, and punched in the telephone number. "Yes, hello. I'm an advance representative for an American film star who wishes to remain anonymous at this time, and require information."

Darius was impressed.

"My employer is planning a trip to Monterrey on her worldwide tour and wishes to host at least one rather large party. She has her routine security but needs to add to that significantly, probably by at least twenty, for the parties. Can you accommodate her?"

Sedona nodded impatiently. "What is your vetting process? How can I be sure we're getting the best, most qualified, and most discreet?"

She listened for a few minutes while the representative from Sanchez Security ran through his spiel. "Please forgive me, I intend no disrespect, but is it possible for me to speak directly to Mr. Sanchez?"

Sedona gave Darius a thumbs-up. "Fine. Have him call me. But I'll need to hear from him within the next fifteen minutes. If I don't hear from him by then, I'll have to move on." She gave the phone number and disconnected the call without saying goodbye.

Ten minutes had barely passed before Darius's phone rang.

"Thank you. That's good to hear, Mr. Sanchez," Sedona said. "I'm comfortable with your process. It sounds very thorough. But all of the additional security need to be black. And no suits. My client doesn't want them to stand out and make her guests feel uncomfortable. We are willing to pay double your usual fee. Can you accommodate us?"

There was a hesitation. Darius held his breath. He'd submitted his own application to Sanchez Security ten minutes ago.

"Yes," Sedona said. "I can wait a few more minutes. But please, no more than twenty."

* * *

Darius sat at the table in the hotel restaurant twirling a fork between his fingers. He wanted to call his wife, but Pamela would hear the stress in his voice and that would not be a good thing. Instead he ordered another drink and fiddled with his silverware.

Unable to stay away, Mex returned to the table, but checked out by closing his eyes. Darius knew he wasn't sleeping, just disinviting conversation. Also good.

Sedona sat stiffly at the table, obviously uncomfortable and unsure of what to say. Truthfully, it was a good thing she said nothing; Darius wasn't sure he'd be able to stop Mex in time if he cut loose more of his feelings regarding his sister. They needed Sedona.

The phone rang and Darius put down his fork. Sedona looked toward Mex who didn't move, then Darius. "It's the security company."

Darius stood and indicated that Sedona should walk with him toward the lobby to take the call. She answered as Darius led her to a quiet and secluded corner.

"Thank you," Sedona said. "I appreciate your regard for my time constraints. Please send me the profiles for our internal review."

She rolled her eyes as the person on the other end presumably expressed an objection. "It is the policy of my employer that we at least do a cursory vetting of every person in her employ, even through a contracted firm such as yours. If you can't provide us with the information we can go elsewhere."

Sedona settled into a chair. "Thank you. I'll let you know once we have reviewed the profiles and photos of the twenty guards you propose to provide."

"That file is going to be too big for your phone. Do you have your laptop?"

"It's in my car."

"Get it. I'll wait here."

"What about Mex?"

"He's okay. I think he needs alone time."

As Sedona made her way to the hotel entrance, Darius located his cell and called Mex. "The security company is sending Sedona twenty profiles. She's getting her laptop and we'll look at them from here."

"Let's hope one of them matches you."

"Surely they don't have twenty black guys on their roster."

"You'd be surprised how extensive these rosters are."

Darius hesitated. "Mex?"

"Yeah?"

"Sedona is handling this like a pro. She can think on the fly and make her case."

Silence.

"You might be able to use her again in the future. She's a natural."

Silence.

"It's only a thought," Darius said.

"Let's just get through this case, shall we?"

"Gotcha. Here she comes. Let's see what we've got. I'm hoping to see my mug in the lineup."

Sedona came back to their corner and powered up her laptop. "What's your Wi-Fi code?"

Darius dug out his keycard envelope and gave Sedona the code.

"Here we go," she said.

They sat next to each other as Sedona scrolled through the guards the security company was offering. She backtracked. Went forward again.

"You're not there."

Darius couldn't believe it. "I'm not? They didn't choose me?"

"Get over yourself," Sedona said. "What do we do now?"

"Okay. Let's go through these guys. Too old? Too fat? Too whatever? Tell them there are a significant number of guards who don't fit your profile. You're good. But tell them enough of their guys won't work so they'll be forced to present candidates they really don't know."

"In other words—you."

"Yeah. Darius the Dregs."

Sedona laughed, and in spite of himself, Darius joined her.

"Make sure you cull out enough that I have a chance," Darius said.

"Leave it to me."

With a fierceness that surprised him, Sedona attacked the proposed security guards. He sat back in his chair and thought about what the next few days might bring. He also thought about the new book he would write based on this experience. It would only sell if it ended successfully. It would be up to him to make it happen. This part, anyway.

"I rejected nine of these guys. My American actor is a bitch. You okay with that?"

"She can be the queen of the bitches as long as I get included in the new group."

"I guess in the next few minutes—I gave him ten—we'll find out exactly how pitiful you are."

"Does Mex know what a task master you can be?"

Sedona hung her head. When she finally looked up at him, Darius realized he'd never seen eyes so sad. So lost. Eyes that looked so much like her brother's brimmed with tears. "I'm the reason Mex lost his family. That's all he cares about. And he's right."

"Look, Sedona, for what it's worth. If you can help Mex save this young girl you'll have put some good numbers in your plus column."

"There aren't enough numbers in my plus column to make up for what I did."

"That might be true. But what columns can't factor is the fact that you're family. And you're trying your best to come back to him. And Mex is one of the best men I've ever known. He has incredible depth."

"Not depth enough to forgive what I did."

"Maybe, maybe not. But I wouldn't count it out."

The two sat silently, each lost in their own thoughts.

A pinging sound signified a new email in Sedona's account. She punched a few keys and Darius drew close to watch.

The security company had sent optional staff based on Sedona's requirements. Nine of them. She went through them one by one. "Shit, these guys fit every parameter I demanded." She scanned through the third, then the fourth.

"Keep going," Darius said.

With every click of the keyboard, Darius's hopes sank. Not only was he going to have to deal with not advancing this case, he'd have to deal with the feelings of inadequacy not being selected would evoke. It didn't matter that he couldn't possibly have been vetted by the security company. It was a matter of pride.

"Look! There you are," Sedona said. "The eighth replacement. We're golden."

Darius snapped his attention to the computer screen. Yep, it was him. And not number nine. His eyes flew over the profile and photo they'd submitted. Damn, they made a good choice. He would've selected him.

"Let them know we're ready to move forward," Darius said.

"Already on it," Sedona said as her hands flew over the keys.

Brian Williams was found guilty Thursday of human trafficking of a minor for sexual servitude. ...Greeley police detectives originally opened the investigation into Williams after a traffic stop with one of the victims in the fall of 2014. During a roadside interview, the victim made reference to the sex trafficking ring.

The investigation spanned months after that traffic stop and stretched from Fort Collins to Colorado Springs. In addition to the Greeley police department, the FBI's Rocky Mountain Innocence Lost Task Force, the Fort Collins and Colorado Springs police departments all handled the operation.

by Tommy Simmons, for the Greeley Tribune, *September 1, 2016*

CHAPTER FIFTY-SIX

Darius received his instructions and worked to blend in. The next part of their plan was about to play out. He needed to be ready.

Sedona had managed to pack the rented mansion with people. They were wall-to-wall. Thanks to Mex's money, no expenses were spared and waiters and waitresses moved among the guests providing drinks and hors d'oeuvres to whoever wanted them. If they were successful in the end, Steven Halston might get one hell of a large expense item. If they weren't successful, there was no doubt in Darius's mind that Mex would eat the expense out of guilt.

Then he saw her. Mex had chartered a private plane to provide both speed and image.

Cade moved in with an entourage, dark glasses and large hat in place. The American movie star. No doubt there would be photos and videos taken. She needed to play the role. And remain anonymous. The guests began to buzz and then swarm.

The plan did not have her on the stage for more than a couple of minutes. Darius split from his position on the floor and moved closer. Got ready.

Suddenly a figure sliced through the crowd toward Cade. Darius applied what he thought of as his Denver Bronco linebacker sacking mode and went on full intercept. The guy was going down.

Seconds later, Darius jumped up from the floor hauling a man with him and shoving the guy out the door. He didn't pose like he would've as a Bronco linebacker, but instead propelled the supposed perpetrator ahead of him and out of the party that, with Sedona's encouragement, would continue as if nothing happened. He felt more than saw the security team surround Cade and hustle her from the scene.

Video done. Social media taken care of. And Sedona made sure the right guests were in the right part of the room to view Darius's heroics. Darius hoped that the actress, whose name they had borrowed, would believe in the 'all publicity is good publicity' philosophy.

The party might be over but it was a win for their team.

At least that's what they hoped.

One teen from Humboldt County [California] said she started working for a local grower [of marijuana] when she was 12. He gave her methamphetamine to speed up her trimming work, she said, and passed her around to pay off his debts. ...The girl eventually ran away, reaching a youth homeless shelter in the county seat of Eureka, only to discover that pimps were using it as a hunting ground. At 14, she said, she became their recruiter.

—In secretive marijuana industry, whispers of abuse and trafficking,

by Shoshana Walter, for Reveal News, *September 8, 2016*

CHAPTER FIFTY-SEVEN

Cade had loved her role in the evening's plan. It was radically different from her normal extraction tactics and she felt an added dimension of danger. From the quick and dramatic takeoff out of DIA to being whisked through the streets of Monterrey, she'd been invigorated.

With the departure of the American film star, even the free alcohol and tasty treats weren't enough to keep the elite of Monterrey occupied. Within an hour the mansion was deserted, but Mex and Darius made a quick search to make certain no amorous couples had sneaked off somewhere for privacy. The caterers were busy packing up and the cleaning crew followed in their wake.

Mex, Cade, Darius, and Sedona sat at a table in the far corner, filled plates and open bottles sitting in front of them. Darius was checking out the internet to see what was available. Several of the individual cellphone videos were too blurry to really see anything, but three of the four pros Sedona had brought in got it all. She hadn't told them why they were being hired, simply to document the evening and the people. A bonus was promised to every photographer who provided them with stellar video. Three bonuses were in order.

Cade took a sip of her wine. "I, for one, think it went well." She looked pointedly at Mex. "You?"

Mex sniffed.

Cade wondered exactly how many buttons she needed to push to get Mex to acknowledge Sedona's help. "Excuse me? I didn't hear you."

"It cost a hell of a lot of money. And we don't have any results."

"Bingo," Darius said. "It worked."

Mex glared at him.

Cade and Darius looked at Sedona, who was having a hard time hiding a smile.

"Details," Mex demanded, his voice gruff.

"I've been contacted directly by an underling of Montonaldo's." Darius checked his email. "Someone named Garcia. Anyway, Montonaldo is having a big party in two days and needs to expand his security staff. They want me."

"I think you have to be hard to get," Cade said. "If you're this good, you can't be readily available in two days."

"But we need to get Alexis," Mex said. "We need to get to her now."

"You're right. But think, Mex. Would you be suspicious if someone fabulous you wanted to hire was instantly available?" Cade asked.

"Cade's right. Montonaldo will get me, but it can't be on his first pass," Darius said.

"Okay. But he'd better come back for a second," Mex said.

Darius replied to the email. **Sorry. Booked elsewhere for the date you require.** He pressed Send and held his breath.

"Breathe, Darius," Mex said. "You're no good to us passed out on the floor."

"Yeah, I've got that."

"Mex," Cade pressed, "don't you now agree that our staging was successful? That your sister came up with a scenario to make it happen?"

"We're still waiting. Montonaldo hasn't hired Darius."

"Only a matter of time, my friend," Darius said. "Only a matter of time."

Sedona eased into the conversation. "I have a good feeling about this," she said quietly.

Darius's laptop pinged and he accessed the message. "Yes!"

"Yes, what?" Mex asked.

"They want to know if I'd be willing to take twice whatever my other client is paying." Darius looked at Cade and winked. "This could be a great gig."

Mex coughed. "You've gotta remember how you got there— all smoke and mirrors." Mex splashed more Don Julio tequila into his glass.

"Take it," Cade said, looking at Darius. "But wait for a few minutes before you do."

Examining the ads and what they appear to be offering, I ask an obvious question: "Isn't prostitution illegal?" [Backpage.com's lawyer (and chief defender) Liz] McDougall's answer: "Prostitution is illegal, and we don't permit illegal activity on the website." But then what are they selling? "Legal adult entertainment services," says McDougall.

I read her a different ad from another 19-year-old: "Make me beg. Smack me. Spit on me. Degrade me."

—A lurid journey through Backpage.com, by Deborah Feyerick and Sheila Steffen for CNN

CHAPTER FIFTY-EIGHT

ALEXIS

I'm tired. I want to crawl away into a dark corner and die. But I sense if he sees weakness, my choice to die or to live will be taken away.

And damn it, it *is* my choice. I don't have much else to keep me going. I've been stripped bare. My spirit has been twisted and I'm not at all sure I can ever straighten it out. None of my old friends would recognize me now. And to tell the truth, there are pieces of me I like better.

Sergio Montonaldo, whose name I only recently learned when I overheard a delivery person, is a monster. And he's turned me into one as well.

I hate him. Right now, for tonight, it's that hate that's going to keep me alive. Hate has taken me from wanting nothing more than a dark corner to wanting to win. Needing to win.

At least for one more night.

He's throwing another party. This one is bigger than the others I've been to. Somehow it's more important. He's proving something to someone and, although I'm not a centerpiece, I will be a trophy on the back wall. While I bite enough to stay alive, I know allowing him to parade me adds to his mystique, and the number of days I'm still breathing.

I suddenly realize that moving from a centerpiece to the back wall is a bad sign. He knows I'm degraded. He knows I've almost given up. Quit.

It's only a matter of time.

I look at the dress that's hanging by itself in the wardrobe. There's never more than one thing now. Every day. It's wear what he gives me or go naked. I remember the first day I was here. At least there was a choice between three things. Was that a week ago or months ago? The days have melded together.

My hate for him mingles with the new hatred I've discovered for myself. Early on I felt strong and in control. But I've done things no self-respecting person would ever do. I've let him do things to me I can never forget. Because I thought I could remain proud and significant. Because I thought I could win.

It's only a matter of time. I know this now as I look at my costume for the evening.

I bring the dress out and lay it on the bed. It's really quite attractive—the nicest thing he's ever given me to wear. While I can see it will be form-fitting, it doesn't scream whore. The color is a deep, almost-black burgundy, and while there are revealing gaps in strategic places, there's an underlying layer of sheer fabric that exactly matches my skin tone. I will look exposed without truly being so.

This is the kindest thing he's done for me.

He will kill me soon.

Does he already have another girl picked out? Is he going to kill me tonight after the party?

It's been a while, but Donny's face suddenly appears in my mind. The hate I feel grows even hotter. I want to make him pay. He sold me into this and has continued to live his life without a care in the world.

Damn him. I want to be the one to hurt him. Turn him in. Sell him into male prostitution. Haunt his dreams.

There's a knock at my door. Like I live in civilization.

The door opens.

"Twenty minutes, Miss Alexis."

* * *

Darius scanned the huge room. It wasn't the only room on this floor, not to mention the grounds in the back of the mansion. How the hell was he supposed to find their target? There were at least a hundred people here already and more streaming in every minute.

He hit the button on his ear mic that most people would assume connected him to his security supervisor if they even noticed. "This ain't gonna be easy."

"What do you see?" Cade asked.

"A big honkin' room."

"Stairs? Something for an entrance?"

"Nope."

"That's not it then. Move on. You're looking for somewhere Montonaldo can show off his acquisitions."

Darius clicked off and began scouting.

He moved quickly through the three rooms connected to the main salon. Nothing. No staging area at all. There were plenty of shady characters with armed guards standing by. People he'd like to interview for a book. Bowls filled with white powder that could only be cocaine sat on tables. The partygoers stood around them politely waiting their turn, engaging in small talk as if they did this every day. Waiters moved effortlessly offering appetizers and delivering requested drinks.

Shit, Darius thought. This could be a party held by anybody anywhere, including Aspen.

Had they been wrong? Was this just another party given by a random rich guy in Monterrey?

Had Sedona been wrong? Or had she scammed them one more time?

Darius moved past two indoor fountains and through wide doors that led him onto a terrace. He surveyed the area.

Beyond the terrace the grounds dropped off to showcase gardens that would make an Englishman proud. To the far left were tennis courts and what looked like a golf course. While Darius thought it was probably nine holes, he wouldn't have been surprised to learn it was a full eighteen. Knowing what he knew about Sergio Montonaldo, his stomach heaved. The gardens, the tennis courts, the golf course... they all looked wrong. Tainted.

To his right was an elevated stage. A manufactured clamshell stood behind it and he thought of the natural amphitheater that Red Rocks provided back home, followed quickly by the realization that if there was a targeted place tonight, this was it. This would be the place Montonaldo would hold court.

While he moved to see what was behind the stage, he pressed a button. "I've got it. A stage area at the back of the house. Not much containment, but I'm heading there now to find out what's behind it. It has to connect somehow."

"That's it," Cade said. "Can you see an exit strategy?"

"Not yet. I still don't know how it connects to the main house."

"Okay, Darius. I get you haven't done this before, but while you're walking toward the stage, look for a way out. Do this now. The sun is setting. Figuring it out later might be too late."

"Shit."

"Yeah, shit. Now talk to me. Tell me what you're seeing as you approach."

"Okay. Not much. There are woods one way and cars parked along the drive on the other."

"What's on the other side of the drive?"

"More woods."

"Damn."

"Thanks. That makes me feel all kinds of confident."

"We're what?" He heard Cade ask Mex. "About twenty minutes from there?"

"Twenty or twenty-five, depending on traffic," Mex said.

"Twenty minutes? Why so far?"

"We got stuck in one of Monterrey's infamous roadblocks. They waved us through but it still delayed us. We'll get there as soon as we can. Just know you've got up to twenty minutes that you need to stay hidden. Head through the woods and then to the drive."

"You know what I'm driving, right?" Cade asked Darius. "The Audi?"

"Yeah." Darius remembered the dark blue rental.

"Let's make sure our watches are in the right time zone. What time do you have?"

Darius, who had a habit of looking at his watch even when it wasn't important, closed his eyes. "Are you kidding me? I can tell you without looking that it's 6:38."

"Fine. Keep this line open. When you see Alexis and know you can nab her, tell me immediately. Mex and I are on our way right now. We're twenty minutes out, but if you see the opportunity in the next minute, take it."

"Why didn't we do this before?"

"Because we didn't know what we were dealing with before. Chill, Darius. We can get this done. You with me?"

Darius considered his options. "Yeah, I'm with you."

Operation Cross Country X, a nationwide law enforcement initiative led by the FBI, took place last week throughout the U.S. The effort focuses on underage victims of prostitution. Nationwide, FBI Director James Comey announced today, 82 minors were rescued and 239 traffickers and their associates arrested as part of the operation.

—10 Alabamians - including 5 accused pimps - nabbed in nationwide human trafficking bust, by Carol Robinson, for the Alabama Media Group, October 17, 2016

CHAPTER FIFTY-NINE

ALEXIS

I'm ready when the knock comes at my door and it opens. The uniformed man stands politely as I check my makeup one last time and then look him in the eye.

He nods and smiles.

"How are you this afternoon, Miguel?"

"Thank you for asking, Miss Alexis. I am well. And yourself?"

I meet his sad eyes. "Couldn't be better." I reach out to pat his hand, having long gotten over the fact it only has a thumb and first finger. One of those lost fingers was my fault. And yet he continues to smile at me.

I like to pretend that Miguel will help me when the time comes, maybe even lay his life down for me. But I know better. He has a family to support.

I'm only passing through.

"You look lovely, Miss Alexis."

"Thank you, Miguel."

We survive partly because we don't talk about what really matters. We pretend that because we are in a beautiful home, wear clean clothes, and have enough to eat, everything is okay.

We pretend we're in control.

I walk down the long hall toward the staircase that descends to the main level. My master will have people set up there to see me. To envy him. He'll watch from a distance and not make a move toward me. I'm on my own.

I'll mingle. Accept the praises for both me and my captor. Move through the crowd. Pretend like I'm a queen.

Queen of the prison. But no one must know that. Keep my parents safe. Wake up tomorrow in a bed and not die in a torture chamber.

I reach the staircase and feel my back straighten of its own accord. My straight posture has nothing to do with Sergio Montonaldo and everything to do with Alexis Emily Halston. If I'm to die soon it will be with a strong belief in who I am, what I've learned, and what I want to stand for in the end.

"Do you wish me to escort you down the stairs, Miss Alexis?"

I turn to him, instinctively feeling this will be the last time I see him. "No, Miguel. I'm fine. But I want you to know how much your concern has touched me. Whatever happens next cannot take away from the kindness and respect you've given me on a daily basis. You've provided a steadiness in my life here. Without it I would surely have died much earlier."

Again his sad eyes meet mine. "Today, Miss Alexis, you are truly beautiful." He leans over and brings my hand to his lips. Then steps away.

I descend the stairs, taking each step slowly, not because that's how I've been coached, but because I think each step is one step closer to the end of my life. While part of me wants to run back to my room and hide, possibly resulting in the loss of yet another of Miguel's fingers, the bigger part of me wants to meet this head-on. Strong. Confident. One step at a time.

I can do this.

From nearby groups I can hear the whispers. While they can't guess my fate, people marvel that I'm still in the favor of the awe-inspiring Sergio Montonaldo. Did they know of or suspect the fate of the young women who have gone before me? Will they remember me in a few weeks when someone has taken my place? Not likely.

One step at a time.

I hit the last step and look around me. It's a curious combination of stares and studied avoidance.

Screw them.

I move through the room, stopping when expected to say the right thing.

"What a lovely party," says anyone.

"Sergio knows how to please," says me. Once or twice I even wink. Who knew that years of covering up parental neglect could come in so handy?

The vast doors are ahead of me. Multiple double doors are open to the veranda. That's the next visual Montonaldo expects.

I can't think of one valid reason to deny him and that makes my heart sink. Have I grown that compliant? If so, my fate is surely sealed.

While many American have heard of human trafficking in other parts of the world—Thailand, Cambodia, Latin America and Eastern Europe, for example—few people know it happens here in the United States.

The FBI estimates that well over 100,000 children and young women are trafficked in American today. They range in age from 9 to 19, with the average age being 11.—Teen Girls' Stories of Sex Trafficking in U.S. ABC News, February 9, 2006

CHAPTER SIXTY

Darius saw her. It took everything he had not to wave and shout.

He replaced the agency earpiece for the Bluetooth. "I've spotted her. How far out are you?"

"We told you, we're on our way," Cade said. "Look, Darius, I've had a lot of experience extricating people from cults. This isn't much different. You trust me, right?"

"I guess. But she's right there."

"I get that. The thing is, you'll only have one shot at this. If you get it wrong, you're both dead."

"Okay, I don't want to get it wrong, but she's right there."

"Tell me what's happening."

"She's moving down some steps. People are moving toward her."

"Excellent. The more interaction the better. Nothing bad is going to happen while people are focused on her."

"So I should be ready to move when their attention shifts?"

"You are a smart cookie. But be ready to move fast. How far away is the drive from where she is right now?"

"A couple hundred yards, maybe more."

"Is there somewhere closer? An outbuilding?"

Darius looked around. "There's a metal building almost hidden behind a bunch of trees. It's about half the distance to the drive."

"Good. Not great, but good."

"I don't see Sedona," Darius said.

"Don't worry. She's got it handled. She'll start the distraction at the most opportune moment. Be ready."

Silence.

"Darius? Are you with me?"

His mouth was dry. He couldn't answer.

"I've done this hundreds of times, often without the aid of a diversion. You can do this."

He tried to force saliva into his mouth.

"Darius?"

"Yeah, I'm here," Darius forced. "But Cade?"

"Yes?"

"When you performed your extraction jobs, were there armed men patrolling the perimeter?"

"More than once."

"Okay. We'll get to the metal building and then make our way to the drive." He tried to scout a landmark for them. "Look for the brown and black motor home parked on the side of the road. I don't see another one in the area. When you're almost to the party, look for the RV. It's huge."

"Got it. Good planning. Now get ready."

* * *

"Seriously?" Mex asked after Cade tucked away her phone. She'd had it on speaker so Mex could hear everything.

"What?"

"Hundreds of times?"

"Maybe not hundreds, but it made Darius feel better."

"Even more—you've snatched people out of cults with armed men patrolling?"

Cade tilted her head and grabbed Mex's hand. "Many times. And I was wearing heels and dancing backwards."

Mex chuckled and then took his hand from hers. "This has to work. It's our only chance."

"Sorry. I didn't mean to be flippant. It will work, trust me."

He didn't say anything.

"Carlos Alberto Del Castillo Cabeza Y Vaca De Anderson, do you trust me?"

"How could I not trust a woman who knows my full name?"

"Okay, you're saying that in addition to the years of experience I've had, the successes I've enjoyed, the families I've reunited, the plan that is almost foolproof, *this* is your deciding moment: the fact I know your full name?" She swallowed, sniffed, and pretended to wipe away a tear. "So you trust me?"

"Just get us there."

Cade pressed down harder on the accelerator. She was feeling the same urge.

Authorities allege Lawrence Campbell Jr. met two 16-year-old girls online and purchased bus tickets to bring them to Waterloo about a week ago. The teens lived at Campbell's home on Clearview Street and were directed to have sex with men for money and steal items from local stores, police said.

—Wife now arrested in human trafficking investigation, by Jeff Reinitz, for The Courier

CHAPTER SIXTY-ONE

ALEXIS

These people pretend to be my friends because they want Sergio to be *their* friend. They make me sick, but I've learned to smile and kiss cheeks and endure the occasional unwelcome squeeze of any number of body parts.

I've learned a lot in a relatively short time.

The steps end and I slip off my heels to walk on the lawn. The first time I did this, Sergio was terribly angry.

He grabbed me by my elbow and hauled me aside. "How dare you remove your shoes in front of other people!"

I almost laughed. This from the guy who had me appear naked at breakfast, wearing only a pair of heels? Okay, there was nobody there, but still. He had been conditioning me.

That day, after everyone left, he took me down to his room of horrors and demanded I choose the device I wanted him to use for my punishment.

"I understand you need to keep me in line, but your line is warped."

He seethed with rage. "How dare you?"

"Do you have any idea how much these shoes cost? I know you can afford them, but I can't believe you actually think I'm worth it."

When he stared without commenting, I continued. "Did you pick these shoes out? They're Stuart Weitzman. You're lucky they aren't two or three million, because trust me, Weitzman makes shoes that cost that much."

"How much did those shoes cost?" he asked in a whisper.

"Assuming the stones are real, and I can't imagine you allowing a member of your staff to buy anything fake, these shoes run five-hundred thousand."

His eyes widened.

"I can ruin them if you want. I just thought I was protecting your property."

His face turned red and I held my breath.

"Get out of here."

The noise and movement of the party bring me back to the present. I take my shoes off without fear of retribution. Of inflicted pain. It's become a mark of victory for me.

My first step into the cool grass is fabulous and I feel defiant.

Suddenly, around the far side of the house a helicopter appears, it's blades whipping loudly. When it lands, the security guards begin rushing toward it, an obvious surprise to them.

A woman I've seen before rushes toward the guests. She's yelling something and it takes a minute to hear what she's saying.

"She's here! She's here!"

I'd heard from Miguel about an American actress who'd been whisked away from her own party a couple of days ago.

Maybe this is her. Maybe she can help me get home. I move to follow the crowd of guests pulsing in the direction of the helicopter when I'm grabbed backwards and practically hauled off my feet.

A black man, one of the security guards, puts a finger to his lips. "Come with me. I'm getting you out of here!"

Thoughts are tumbling over each other. Can this be happening? Is it real? Or is this some kind of sick test?

"Go!" He pushes me away from the crowd. "Go, now!"

What the hell. If I'm going to die anyway, let me die thinking I'm going to survive. I take off running and hear him pounding behind me.

"They gave drugs to the girls [at least one was fourteen and one fifteen years old] in order for them to forget about having sex with the men," said Orlando police Det. Michael Fields during a news conference last Wednesday. He added, "The girls felt threatened, they were shown guns, firearms and told that bad things would happen to them if they were to tell."

—2 arrests in case of human trafficking, death of teen, Fox 35 Orlando, U.S. World News,
October 17, 2016

CHAPTER SIXTY-TWO

Sedona's diversion had worked. Now it was up to him.

Darius heard nothing but a roar in his ears as he led Alexis to the metal building on the property. If they could get behind it without being seen they had a chance.

The journalist in him was screaming. *Verify! And verify again!* Why the hell hadn't he checked out what the building housed? What if it was a barracks and he was leading the girl he was trying to save into a trap?

Too late now. They were committed.

Alexis was keeping up with him and for that he was grateful. He'd completely freak if he had to drag her with him.

The building was about fifty yards ahead of them and he angled for a corner. Breathing more heavily than he wanted, he cursed himself for not staying in running shape. But then he'd never been a runner so there was no "staying" in the equation.

He spared a glance over his shoulder. Almost everyone was still seemingly attracted to the helicopter and whatever excitement it promised.

Almost everyone.

He saw a security guard, rifle at his side, look in their direction. He was two hundred yards away but starting to run.

Fast.

Would he shoot? The guard had to know that Alexis was Sergio's personal "property." An acquisition. Was the guard a sure enough shot that he could easily take out Darius and return Alexis to her master?

Even though he had very little more to engage, Darius dug deep for whatever additional speed he could muster. Alexis, thankfully, kept up.

They rounded the corner of the metal building when the first shot rang out.

Quickly they made their way to the other corner. Darius looked frantically toward the drive, hoping beyond hope to see the Audi waiting for them.

Nothing.

It would only be a matter of time before the security guard got to the building. But where they were they were sitting ducks.

Alexis looked at the shoes she was carrying and shrugged her shoulders.

"Not exactly running shoes," Darius observed.

"Not exactly."

Darius signaled Alexis to crouch low and they rounded the corner nearest the drive. They'd be exposed if the guard came up on the opposite corner where they disappeared.

He removed his Glock from its holster and spoke softly. "Stay behind me and stay low. If I signal you to run," he flicked his hand forward, "run like the devil is on your ass."

"Because he is," Alexis whispered.

"If something happens to me, look for a blue Audi to drive up near that RV in the driveway. See it?"

Alexis glanced where Darius pointed, then nodded.

"Do not stop to help me. Get your butt to that car. Understood?"

Another nod.

"Okay, then. Let's see if we can't both get out of here alive."

Darius moved forward and felt a tug on his arm.

"In case we don't?" Alexis swiped a tear from her cheek. "In case you die or I die or we both die? I've never been more grateful to anyone in my life."

"Save it for later. We're getting out of here."

Darius thought of Pamela. He thought of their family. Then he boxed those thoughts away and focused. "Behind me and low. Got it?"

"Got it."

The pair rounded the corner of the building, Darius ready to fire if the guard came into sight.

When they edged up the side, Darius put a finger to his lips like he had before. Alexis nodded.

He searched the drive. No sign of Mex and Cade. But he could hear the security guard hit the building at the opposite end.

"Go!" he said just loud enough for Alexis to hear.

The two set off on the sprint of their lives.

As they got close to the motor home, the sound of gunfire pierced the air. Darius and Alexis instinctively altered course, zigged and zagged and ducked. He put Alexis in front of him, hoping to act as a shield.

Alexis screamed. She'd been hit in the shoulder and she stumbled. Darius came up behind her and hauled her body into his, still heading for the temporary protection of the RV.

"We can do this!" he shouted, as much to himself as to Alexis. "We're almost there!"

The motor home was taking a beating, any one of those shots potentially ending everything. Then they were there, limping, and had for a moment at least, cover.

A car screamed up the drive and braked in front of them. Darius didn't care at that moment if it was an Audi or a Chrysler. He and Alexis were getting in.

A door flung open and he slammed the girl into the backseat, falling on top of her. No time to make a three-point turn, Cade plowed onto the shoulder on the other side of the drive and squealed away, the momentum finally forcing the door closed.

"You okay?" Mex asked.

"She's been hit," Darius said. "Shoulder. Get us out of here."

Alexis began to cry. Her cries turned into wails. She rocked and shook and kicked.

Darius put his arms around Alexis and held her tight, rocking with her. "Everything's okay, Alexis. Everything's okay."

Cade rocketed the car down the drive. "Ya'll cool if we skip the tourist spots and head straight to the airport?"

I confirm and represent that I am 18 years of age or older (and am not considered to be a minor in my state of residence) and that I am not located in a community or local jurisdiction where nude pictures or explicit adult materials are prohibited by any law. I agree to report any illegal services or activities which violate the Terms of Use. I also agree to report suspected exploitation of minors and/or human trafficking to the appropriate authorities.

—From Backpage.com

CHAPTER SIXTY-THREE

JAYLA

We've bumped along the highway in the windowless van all day. The piss pot in the corner is overflowing and we're all tired. If we felt like we had the freedom, we'd be grumpy.

I'm not even sure what city we left. At least when we're somewhere for a sporting event, football or NASCAR or golf or whatever, we know the name of the city. There hasn't been a major event in the last week or so which makes my geography-sifter worthless.

Finally we pull over and stop. Not just a stoplight stop. A real stop. I hear the engine sputter and die. When the doors are thrown open it's dark outside. We must've been on the road for at least twelve hours.

Each of us moves our cramped bodies outside to stretch.

And I smell it.

Never in my wildest dreams would I believe I could discern this. But I know it for a fact.

I'm home. I'm in Denver.

Without looking around for a landmark, thereby calling attention to my awareness, I try to figure out where we are. I can't. We could be anywhere. Maybe we aren't really in Denver and I'm delusional.

And then I see a car with Colorado plates. And another. And another.

My chest fills. If I can manage to walk away, to escape, I have options. For the first time since this nightmare began, I actually feel like I might wake up from it. All I need is a minute or two when no one is paying attention.

"Well, look at you, Cherie."

Someone grabs me by the arm.

"Haven't you come a long way from that first day?"

I look at the woman. Familiarity buzzes. "I know you."

"Damn straight you do. I'm the one who told you your friend sold you out. The one who set you straight. I'm the one who told you how to survive."

"You're Ginger."

"That's what they call me."

I consider a moment. "Do you have another name?"

"Look, honey, I'm here to make sure you keep it together. To make sure you don't get any ideas. Think of me as your friendly warden—who you don't want to piss off."

I force each word, "Do you have another name?"

"If I tell you do you swear you won't run off?"

I hesitate. I've told enough lies in the last six months to fill a lifetime. I'm tired of lying. But I really want to know her other name. Somehow it's become the most important thing in my life.

"I can't swear. But I desperately want to know your name."

"Swear to me or fuck off."

"Okay. I swear. I won't run off."

Ginger looks off into the distance. She blinks a couple of times. There are no tears, only a bottomless sadness. "People used to call me Leah."

"There's someone I want to see, Leah."

"Never call me that."

"I want to see the person who put me into this life. Can you make that happen?"

Ginger turns her head away and closes her tired eyes. "Does Daddy have you set up for in-call or outcall?"

"Both, but he does all the scheduling."

"Leave it to me."

"Why are you doing this?"

"Maybe because I never got the chance to look the person in the eye who did the same to me." Ginger shook her head. "Be ready to leave at ten o'clock."

I hang my head. It's funny what I'm ashamed about these days. "I don't have a watch. What time is it?"

"Eight-thirty. Daddy will be happy you have an appointment so soon. Especially one that's a referral."

"Will you drive me?"

"I'm guessing that's what I'm here for. He didn't tell me you were doing outcalls, but then he doesn't tell me much."

"Why all this attention on me?"

"Because, Cherie, you're home. You know the city. I don't know why he brought you back so soon, but here you are."

"What'll happen to you if I run?"

"Stupid question, and you're not a stupid girl."

"Okay. I won't. I promise." And I mean it this time.

Ginger takes me to a hotel room. "This is where your intakes will be for the next week. It's not much, but I'm willing to bet it's better than most you've seen."

I look around. It's clean. Boring, but clean. There are actually soaps and shampoos and even a tube of toothpaste in the bathroom. Daddy must be expecting pickier customers than usual.

"What's going on? An event I haven't heard about?"

"Nothing I know of." Ginger walks to the door, key in hand. "Clean up. Rest. I'll be back in an hour to take you to your appointment."

Alone in the room I sit on the bed and think about Chris. He'd been my friend. I'd trusted him. Why did he do this to me? What will I say to him?

How will I feel when I see him again?

"To those scouring the web or apps in search of sex with our state's children, let me say this: Be warned," says [Tennessee] speaker Harwell. "This is an agency, a movement, a state that is gaining momentum in its effort to insist it ends right here, right now."

—*41 Arrested in Nashville Human Trafficking Operation, TBI Newsroom, August, 2016*

CHAPTER SIXTY-FOUR

"What if he moved?" I ask Ginger as she follows my directions to Chris's apartment.

"He hasn't."

"How do you know?"

"I used to live in Denver too. I still know a few people."

"Denver's your home?"

"Honey, I no longer have a home. Denver's just another place on the map."

"Do you have family here?" I know it's none of my business, but I can't seem to stop. My skin is tingling with memories and my eyes feed it while we drive. I'm ready to burst. I can visualize splitting with pieces of me flying off because all I want to do is find a place to land. To be safe. Or not. At least I'll be home.

"Don't know much about any family." Ginger drives up to a four-way stop and waits for the other cars to pass in front. "I have a couple of contacts who are still willing to get me some answers is all."

"Would you like to stay here?"

Ginger gives the car more gas. "And do what? Apply for welfare? Fuck that."

"At least it would be your life. Your choices."

She was quiet for a long time and I worried I might have pissed her off. Maybe she'll change her mind and not take me to see Chris.

"Here," I say. "This is it." I feel clammy. I look at a drab apartment building and remember the abject horror of that night over six months ago. This structure should look evil. The red brick should've turned gray. There should be at least two gargoyles peering over the entrance.

I start to shake. Tears roll down my face. Nothing makes sense. And then it hits me. It's the very normalcy of the place, the blandness of it, that feeds my terror. How was I supposed to know? How is anyone supposed to know?

Ginger turns into the parking lot and finds a spot. She shuts off the engine. "Are you gonna be okay? Do you want me to go with you?"

"No. I've got to do this on my own."

"You promise me you won't run?"

"Leah—and I mean Leah—I've got enough bad karma for a dozen lifetimes. I'm not gonna add to it."

"How much time do you want?"

I think of my tricks and the times and fees associated. "Give me an hh," I say, street code for half an hour. "If I'm not back in thirty-minutes come find me. There might be a body involved."

"I'm not down with hurting someone."

"Okay to run if I kill him?"

A small smile crosses her face. "Yeah, that I could probably survive."

I look over at Chris's beater sitting like an abandoned piece of junk. Apparently he hadn't sold me for enough money to get a new ride.

Why *had* he sold me?

"See you in thirty." I shove the door open and haul my body out. I feel like I'm fifty pounds heavier.

I hadn't thought about how I'd get through the security door, but a tenant was either moving out or in. The doors were braced open and I walk straight through and punch the elevator.

So far, so good.

As the old elevator rumbles into action, my stomach matches it groan for groan, yank for yank. I'd forgotten I used to climb the stairs. When it jerks to a stop there's this huge pregnant pause before the doors stagger open like a drunk about to hurl. I'm right there with it. The only reason I step into the hallway is that I don't want to stay in the elevator a moment longer and lose my cookies.

I can see Chris's door down the hall to the right. It looms in front of me. Since I didn't use the buzzer I will most definitely be a surprise.

It feels like I'm wading through a waist-deep river. One step. Then another. The water rising.

And then I'm at his door.

Chris. My friend. My fucking friend I was so worried about when I first woke up on that cement floor half a year ago.

I stand there, an arm's length away from the door. I'm welded in place. Do I really want this? Do I want to see him? What good will it do?

My feet unstick and I begin pacing the hallway. It's not long, and even though Chris's door is at the end, I come close to it three times and still can't decide what to do.

I'm at the other end of the hallway when I hear a door open. It's Chris's. The lights at my end are dim and he doesn't notice me.

He's so different. Slack-faced and slump-shouldered, he shuffles to the elevator and slaps a palm on the call button.

I approach him. Instead of being surprised, he lifts flat eyes that seem to look through me.

What's happened to him that he's not only given up but is so haunted? Automatically I reach out and touch his arm. The difference between standing at his apartment door and seeing him right in front of me is striking, and my barriers crumble to the ground.

He startles at my touch in a numb and confused way. Then he looks me in the eyes.

You might think that when a trafficking victim escapes, their life is saved. In reality, though, survival is much more complicated.

—Why Human Trafficking is a Public Health Problem, by Margaux Gray, for the CNN Freedom Project, 2016

CHAPTER SIXTY-FIVE

I watch as Chris realizes who he's standing with at the elevator. He squeezes those flat, dead eyes closed and then opens them again. The shaking starts in his hands and within seconds he's on his knees. He doesn't utter a sound for a few seconds and then an anguished cry crawls up from deep inside of him.

"Oh, God!" He sprawls on the crappy carpet in front of the elevator and sobs. Deep, heaving sobs.

I join him and hold his face in my hands. His eyes have gone from listless to red-rimmed. At least there's emotion there. A person beyond the stare.

"Oh god oh god oh god oh god."

"Can we go back to your apartment?"

He freezes.

"Chris, I want to talk to you. Can we go inside your apartment?" I stand and offer him my hand.

He shakes his head and forces himself to stand. Without a word he turns around and moves like an automaton down the hallway. Drives his key into the lock and throws open the door.

I take the keys out of the lock and follow him in, closing the door behind me.

What the hell? I think as I look around the dark, dingy and dirty place. While not a palace before, at least it had been clean with wonderful natural light coming in the now shaded windows.

Chris stands next to the countertop he'd cleaned and re-cleaned the night my life changed forever. Only now there was a buildup of grime and styrofoam takeout containers. Dishes were piled in the sink and something smelled dead.

"Why'd you do it, Chris? Why'd you let that person take me?"

"You escaped, right? You're okay now?"

"Answer my question, Chris. I deserve to know."

"Do you want something to drink?"

"I want an answer. And then you can tell me what the hell has happened to you." I gesture to the filth.

Chris follows my arm like he's seeing his apartment for the first time. "I, uh..."

"Did you sell me?"

Chris blinks and scratches his chest. "I, uh..." He rubs his face.

"Did you?"

"I owed someone money."

"How much, Chris? How much did you get?"

"Two thousand."

"You sold me, my life, for two thousand dollars?" I shove him. "I thought you were my friend!" I shove him again. "I was worried something bad had happened to you!"

I shove him again and again. He stands there and takes it. I realize I'm crying and that pisses me off even more.

"What the hell did you think was going to happen to me?"

"I thought it was a joke. A prank." His eyes brighten and he looks at me eagerly. Like I'll believe him and we'll have a good laugh. Share a beer. Even though I'm not old enough to drink.

"Fuck you. You knew."

It's like his face turns to glass and breaks from the inside out. I feel a surge of satisfaction.

"You know I confessed, right? I start serving three years next month."

"Like that makes it okay? It should be more."

"But you're out now, right?" His nose drips and his mouth twists. Like he's the one who was sold.

"No, Chris. I'm not out. In fact I have to leave now. Time is money, which I guess is something you know all about."

"Will I see you again?"

I turn and walk away.

FBI personnel conducted research before and after World Cannabis Week in 2015 and noted a 35 percent increase in the number of online escort postings. Also, during this year's event, nearly 40 percent of escorts told police they traveled to Colorado for the special event....One of the recovered minors, a 15-year-old victim, had been transported to Colorado from California by traffickers specifically for '420 Week.'

—Dozens arrested in sex trafficking bust in Colorado, by KRDO.com Staff, Colorado Springs, Colorado, 2016

CHAPTER SIXTY-SIX

"You're exhausted, Mex," Cade said as they stood in front of the ticket desk at the airport in Monterrey. "Give it a day."

"Can't. Every day Livvy is where she is, she's in hell." Mex cleared his throat. "Plus, we can't know she'll have another day." He signed the credit card bill and waited for a boarding pass.

Cade had called ahead to Rachel, the newly-minted team member who'd met with Alexis's mother, and asked her to meet them at the Westin DIA where she'd arranged a suite. This wasn't going to be an easy transition for anyone, and she wanted to take all the right steps.

When Cade had called Steve Halston to let him know they'd rescued his daughter, he'd been in Europe on business. While he sounded relieved they'd rescued Alexis, the raw concern he'd expressed earlier was gone. He said he'd make every attempt to return to the states as soon as possible, but

Cade got the distinct impression "as soon as possible" meant "as soon as my business here is complete."

Business must be pressing, Cade thought sarcastically, and the problem at home had been resolved. His daughter was safe.

Adele Halston had been almost non-responsive, the drugs and alcohol numbing her. It wasn't hard to get the woman to agree not to see her daughter the moment she landed. Cade's heart went out to Alexis. Her support system was seriously cracked.

Right now Alexis was asleep in a private room within the airport after receiving medical attention for her bullet wound. It helped having both Mex's connections and his money.

Darius's contacts had been able to pin down the location of the computer Livvy's "online love" had used. It had been opened recently and repeatedly from an apartment building in Phoenix. Darius was then able to track down a Backpage ad showing Livvy, using a pseudonym, clearly all of twelve years old, and advertising herself as that magic age of eighteen.

While Cade hugged herself and turned away from him, Mex called the number and made an appointment with Livvy for midnight. She was receiving "guests" at a fleabag motel less than a half mile from the stadium.

His flight from Monterrey would get into Phoenix about eleven. The motel was only about six minutes from the airport. It would give him enough time to pick up a rental car and scout the layout of the motel.

Neither Mex nor Darius had been able to come up with any information regarding security. The three of them guessed there wasn't much, but there was no way to know for sure.

Cade paced away from him and then marched back. She nuzzled into his arms. "Do you promise me—*promise me*—not to do anything if something feels off? Do you promise me to pay attention to your gut? To pay attention to your tired, beautiful gut?" A tear slipped down her cheek.

Mex offered a rare smile as he brushed her tear away with his thumb. He leaned down and kissed her cheek. "I promise. Plus, my tired, *handsome* gut will sleep on the plane. Everything will be fine, and we'll have another girl home with her family."

"If this goes south, Mex Anderson, you'll have hell to pay. And I'll be collecting."

"And if this goes as planned, Cade LeBlanc, you'll owe me, and we'll both be collecting." He winked.

"Fuck you," she whispered.

"Exactly."

Miya's parents soon learned from police that more than approximately 30 other girls had been approached by the same couple in that mall and in surrounding areas—the same couple, apparently, who were seen with Miya and who claimed to be recruiting models.... Within days, Miya had been moved several times, farther from home, and she said she was too scared to try to escape. "I mean, I was really far from my house, and I didn't know where to go," she said.—Teen Girls' Stories of Sex Trafficking in U.S., ABC News, February 9, 2006

CHAPTER SIXTY-SEVEN

ALEXIS

There's a soft light in this room. The linens are fresh and a lavender scent fills the air. All meant to relax a weary traveler.

But I'm more than simply a weary traveler. I know I'm going home but I can't quite believe it's happening. Every time I fall asleep I visualize the room with all of the torture equipment. I'd managed to avoid permanent physical damage, but only because someone else took the pain.

A doctor attended to my wound. Nothing serious he tells me. I'll be sore for a month or so fully recovered in three to six.

The madness is over, but is it?

Will my dad be there to greet me? My mom? A tear slips out of my eye as I realize how terrible it is to have to ask those questions.

This Cade person seems nice. I recognize that the old Alexis would be hung up on her casual appearance, but I'm so far beyond that girl. I realize I'm no longer one to judge someone else. I feel a rush of relief when those words come into my head.

A memory of Miguel's sweet smile flashes, and I think of the fingers he lost, knowing his weren't the only ones. I wonder what will happen to him now. Will he be held responsible for my escape?

Another image slips into my head. Those used sandals from the closet when I'd first arrived at my jailor's residence. Used by whom?

How can I possibly judge another person ever again?

There's a soft rap on the door and Cade enters.

"How are you feeling? How's your shoulder?"

"I'm okay. When can I go home?"

"We have chartered a plane that will be ready to go in forty minutes."

"Are you coming with me?"

"Yes. Darius, the man who rescued you at the party, and I will both fly home with you."

"Will my parents be at DIA?"

Cade swallowed. "Your dad is in Europe, but I'm sure he'll be home as soon as he can."

His only child has gone missing and my dad is still focused on business. I wonder if his business associates even know about me. Even know I was abducted. And hey, it's not like I'm his son. His Samuel.

"And my mother?" I ask this question even though I know the answer. My mom is the Self-Medicating Queen. After the whole ordeal of my older brother, she pretty much checked out. I don't blame her. I might do the same thing. Who cares if there's a new baby?

"Your mother understands you need time to decompress. A woman is meeting us in Denver who you might feel especially comfortable talking to."

"Really? Was she one of Sergio Montonaldo's girls?" I smirk. "Oh, wait. None of the girls before me lived, at least none we know about." I'd heard more than they thought I'd heard in this tiny room with all of the law enforcement people talking. I might not know a lot of Spanish, but I know enough. I could also put together a thing or two on my own.

How the hell can I talk about this to anyone?

And I have the answers about my parents. No surprise.

Why should I care what happens to me? I want to cry, but I can't.

They should have left me in Monterrey.

The initiative, from Thursday through Saturday, was an intensive effort that spanned hotels, truck stops, street corners and social media applications. The youngest recovered victim was 14 years old.

—FBI recovers 9 child sex trafficking victims in Colorado, Wyoming as part of national operation,

by Jesse Paul, for The Denver Post, October 18, 2016

CHAPTER SIXTY-EIGHT

LIVVY

The sun is beginning to set. In Phoenix there's color to sunsets but not a lot of drama. I miss my mountains.

It's not that I hate it here. It's only that it's not home.

And my life isn't right.

And so yeah, I pretty much hate it here. Palming the pills Ian gives me keeps my head clear. I don't like what I see and feel, but at least I know what's going on.

When I first stopped taking his "pony" pills it was hard. But at least I'm not addicted. Other girls I see seem lost, and I don't want to be more lost than I already am.

I'm beginning to give up on a lot of things, even without needing the pills. What hurts the most is the idea of never seeing my family again, even if my brother and sister are pains in the you-know-what. The memories I have with them slip into my dreams and make me cry. Sometimes a memory is more of a hurtful thing than a sweet thing.

I guess it depends on where you are at the moment you get the memory. Are you in a classroom with your friends or are you in a dirty hotel room with a man who could be your dad. Or your uncle. Or your grandpa.

It depends on where you are.

And maybe I don't deserve to ever see my family again. How could they still love me? With what I've done? With what I've become?

If I can't see my family how can I be a vet? How can I be anything?

I think maybe a person can lose everything. And it's not their fault. I'll never look at a homeless person the same way again.

Except I don't believe that—about it not being my fault. I was the one who believed everything Ian told me. It was me. No one else.

Everything that's happened to me is my fault. Maddy tried to tell me different and I didn't listen. What did she know? I was so sure I'd found my Romeo.

My thoughts circle around these words, making my stomach hurt.

The door flies open.

"I've set you up with three appointments," Ian announces. "In between those, hit your track. Pull your weight. Your appointments aren't enough and you know how unhappy I get when we don't have enough."

"Are the appointments all for here?"

"Yep. Your first up is in thirty minutes." He looks at me. "Get ready. Except for being twelve, you look like shit." Ian walks out of the room, not bothering to close the door. It swings closed but doesn't latch. Anyone could walk in and kill me.

Maybe that wouldn't be such a bad thing.

Something inside of me cuts away. Cuts off.

Cuts.

I nod even though Ian is no longer there. "I'll be ready."

What that means, I'm not exactly sure. I only know that going along with Ian saves me from getting punched. Or worse.

Thirty-five minutes later there's a knock at my door.

I'm wearing the pink outfit Ian told me to wear tonight. I guess it makes me look young and fresh. Two things I'll never feel again.

When I open the door I'm prepared for anything. In a few days I've already seen a lot. I know a bad reaction can mean trouble for me later on so I focus on my face.

Smile, Livvy. Smile.

Standing in front of me is a man old enough to be my dad. Maybe even my grandpa. His face looks sad, but as I look at his eyes, I see his meanness. This will not be a quick and easy appointment. I'll need to stay sharp and pay attention to avoid getting hurt. Badly hurt.

I open the door wider. My smile stays on my face.

"Welcome to your amazing experience," I say as I've been coached. "My name is Desiree, and I'm here to fulfill not only your needs, but your fantasies as well."

The man moves into the room.

"What's your name?" I ask.

The man glares at me then puts his fist through the wall.

Rather than respond, I close my eyes and bow my head. I've learned that this is my go-to position when confronted with this amount of anger. I can hear him unbuckle his belt.

I don't automatically undress. I wait. I keep my eyelids closed and my face down. It's my safest move.

This guy is one of those johns who likes to tell me when I can do everything. Sort of like Ian.

I might only be twelve, but I'm not stupid. I've learned a thing or two.

"Undress," he says gruffly. "But slowly."

* * *

After I clean up I drag my butt out of the room. I pray for energy. I pray I can make enough money to keep Ian happy.

I pray for something else to think about. Like figuring out how to get out of here.

"Good," Ian says as I exit the lobby. "I've got another appointment for you. Midnight."

A horrible taste shoots into my mouth. I work to swallow it back down. It burns. "Is it okay if I stop after that one?"

"Why not? As long as you've made your quota. I'll expect you to look better tomorrow. And remember, I'm watching you."

I walk out to the street.

"Don't you have something to say to me?" Ian asks.

I swallow more of that bad tasting stuff that comes up my throat.

"Speak up girl."

"Thank you."

"You owe me."

Don't I always?

The next few hours move by with same old, same old similarity. The other girls catch my mood. No one talks to me.

How can it be same old, same old this fast? What happens in a month? A year?

Maybe I'll save those pills, pocket them or something, and swallow them all at once when I can't take it anymore.

I'm suddenly relieved, even as a tear slides down my cheek. I've finally figured out my way to get out of here even though I don't want to think about it.

It's almost time for my last appointment. I'll be able to go to sleep afterward, so I'm ready. Anxious even, to get this over with.

There's a light knock on my door. I panic and look at the clock. No, it's not midnight. I've still got five minutes.

The dim light in the hallway frames a small shape. A girl.

She looks quickly in both directions then steps into my room and closes the door.

Isabella. The girl from Guatemala.

"*Por favor*. Please." She'd used her one English word and continued in rapid Spanish. I understood enough simply looking at Isabella to see her panic. Her terror. She was asking, no, *begging* me to hide her.

I put my arm around her. "*Si, si.*" I look around the tiny room. If someone's looking for Isabella, they'll look in the obvious places. The bathroom, the closet. She'll have to go under the bed. I motion toward the tight space and she shoots me a look of gratitude.

For a moment I feel like a hero until understanding filters through. If Ian finds out there's no telling what he might do. We are totally breaking the rules.

Isabella slides under the bed at the same time there's a loud pounding at my door. Whoever's there obviously doesn't know he can just walk in. I open the door and a man bursts into the room.

"Is she here?"

I take it as a positive sign he didn't ask where she is. We might make it through this.

"Who?" I ask.

"The little spic bitch." He lunges into the bathroom, angrily slamming the door against the wall.

"You're scaring me," I say. And it's true. This man is in a rage.

"I could give a fuck. Is the little cunt here?" He tears the closet door off its hinges and throws it to the ground.

"She's not here, can't you see?"

A figure fills the doorway. "Do you seriously think I'll be okay with you taking any of my time?" His voice is smooth and soft but threatening.

The angry man whirls and takes a swing at the man behind him. Suddenly he's face down on the floor with his arms pinned to his back.

"Unless you want to leave here with something broken, I suggest you promise me right now that you're going to get up and walk out of here like the gentleman you were never raised to be. If you don't nod in the next three seconds, you'll hear, and feel, something snap."

The man can't nod enough.

"Good. I'm going to let you up, but I'll keep hold of you. I don't trust you to know how a gentleman would act."

Another nod.

Within seconds the crazy man is on his feet and out the door. When the door closes I'm suddenly terrified. What is this man going to do next? The phone Ian gave me is across the room. If I push a button, Ian will be here. At least that's what he told me. He also told me that if I push the button and I'm not almost dead, I'll wish I was.

Adams County social workers and an FBI victim specialist interviewed the girl at the Innocence Lost Task Force Office, where she told them she had met Castillo over Facebook and that her father had told her to call Castillo "uncle."... She also told the workers Castillo had sent her father, who lives in Mexico, money on several occasions and helped pay for her bus ticket from Las Cruces, New Mexico to the Denver area.

—Records: Father sold girl, 15, to Thornton man for sex: girl now pregnant, by Ryan Luby and Blair Miller, for KMGH Channel 7, October 19, 2016

CHAPTER SIXTY-NINE

"Quickly, Livvy. Put this on." Mex tossed Olivia a dark hoody.

"Who are you? How do you know my name?" The young girl freezes. "Does Ian know you're here? I should call Ian."

"I'm here to take you home. Do you want to go home?"

Livvy nods, but doesn't move.

"The car we're using is about a block away from here. I used another car to drive into this parking lot in case I was being watched, so don't worry. We'll leave out the back but we need to leave now."

Still Livvy doesn't move.

"Come on, girl. Let's go."

"I'm not alone."

Mex spun around the room, checked the closet and yanked open the bathroom door. Empty. "What do you mean? Where?"

Livvy looked toward the bed, then shook her head like she was trying to disguise her tell.

Mex dropped to his knees and lifted the soiled bed skirt. Two frightened brown eyes met his gray ones. Latina, he thought. "*Es bueno,*" Mex said softly. "It's okay. I'm here to help," he continued in Spanish. "Come out."

Hesitantly, the young girl emerged from under the bed but she didn't move to stand.

"Get up," Mex stood and offered his hand.

"We need to take Isabella too," Livvy says. "I can't go without taking her. She'll die if she doesn't come with us."

Isabella tried to brush the dust and dirt and who knew what else from her clothing, but succeeded mostly in rubbing it in even more.

"Do you have a hoody for her too?"

Mex looked at the two young girls in front of him. "Isabella is an unexpected surprise, but I think I know how we can do this."

A minute later Mex popped his head out of the room and scanned the hallway in both directions. He nodded, held out his hand, and a second figure appeared next to him. They moved quickly down the hallway to the back entrance of the hotel.

The sign on the door said it's locked at ten o'clock, but Mex had checked at eleven-thirty and it was open. They shouldn't sound any alarm as they moved through it. At least that's what he hoped.

He looked down at Livvy. "Be ready to run if an alarm sounds. If there's no alarm, we're going to just walk casually to my car. Do you understand?"

Mex felt her squeeze his hand.

He pushed the bar to open the door and held his breath.

Nothing. It didn't mean that an alarm didn't sound somewhere else, but he'd begun to feel better about it.

Holding Livvy's hand, he angled across the parking lot in a beeline for the street. If we can get off the motel property, he thought, we might have a chance.

The parking lot was filled with potholes. Litter tossed around them as dry desert gusts of wind swirled. The lighting at this end of the hotel was nonexistent. Dark shadows poured over their own shadows providing protection.

"Hey there!" someone shouted. "Wait!"

Mex had a split-second to decide. Should he tell Livvy to run? The wrong decision could mean the end of her chance to see her family again. The wrong decision could kill her.

He held Livvy's hand tightly in his own and turned. "Yes?"

"Your daughter dropped this." The man held out a tube. Mex indicated that Livvy take it.

The man looked suspiciously at the obviously dissimilar adult and child.

"Thanks," Mex said.

"Hey, I know what my kid would do if she lost her lip gloss."

"Step-kid," Mex said. "You saved me, buddy. Thanks again."

Mex turned and they continued toward the street. He'd come that close to blowing everything for the sake of a tube of pale pink lip gloss.

Once they'd exited the motel property and had walked a few yards on the sidewalk, Mex let go of Livvy's hand and opened his coat. Isabella dropped her feet to the ground.

"We're not safe yet," he said in Spanish and then English for Livvy. "Hurry."

The trio hustled up the block and Mex pulled a fob out of his pocket. The unlocking noise sounded loud in the post-midnight quiet of the block.

When the girls were in the back seat, Mex climbed in front and started the engine. "Livvy, get your seatbelts on and stay down as low as possible. If anyone's watching, it's only a man driving home from a late night."

He found his cell and thumbed the phone. He waited. "I've got them. We're on our way to the airport."

"Them?" Cade asked.

Mex had forgotten Isabella wasn't part of his mission.

"Them who?" Cade asked again.

"We have what you might call a stowaway. Can you call the airline and make a third reservation?"

"Okay. What's her name?"

"Isabella."

"Isabella what?"

Mex caught his breath. He didn't know her last name. He arched his head to ask her, then changed his mind. "Isabella Anderson."

"What?" That one word coming from his lover conveyed many more questions underneath.

"Let's go with that name for now. Like what, they're gonna ask for ID?"

"The first time I was trafficked, I was five years old. I was handcuffed to a truck stop bathroom, and I was raped and sodomized for six hours, and given cocaine and alcohol," said Elam.... "The way he kept my silence was he told me that if I said a word, he would kill my mother," Elam remembers.
—11 Call for Action Investigation: Human Trafficking in Southern Colorado, by Danielle Kreutter

CHAPTER SEVENTY

LIVVY

I'm home. I'm really home. My mom and dad practically shove people aside at the airport to get to me. I know they hugged me before, but they never hugged me like they're hugging me now. They never hugged me hard, laughed and cried at the same time. They never hugged me and couldn't get their breath.

Sarah and Ethan stand awkwardly to the side until I wave my hand toward them. Suddenly we're this big lump of arms and heads and backs and people, all of our body parts are flopped together and perfect. All of us are crying.

I wouldn't care if time froze.

Perfectly loved at this moment, they don't know how horrible I am. Perfectly loved, they don't know what I've done. They love me so much they can't get their breath.

They won't love me when they know. When they know, they'll gasp and let me go.

A woman comes up to us, wraps her arms around our huddle, and then steps back.

"My name is Cade LeBlanc," she says. "You don't know me, Livvy, but I know a lot about you. Your family trusts me, and I'm hoping you can too."

"Do you know Mex?"

"I do."

"Where is he?"

"He's resting right now."

"And Isabella? Where's she?"

"She's being looked after. She's safe, thanks to you."

"Me and Mex."

Cade smiles. "Yeah. Thanks to you and Mex."

"What do you want me to do?"

"Right now we're going to take you to the hospital to make sure you're okay. You won't be alone, I promise."

Cade reaches out and hugs me again. "You're so brave." She squeezes my arm. "Would it be okay with you to talk to someone from the Aurora Police Department? Her name is Elizabeth Rider and she's nice. Plus, I have a friend who's been through what you've been through. If it's okay with you, I'd like you to talk to both of them. And of course your mom and dad can be there too."

"Someone who's been through what I've been through?"

"Yep. Her name is Rachel."

"Will you stay?"

"I'll stay."

"Do you know my friend Maddy?"

"I've met Maddy."

"When can I see her?"

"Let's get to the hospital first, then talk to the police. Later, if you're not too tired, we'll bring Maddy to you. I'm sure she's excited to see you again."

"She was right, you know."

"Right? About what?"

"About Ian."

"Let's take this a step at a time, shall we? And sweetheart, we all make mistakes. We've all trusted the wrong person."

"But I trusted the wrong person in a big way."

"Yeah, you did. But you're not the first person to do that. You're not alone. Not then, and definitely not now."

I wonder if I should trust her, but she knows Mex. And I wouldn't be here without him.

"Okay. I'll talk to the police. But can it only be my mom who stays? I'm not ready for my dad."

Cade looks at my dad. He looks sad but he nods.

"Sure, if that's what you want," Cade says.

My dad comes up and holds me close. "Whenever you're ready for me, Livvy, I'm here."

I can only nod.

Backpage claims to combat human trafficking, saying that it screens posts for illegal activities. But a subcommittee investigation says Backpage actually aids sex traffickers by helping to shield them from detection.

For instance, the Senate investigators found Backpage screens posts before they appear online, and the site removes key words from ads that could tip off law enforcement officials to illegal activity.

—Supreme Court refuses to block Backpage subpoenas in sex trafficking investigation, by Jackie Wattles, for CNN, September 2016

CHAPTER SEVENTY-ONE

JAYLA

Daddy says we're moving on in a couple of days unless business picks up. There's a big convention in Salt Lake next week.

I smile inwardly at the irony of hoping for more sexual encounters with strange men so I can stay in Denver. So I can breathe familiar air, see familiar buildings and mountains and... well, never mind.

My last appointment was one of those guys who plays all macho until the moment. Then it's over, he's embarrassed, you say nice things to him to stroke his ego and bring him back because he's the john all girls want, and then he's gone. You've either got time for yourself or time to hit your track again if you haven't made quota.

Well, I've got more than enough money to keep Daddy happy and my appointment is over early, so I slip out of the room. Ginger is asleep on a chair in the lobby, undoubtedly thinking she can catch a few zees while I finish my last trick. It would be so easy to walk out the door and keep on walking. In a strange city, I wouldn't know where to go. In Denver? I have options.

Almost fifty percent of the cells in my body are luring me toward the doors that spell freedom for me. *Almost* fifty percent. The other fifty percent-plus know the price Ginger will pay at the hands of Daddy if I leave. I've seen him in action. Hell, he makes sure we've all seen him action so we all know we're either gonna cause pain or receive it ourselves.

Instead of leaving, I sit on the arm of her chair and wait. Her soft snoring humanizes her. Softens her somehow. After a minute or two she shifts and realizes someone is near her. With reaction born of personal history, Ginger shoots up ready to fight off an aggressor.

"It's me," I say. "Just me. You're okay."

"What the fuck?" She looks at her watch then connects her gaze to mine like her life depends on it. "What happened?"

"Nothin'. The appointment ended up being a john with a stamina fantasy," I smile down at her.

She looks around the empty lobby. "You could've left."

"Yeah. I thought about it."

"But you didn't." She stands and smooths her rumpled clothes. "What the hell kind of moron are you?" she asks me *sotto voce*, her face angled close to mine. "Why didn't you run?"

"You and I both know why." I shove off the chair's arm and head to the elevator. "And you're welcome."

* * *

I can't sleep. I've turned the chair so I can sit in it and look out the dirty window at the night sky. From this angle, with this view, I could be anywhere, but I know I'm in Denver. I know I'm home and for now that's all that matters.

With appointments booked through tomorrow night, I'm pretty confident we'll stay for at least one more day. And then what? Salt Lake City? Albuquerque? Las Vegas?

Thoughts of LaTisha drift through the window. I don't think of her as Amber. That was her street name. Her slave name.

I remember holding her while she died. She was tiny and frail—and pregnant. She hadn't wanted to die alone. I watched her lips turn blue and her breathing grow more shallow with every breath. Before meeting me that night she'd overdosed on heroin.

Maybe she's one of the lucky ones.

There's a quick knock at my door before it opens.

"I wanted to come and say thank you," Ginger says. "There's a lot more to you than most of these girls."

"Don't underestimate them. You don't know them."

The woman nods. "You're probably right. I don't want to know them. I can't afford to know them."

"And me?"

"I haven't decided."

I don't respond. I turn back to look at the sky out the window.

A moment later I hear the door close.

Only one man had made a profit off of me, but there were numerous men who had bought me, and I felt my anger rise and rise. It began to occur to me that the exploitation of girls could not happen without these men.... Yet calling men who buy sex from children 'johns' minimizes the harm they do. At the very least, they are statutory rapists and child abusers.
—Girls Like Us, *by Rachel Lloyd*

CHAPTER SEVENTY-TWO

Darius had called Pamela three times in the last hour, both of them laughing about what a bad john he'd make, calling his wife every few minutes. Still, they both knew that while the security around Jayla might not be as tight as that around Alexis, it was risky. And they both had an idea of the hell Jayla had been through the last six months.

They needed to laugh.

He'd scored a hotel room about twenty minutes away from the base-hotel where they were holding Jayla. Far enough away to have fewer eyes on them but close enough not to draw suspicion.

"How are the girls?" Darius asked for the third time.

"They're fine, DJ. Home from school and complaining about homework while secretly diving in for a good grade."

"And our son?"

"Sleeping for the time being."

"Do you miss having your mom around?"

"I miss having an extra pair of hands. I don't miss having her tell me how to do things."

"Or that you should've married Paul Blair instead of me."

"Yeah, that too."

He could hear her smile.

"Did Mex get there?" Pam asked.

The last time they'd talked, all of fifteen minutes ago, Mex hadn't arrived.

"Yep, he's here along with the DPD detective assigned to Jayla's case and a patrol unit in plain clothes. I'm covered." A lot more covered here than I was in Monterrey, Darius thought.

"Better than Mexico," PJ echoed, as if she'd heard him.

"Tell the girls I love them. Tell them I'll try to be home in time to tuck them in tonight."

"Tell them yourself." Pam called the girls to the phone.

"Thanks for that," Darius told his wife after the two brief conversations were over. "I'm the luckiest man in the world."

"And don't you ever forget it. If you do, I'll be sure to remind you."

There was a knock at his door.

"Gotta go. It's showtime," Darius told Pammy. "Love you."

"Love you more," Pamela said.

"Love you most."

He disconnected the call and stowed his phone before answering the door.

Darius was unprepared for the young girl standing in his doorway. He'd seen pictures of Jayla in her yearbooks, selfies she'd taken with friends, family photos from last Christmas. The overly made up, cheaply and scantily dressed girl in front of him bore no resemblance to what he'd been expecting. Even her ad on Backpage hadn't reflected reality. But the biggest shock to his system was that he knew this tired and sad person waiting to come into his room—who would allow him to do anything he wanted to her—was the same girl.

"I'm Cherie. You're expecting me, right?" She looked doubtful.

He shook off his thoughts and forced a smile. "Sorry. Yeah, yeah, Cherie. I am." He stepped away from the door so she could enter, then stepped into the hallway to look in both directions. Empty.

Jayla had gone immediately to the bed where she sat and began removing her shoes. "Don't worry. It can be awkward at first."

"Stop," Darius said. "Don't take anything off."

Jayla froze. "You don't like me?"

Darius understood that rejecting a girl could result in harsh punishment. "No, no, that's not it at all."

The girl didn't move. She waited like she was waiting for the other shoe to drop. Smart girl, Darius thought.

"Your mom contacted my friend and partner. I'm here to take you home." He knelt on the floor and grabbed her arms.

Jayla's mouth opened. Closed. Her eyes squinted. She snatched her arms away.

"Jayla, I'm telling you the truth. I'm here to take you home."

"What did you call me?"

Darius took her hands in his. "I called you Jayla."

Tears flooded her eyes and spilled into her lap. Still, she didn't make a sound. She didn't move.

"It's true," Darius said. "We have backup in the hotel, but I have to know what kind of security is attached to you. Who's making sure you don't try to escape?"

Jayla closed her eyes and took a breath. Another. "I have a handler because Denver is my home turf. She's in the lobby. Her name is Leah, but she goes by Ginger."

"Is she the only one?"

"Yes. But she needs to come with me. If I leave and she doesn't, her life will be hell. It might even be over."

"I don't want to argue the point, but she's your jailer, right?"

"Yeah."

"And you want to save your jailer?"

"Yeah."

"Got it. Not a problem. What does she look like?"

"Black. Older than me. Red hair. Hard."

Darius took out his cell and swiped. "We've got another stowaway. Look around. Do you see a black woman in the lobby? Might look like she's waiting for someone?"

He gave Mex the particulars. "We're on our way down."

Once in the lobby Mex, Darius, and Jayla approached Leah. The DPD detective and officers on scene were asked to stand down for this meeting. When Mex explained the situation they grudgingly agreed.

Jayla reached out and grabbed Leah's hands. "This is it, Leah. These men are here to save us."

"You mean you."

"No. I mean us."

"I don't understand. Are they arresting us?"

"No. They're here to *free* us."

Leah shook her head. "No. I have nowhere to go."

"We can figure that out," Jayla pleaded. "Please come with us."

"What would I do?"

"You mean who would take care of you," Jayla said.

"No. Yes. Who would take care of me?"

"What if it's eventually you? What if you have help at first, including me and my family? And then you can have your own life?"

Leah stood and turned away. "No. I can't."

"Leah, look at me," Jayla said. "Trust me. Look at me."

Slowly the older woman faced Jayla.

"Is this what you want?" Jayla asked. "To keep working for Daddy? To be threatened? To turn more young girls, *children*, into revenue streams for him? We both know what will happen to you if I leave. You'll be beaten. You might even be killed. And I know you still have a personal quota. Tell me, is this what you want?" Tears flood down Jayla's face.

"I can't leave, Cherie."

"Jayla."

"I can't leave. I have nowhere to go. I don't trust that anyone can help me. I've tried it before." She reached out and hugged Jayla. "You go. You're young enough. You have family." She sobbed. "My family is Daddy."

Darius tugged Jayla away from Leah. "We have to go." Jayla didn't move. "We have to go now."

Jayla looked at Leah for a long moment. "Leah, listen to me."

The older woman shifted, but didn't engage her eyes with Jayla's.

"Listen to me," Jayla repeated. "I understand where you're coming from. I would never blame you for choosing Daddy. He's the evil you know. But if ever you want out, all you have to do is call me. Or Darius. But Leah, I'm leaving. I hate what's ahead for you, but I'm leaving. Are you sure you don't want to come with me?"

Leah and Jayla's eyes met and locked.

"There's nothing there for me now," Leah said. "It's been too long. My life, whatever it is, is with Daddy."

Darius watched Jayla's shoulders slump. He watched her swallow. Once. Twice. He watched as Jayla offered his business card to Leah. "Call him if you change your mind," she said. "You're never alone."

Leah smiled. Reached out for a hug. "I never thought I was."

After the hug she tore up the card.

"Why?" Jayla asked through her tears.

"Too dangerous for all of us if I kept it."

[Brock] Franklin allegedly recruited girls by contacting them through Facebook, and meeting them at hotels and nightclubs, routinely using violence, drugs and sexual assault to control and coerce the victims, according to the indictment.

—Seven indicted by Colorado grand jury in child sex trafficking ring bust, by Hsing Tseng, for Fox 31 Denver and Colorado's Own The CW2

CHAPTER SEVENTY-THREE

ALEXIS

I tug the afghan up to my chin. I'm out on the deck off our family room, sitting in the sun like a pitiful invalid.

The first few days after I got home my phone never stopped ringing. It seemed like I was never alone, so many people filed through my house. But it wasn't that they cared about me.

They were curious.

I get that. I didn't blame them. But I wasn't all that forthcoming. And they sure as hell didn't know the right questions to ask. I got everything from, "Oh, Alexis! Was it romantic?" to "Were you gang raped?" What idiots. But to be truthful, what would be the right question to ask someone who'd been through what I've been through, for one night, or ten, or twenty?

Thank God for Rachel. She keeps me strong even though our stories are totally different. They each hold the horror of bondage. Captivity. Sex and torture. Rachel survived.

I'm not so sure about me.

Oddly enough, one of the other vetted security guards at Montonaldo's party was a cousin of a former Sergio acquisition. Montonaldo was found hours after everyone had left spread-eagled on one of his own torture devices. There was a body next to his, identified later as the cousin, with a self-inflicted gunshot wound to the head.

When I heard about this I thought immediately about those used sandals. A weird part of me hopes she and I shared those shoes. She was at least loved by someone.

My dad got home a couple of days after I did. He hugged me. He told me I was strong and could overcome anything that had happened to me, but he didn't want to listen. No real change from before. He tried, he did. But it isn't part of his personality to spend a lot of time on a problem that has been resolved. Even worse, to connect with a daughter who'd been sold to a man wealthier than him for sex. For power. He was home for less than twenty-four hours before heading out again.

Really? A quick pep talk and that's all he thinks it's gonna take?

I want to know why my daddy doesn't love me enough to fight for me. Why an asshole businessman in Asia is more important than his daughter who is dissolving into a puddle of pain in her bedroom.

I figure out that he's got a void where the family link should be. It's not his fault, it's just not there.

I need him. I've never needed him more.

Damn him.

Mother, believe it or not, gets more credit. Not much, but some. When Rachel and Cade approached her with a couple of names of therapists who might help me, she did her best to pay attention. I went to see a woman in Boulder, Lynda Hilburn,

332

who is working with PTSD patients and having success with a new type of therapy. I guess I qualify.

Rachel drove me up to Boulder to meet with her yesterday. I liked her. She made me work but she didn't make me do all of the work. It's gonna take a while. It might even take longer than college would have. College. Not on my radar any longer. My future consists of visits with a shrink-type from now until whenever.

But it's all I've got.

Right now, sitting out on this deck at my parent's house, I wonder why I survived. There's nothing for me here. There's nothing real about my life before, or my life now. It's all show.

When I was with Montonaldo, I'd held my *attitude* as long as I could. I thought my *attitude* could save me. And now I see it for the freakin' fake it was.

I have nothing.

I am nothing.

I've got another hope besides Rachel. Some girl named Jayla. Seems like we were both held at the same holding pen in Denver. She went one way and I went another.

But we were in the same place.

The women, mostly minors, were lured away from their families by men who appeared to be seeking romantic propositions, but were then kidnapped and subject to rape....Authorities say the women were forced to service as many as 20 to 40 customers a day, with all of the money going to the men....They were either dropped off in brothels or "delivered" to a customer's home by a driver in New York, New Jersey, Connecticut, Maryland, Virginia or Delaware.

—U.S.-Mexico Human Trafficking Ring Busted with Seven Men Facing Life Sentences, *by Barbara Gonzalez, for* Latina *November 4, 2016*

CHAPTER SEVENTY-FOUR

LIVVY

My family is trying. They really are. It's probably harder for them than it is for me because they didn't live what I lived. All they can do is imagine.

I've seen Maddy a few times but I'm still so ashamed. She tried to warn me. All I do is cry. And then she cries. I think we'll be BFFs again, but it's gonna be hard. It's gonna take time. What I know is she loves me. That's all I need to know for today.

Cade and her friend Rachel help hold me together. Even though Cade's story is different, with the cult stuff and all, she sure gets me. She understands what I'm thinking. Rachel has smelled the same smells and felt the same hands on her body as I have. I listen to what both of them have to say, and they listen to me without judging. Two angels on my team. I don't know what I did to deserve them.

But even with my family and Maddy and Cade and Rachel, the person who's really helping me is Isabella. She's staying with us until Cade and Mex can formally adopt her. It's gonna take time for the adoption because the law gets all blind about what's right when all of the proper papers aren't in order. That's good though, because I count on her right now, and Aspen Falls, where Mex and Cade live, is almost four hours from here.

I haven't gone back to school yet. My mom arranged for lessons to be sent home and we're going through them together. She doesn't want me to fall behind. There are days I wonder about the point of it all. Why bother? I'm not the girl I was before all this happened. On the plus side, going over the schoolwork gives Mom and me something to talk about. A bond.

Mex and Cade hired a tutor for Isabella too. We go to different counselors because she doesn't speak much English. Plus, and this is a big plus, Isabella doesn't have a family like I do. From what I can tell, Isabella had been practically starving in Guatemala. That's why she was so desperate. So eager to believe in the story her captor told her.

Her life has sparkles now. She has America. She has Mex and Cade. She's a hero.

I'm still trying to find my way back to Livvy. Back to my life. Back to my dreams.

In addition to their strategies of control and their paternalistic rationalizations, the other thing that pimps have in common, regardless of who they are, are the damaged lives they leave in their wake. To a girl who's been beaten because she didn't make her quota, or put out on the street after a rape and told, "There's nothing wrong with your mouth," it doesn't really make that much difference whether her pimp is a sociopath or not, if he had one girl or ten, if he ever felt bad about what he was doing, if he wished he could do something else with his life. The humiliation, the physical and emotional pain, the trauma, the nightmares all feel the same. The damage is done.

—Girls Like Us, *by Rachel Lloyd*

CHAPTER SEVENTY-FIVE

JAYLA

I think about that image I had more than six months ago at my school bus stop. A crumpled piece of paper caught by the wind, shredding bits every time it hit the pavement. I remember identifying with it then. I wondered if my life was like that clump of paper, tossed around, wearing away at my soul, finally exposing my bones and leaving me to die. Because at that time, if felt like normal life was scraping away at me. Changing me.

Normal life.

What's normal for me today isn't what was normal six or seven months ago. I fully expect my definition of normal to be different a year from now. What's normal for one person might not even be in the same world as the next person.

It all depends on the links.

A friend of mine has an uncle with cerebral palsy. Normal for him would be foreign to me. I haven't spent much time in his world. I haven't moved throughout his days and nights. And yet, having met him, he has a pretty good grasp on my normal. See what I mean?

The links.

I met with a couple of psychologists. Both of them were astounded at my ability to grasp reality. To grasp what's happened to me and not be a quivering mass of neurosis and fear.

What is with these people?

It is what it is. I was a winner and a survivor going in, and I'm a winner and a survivor coming out. But one with a much greater understanding of people. I have a greater understanding of strength I didn't know I possessed because I hadn't had to access it before.

Has my future changed? Damn straight it has. Not only will I be going to college, I'll be volunteering to help trafficked girls, and boys as well. I'll be fighting to increase the penalties for both original sellers like Chris, traffickers like Daddy, and the buyers. I'll be fighting to make sure that resources are put in place so that girls like LaTisha have a sanctuary. A choice. And to make sure they know about it.

The third psychologist brought me to my core. Although I'm strong, I might be able to use help here and there. During our session she showed me it was okay to feel vulnerable. What I think of as weakness isn't always weak. Sometimes it's courage in disguise.

I've got a way to go.

I'm a fighter. I'm smart. Rather than having bits of me scraped thin like that paper, my skin has thickened to an impenetrable toughness. I designed that thickness with faith in myself. And by design, my heart is still accessible. I hope I never have to change that.

And Mama is proud.

It has been more than six months since a 16-year-old girl from Aurora disappeared. [See Chapter Forty]

LaShaya Stine left her house at 2:30 a.m. on July 15 to meet someone, but she never returned.... Aurora police chief Nick Metz said police received information that is cause for greater concern...—Aurora teen LaShaya Stine still missing after more than six months, by Anica Padilla for Fox 31 Denver and Colorado's Own CW2, January 16, 2017

CHAPTER SEVENTY-SIX

Mex took a deep breath and exhaled. Did it again. Earlier he'd dug out the bottle of pills from his bag and set them on the countertop in his kitchen. If he needed them they were there.

He looked out of the floor-to-ceiling windows and watched as five deer grazed by the stream that ran across the back of his Aspen Falls home. They looked peaceful, without a care. Any sudden movement and they'd be off. Not so peaceful after all. Peace was fleeting.

Mex remembered watching a mountain lion take down a deer a few months ago. The mountain lion gained life at the expense of another.

People were worse. They didn't need to prey on others to survive but they did so anyway.

Cade walked in behind him, tossed a sweater on his lap, and gave him a hug. "C'mon, Cowboy. Let's go sit outside and talk for a bit. I've got news. You get the fire going and I'll round us up something to sip on."

"You round yourself up whatever you want. I want a glass of the Macallan."

"Done."

The doorbell rang.

"Mex? Do you mind?" Cade called from the wet bar.

"Make up your mind woman," Mex gave her a wink. "First you have me lighting your fire and then you completely douse the mood by making me a butler."

"You're all things to me, Cowboy."

Mex opened the door. Darius stood there with Sedona.

His smile toward Darius slipped to a frown when he saw his sister. "Damn," Mex said. "The evening was going so well."

He considered closing the door in their faces and getting back to whatever news Cade had to share. Instead, he left the door wide open and walked away.

"Pour a couple more, Cade," Mex said as he walked through the house to the back deck. He didn't bother to tell her who was at the door. She'd see soon enough.

The fire pit blazing, afghans stacked at the ready, the four of them sat gazing at the flames.

"Thank her," Darius spoke into silence broken only by the crackling of the wood on the fire.

"Thank who?" Mex asked.

"Mex, damn it. You don't have to forgive her. I don't know if I could. But she's trying. She can never put things right. But she's trying."

"You said that already."

"Without her help, we might never have been able to save Alexis," Darius said.

The fire waned a bit and Cade added a new log. "He's right, you know."

Mex shifted back into the darkness, away from the warmth of the fire.

Sedona stood. "I should go. Kenneth and his children have been without me long enough. I'm sorry. I should never have come here."

Cade, standing by the fire pit shook her head. "You sit back down. Darius is right. You deserve thanks for everything you put in place to save that young girl."

Sedona didn't move.

"Sit, damn it," Mex said. He waited.

Slowly, Sedona lowered herself.

Mex sniffed and took a long swallow of his scotch. "I'll never forget what you did to my family. I can't imagine ever forgiving you. Not only for what you did but for never saying a word to me. Never admitting the role you played. I don't give a rat's ass that you were strung out. That you were in love. I don't care. You killed my family."

Tears streamed down Sedona's face.

"But Cade and Darius are right," Mex choked out the words. "Without you, Alexis Halston might well have been lost forever. So thank you." He looked directly into his sister's eyes. "I hope you and this Maxwell guy can find happiness together. That's all I've got to say. You can go now."

Sedona stood and Cade ushered her out, arms around the beautiful woman's shoulders.

Mex and Darius sat in silence, staring at the fire.

"You got a start on that new book of yours?" Mex asked.

"I do."

More silence. More staring.

"I should go," Darius said.

"Because you need to take Sedona home?"

"Yep," Darius nodded. "That okay with you?"

"Yep."

When Cade returned she put another log on the fire then snuggled next to him. They sat in silence, enjoying the warmth, the flames, and being near each other.

"So, do you want to hear my news?"

"I don't know. I'm still working on the fact I said thank you to Sedona. Don't know if I can take any more."

"I think you can handle this."

Mex worked to pop his neck. Release the tension. "So shoot, woman."

"First, remember that little boy named Davie from Golden? The one whose parents didn't want us involved, but who Jayla was in contact with?"

"Yeah."

"He hasn't been found and his parents are now asking for our help."

"Okay. Tell them we'll do what we can."

"We're meeting with them tomorrow. They're driving here and should arrive in time for lunch."

"And?"

"I've received an offer on my Louisiana house."

Mex sucked in a breath, feeling everything that had been flat in him two minutes earlier swell. He waited.

"Don't you want to know if I accepted it?"

He waited. He knew the answer was coming.

Then she kissed him.

* * *

Author Notes

I'm plugging this in here because I don't want you to miss it.

I've never researched any topic more heartbreaking, more soul-numbing, than human trafficking. While I can "wrap up" a story, it's important to understand that for many girls, boys, and young women out in the real world, there is no wrap-up. There's only today, tomorrow, the day after and the day after that.

Can you make a difference?

If your conscience is engaged, if you feel any kind of tug, follow it.

In the next pages you'll see a resource list. If you are in need, seek them out. If you can avail yourself as a volunteer, seek them out. If you have funds to support a particular resource, check them out and then let your dollars make a difference.

It takes all of us, using whatever means we have available, to shine a spotlight on both the problem and the solution.

I believe in you.

RESOURCES

Colorado Network to End Human Trafficking 1-866-455-5075
www.combathumantrafficking.org

A statewide referral network for victim service referrals from service providers and law enforcement; survivor support and case management referral; tips regarding potential trafficking situations

Child Sex Trafficking in America: A Guide for Parents and Guardians is available at **www.missingkids.com/CSSTT**

International Human Trafficking Institute www.theihti.org

Provides ways to join the discussion, get involved, and take action on a global level.

National Center for Missing & Exploited Children 1-800-843-5678 www.cybertipline.com

National Human Trafficking Hotline   1-888-373-7888 TTY: 711   help@humantraffickinghotline.org www.humantraffickinghotline.org

A nationwide hotline to provide support and services to victims and survivors of human trafficking. 24-hour access to report tips, seek services, ask for help. Multi-lingual.

Truckers Against Trafficking   1-888-3737-888 www.truckersagainsttrafficking.org

Educates, equips, empowers and mobilizes members of the trucking and travel plaza industry to combat domestic sex trafficking.

The following is provided by Dr. Susanne E. Jalbert.

Colorado's Effort to Stop Human Trafficking
Acronyms and Contacts
Revised January 2017

Colorado and National Actors and Acronyms

ACOVA - A Community Organization for Victim Assistance
ADAD - Colorado Alcohol and Drug Abuse Division
Blue Sky Bridge
Bridges Child Placement Agency
CANPO - is now the **Colorado Nonprofit Association**
CASA - Court Appointed Special Advocates
CBI - Colorado Bureau of Investigation
CC - Community Corrections
CCADV - Colorado Coalition Against Domestic Violence
CCASA - Colorado Coalition Against Sexual Assault
CCIC - Colorado Crime Information Center (at CBI)
CCVC - Colorado Crime Victim Compensation (software program)
CDAC - Colorado District Attorney's Council
COB - Colorado Outward Bound
Colorado Division of the FBI – *contact Ann Darr*
Colorado Human Trafficking Task Force – *Janet Drake, Assistant Attorney General of Colorado is the lead prosecutor in HT cases and member of the Task Force.*
Colorado Legal Services
COVA - Colorado Organization for Victim Ass**istance**
CVAA - Colorado Victim Assistance Academy
DA - District Attorney

DCCV - Denver Center for Crime Victims

DCJ - Division of Criminal Justice

DOC - Department of Corrections

DOJ also **USDOJ** - Department of Justice

DOSS also CDHS - Department of Social Services

DPS - Department of Public Safety

DV - Domestic Violence

DVI - Domestic Violence Initiative (for Women with Disabilities)

Empowerment Program

EVAW - Ending Violence Against Women Project

FBI - Federal Bureau of Investigation

Fracre - www.fracresourcedirectory.com

Free a Child - www.facebook.com/**freeachild**

Focus on Family - www.**focus**onthe**family**.com/

GRASP -__**http://www.graspyouth.org/staff**/Contact Michele McDaniel

HB - House Bill

I-Empathize – http://iempathize.org/

Innocence Lost Task Force

JBC - Joint Budget Committee (of the Legislature)

JD - Judicial District

JJDP - Juvenile Justice and Delinquency Prevention

John School Diversion Program

Laboratory to Fight Trafficking

MADD - Mother's Against Drunk Driving

MHC - Mental Health Center

Mile High Ministries – contact attorney Rene Wright

NCASA - National Coalition Against Sexual Assault

NCJRS - National Criminal Justice Reference Service

NCVC - National Center for Victims of Crime

NOVA - National Organization for Victim Assistance

NVAA - National Victim Assistance Academy

NVCAP - National Victim Constitutional Amendment Passage
OVC - Office for Victims of Crime (Washington, DC)
OJJDP - Office of Juvenile Justice and Delinquency Prevention
PD - Police Department
POMC - Parent's of Murdered Children
POST - Police Officer Standardized Training
PRAX(US) - http://www.praxus.org/
(Project) PAVE - Promoting Alternatives to Violence through Education
RAAP - Rape Assistance and Awareness Program
Rocky Mountain Immigrant Advocacy Network (RMIAN) - http://www.rmian.org/
SA - Sexual Assault
SB - Senate Bill
SAIC - Sexual Assault Interagency Council
SANE - Sexual Assault Nurse Examiners
Shared Hope *sharedhope.org/ Shared Hope* International based in Washington DC is dedicated to bringing an end to sex trafficking through our three-prong approach.
SO - Sheriff's Office
Summit 2 End It - http://www.init2endit.com/home.
The Lab *combathumantrafficking.org /The Laboratory* to Combat *Human* Trafficking is a leading 501(c)3 nonprofit organization in Denver creating an informed social change movement to *end human* trafficking.
Templeton, J. E.
USAID
VW - Victim Witness
VALE - Victim Assistance Law Enforcement (State and Local)
VOCA - Victim of Crime Act
VOI - Victim Outreach Information
VRW - Victim Rights Week

Women of Global Action – Attorney Patricia Medige

Please send your suggestions to the following email address:
coloradovcac@gmail.com

Other National and International Resources
Not intended to be comprehensive

Borodkin, Rep. Alice – Former CO House of Representatives, Chair of Inter Agency Task Force on Human Trafficking created through House Bill 143 Seehttp://www.linkedin.com/profile/view?id=31342446&locale=en_US&trk=tyah)

California's ETR Associates: http://www.etr.org/home (Resource for Dr. Pamela M. Anderson's research)

California's UC-San Francisco program at San Francisco General Hospital – See protocol: www.medschool2.ucsf.edu/files/sfgh/.../SFGH2012orientation bklt-staff.pdf

Center for Women Policy Studies - http://www.sitelevel.com/query?query=Anti-trafficking&GO.x=0&GO.y=0&crid=4384cb6f559cb004 (list 60 AT resources)

Chicago Alliance against Sexual Exploitation – http://caase.org Colorado Resource Directory - https://docs.google.com/spreadsheet/ccc?key=0Ai9AGtUnZr W9dFFVOUgxWVZqOFE2aTl5QzlsTXhvMHc&usp=sharing

Denver University Research - http://www.du.edu/korbel/hrhw/researchdigest/trafficking/In ternationalLaw.pdf

D'Estree, Claude, heads the Human Trafficking Clinic at DU. Email: cdestree@du.edu.

T: 303-871-6286. Note: also heads the Center on Rights Development at Korbel.

Harvard - http://www.hks.harvard.edu/centers/carr/programs/human-trafficking-and-modern-slavery

GEMS - http://www.gems-girls.org/ GEMS, founded by Rachel Lloyd, was talked about a lot at the CO Summit. International Justice Mission

Institute for Inclusive Security - www.**inclusivesecurity**.org/

International Justice Mission - www.**ijm**.org/

Klein Frank Foundation – 303 448 8884

Lust Free Living - http://www.lustfreeliving.org/men/home.html

Man Up Campaign - http://www.manupcampaign.org/ .This is run by Beth Klein's friend

Jimmy Briggs (he was a 21 leader with me, and his reach in giant) He stopped South Africa from legalizing prostitution during the World Cup.

Miami-Dade County Public Schools - http://studentservices.dadeschools.net/HTAC/

Moldova Anti-Trafficking Web Site: http://www.atnet.md/index.php?l=en (Project and site designed by S. E. Jalbert, Ph.D. through USAID/Winrock International and Antonia

DeMeo at OSCE in 2005-2006)

National District Attorneys Association - http://www.ndaa.org/ncpca_bios.html

NV, Las Vegas Anti-Human Trafficking Unit – contact Chris Baughman, also see his book: *Off the Street*

OSCE - http://www.osce.org/cthb

Polaris - http://www.polarisproject.org/what-we-do/national-human-trafficking-hotline/the-nhtrc/overview - contact Becky Owens Bullard, Project Coordinator

Portland's Sexual Assault Resource Center - http://www.sarcoregon.org

Protected Innocence Challenge Report Card

Sage - http://sagesf.org/ is a San Fran group that really transformed the conversation.

Shared Hope – www.**sharedhope**.org/

Texas' UT Medical Branch Galveston, School of Nursing – see Patricia A. Crane at: http://son.utmb.edu/faculty/crane.asp to inquire for reporting protocols

Truckers Against Trafficking - http://truckersagainsttrafficking.org – They had a display at the Summit. It is run by Kendis Paris from Denver. They reach 3.5 Million, and have distributed hundreds of thousands of awareness cards to drivers. The drivers are doing a great job working with the FBI when they spot a probable victim.

United Nations Association, UN Women, and the United Nations in general.

US Department of Defense – http://ctip.defense.gov/ contact Linda K. Dixon, Program

Manager of DoD's Combating Trafficking in Person (CTIP)

US State Department (TIPS report) and USAID: www.state.gov/j/**tip**/rls/**tip**rpt/

Zonta International - http://www.zonta.org/

Videos

http://www.youtube.com/watch?v=xSpQxvtTbFU

http://www.youtube.com/watch?v=4DlGQJrGJMs

http://www.youtube.com/watch?v=ZdSxGDrbysE (AAS)

http://www.youtube.com/watch?v=FGqeC5gML-0 (COVA)

http://www.youtube.com/watch?v=nmSgsWZkvMY (Sullivan)

http://www.youtube.com/watch?v=WsoJ_01JASw (HT 2012 arrest)

http://www.youtube.com/watch?v=9ij_6iMi9gA (Rachel Lloyd's TedX on GEMS, also see her book *Girls Like Us: Fighting for a World Where Girls Are Not for Sale: A Memoir*)

http://www.kickstarter.com/projects/2031445933/10000-men (A Jane Wells production) Also see: www.10Kmen.com/

http://www.amazon.com/Sex-Among-Allies-Katharine-Moon/dp/0231106432 (Katharine H.S. Moon)

Questions

Violence against women is pandemic, and is recognized as a trafficking-in-women and children push factor.

What is your focus area:
Root problems: domestic violence and poverty
Protection – awareness campaigns, outreach, hotlines
Prosecution – legislative, court system, and police
Rehabilitation – health, social, psychological, economic

How will our leaders of foreign policy establish a priority solution?

How will awareness be raised in our state to combat trafficking-in-persons?

What are law enforcement agencies actively doing?

Are the current laws appropriate and adequately implemented?

The Four "Ps"

Governments and international organizations have declared that an effective response to human trafficking must include four key elements (US State Department & UNODC):

1. **Prevention**—decrease the number of people trafficked.
2. **Protection**—increase protection, support to victims and survivors.
3. **Prosecution**—investigate and prosecute traffickers,

strengthen laws and legal responses.

4. **Partnerships**—to bring together diverse experiences, amplify messages, and leverage resources of law enforcement, service providers, community members, and survivors.

About the Author

A Colorado native, Peg Brantley and her husband make their home southeast of Denver, sharing it over time with the occasional pair of mallard ducks and their babies, snapping turtles, peacocks, assorted other birds, foxes, a deer named Cedric, and a bichon named McKenzie.

With the intent to lend her stories credibility, Peg is a graduate of the Aurora Citizens' Police Academy, participated in the Writers' Police Academy, has interviewed crime scene investigators, FBI agents, human trafficking experts, obtained her Concealed Carry Permit, studied diverse topics from arson dogs to Santeria, and hunted down real life locations that show up in her stories.

At this very minute (well, not *this* very minute) she's busy turning her standalone books into two separate series because that's what her readers want.

Peg's third book, *The Sacrifice*, was a finalist for two 2014 Colorado literary awards.

You can learn more about Peg's books at http://www.pegbrantley.com or meet up with her on Facebook at http://www.facebook.com/pegbrantleyauthorpage or follow her blog at http://www.suspensenovleist.blogspot.com

It's all better with friends.

46413973R00204

Made in the USA
Middletown, DE
31 July 2017